THE BEACHFRONT SURPRISES.

'SCONSET BEACH BOOK TWO

AINSLEY KEATON

CHAPTER 1

AVA

The kiss with Deacon was on Ava's mind the entire night. She was nervous and excited and really wanted to see where it would go with the handsome young contractor.

Yet, she was also extremely apprehensive. She had a hard time just going with it. Her head always got in the way. And, it was definitely getting in the way here because he was just too young. Ava always had a hard time getting involved with somebody if she didn't know where it would go. There were too many questions about Deacon in her mind. Did he want children? Was he looking to get involved with her, or was it just going to be a fling? Did he just kiss her because he was drunk?

Worse, she didn't know when she would see him again. He had left early that morning, after the house was completely cleaned up spic-and-span. He didn't indicate when he would be back or even if he would be back. She hated not knowing if she would even see him again.

But, just when she was going to pick up the phone to call Quinn, or Sarah, or Hallie, her mother appeared.

"Hey, Ava," her mother, Colleen, said. Colleen had been staying in one of Ava's eight rooms while she was in town. She'd only come to town to watch her granddaughter Siobhan while Charlotte, Siobhan's mother, helped out in the kitchen. Charlotte's husband Matthew was the chef for the party. He was shorthanded getting the food ready for Ava's big open-house shindig, which was a rousing success.

Ava just nodded her head. She never got along with her mother, but she never knew why. Her mother was just always very cold with her, right from the start. Yet, with Sarah, Ava's gorgeous sister who Ava always thought had it all but really didn't, Colleen wasn't cold. In fact, Colleen went out of her way to help Sarah move to Nantucket.

And, no matter what, Ava always felt like she was five years old around her mother. Yes, Ava had graduated from Harvard, had worked at a very high-powered law job for many years, and currently was running her very own bed-and-breakfast in the small village of Siaconset on the island of Nantucket.

Yet, whenever Ava was around her mother, she was that little girl who was dying for her mother's positive words. It was almost as if she was holding her breath, waiting for Colleen to say something nice to her.

But those kind words never came.

"Mom," Ava said. "Thanks so much for watching Siobhan. You were a lifesaver."

"Happy to help. Charlotte needed me, so I came. Of course, I would've loved to have been in the crowd, enjoying this gem of a house that came together thanks to me and my money, but it is what it is. I'm just happy last night's party was a real barnburner. That means I'll be making major bank off this place without even lifting a finger. That's my favorite way of making money. Passive income. You're going to be putting in your blood, sweat, and tears. Better you than me."

THE BEACHFRONT SURPRISES.

Ava nodded her head. She had mixed emotions about her mother having to invest in her place. On the one hand, she was extremely grateful that Colleen could give her the money she needed to get the place renovated and ready to go. On the other, well, she didn't want to be so tied up with her mother, for obvious reasons. It put great pressure on her to ensure that the place was super successful. Because, if it wasn't, she would never hear the end of it.

Ava was also apprehensive that Colleen demanded a note for $200,000 of the $500,000 she had given Ava to invest in the place. Ava knew she would adhere to the terms of the note, no problem, but it had an acceleration clause, which meant that Colleen could call in the note whenever she wanted. And that made Ava terrified.

"Well, looks like I'm going to have to make myself scarce. Don't screw this up, Ava. I'm warning you," her mother said with a wag of her finger.

Ava sighed. She had enough therapy over the years to realize that part of why she was such an overachiever was because she never wanted to disappoint Colleen. She strove for straight A's in undergrad, which she got, graduating *magna cum laude* from the University of Missouri with a degree in political science. Then, when she determined she wanted to go to law school, she took her LSAT practice tests so many times that she had all of the analytical games memorized, which was why she got such a high score on the test. After all, the analytical games were what tripped up most students, for good reason - they were damn hard to figure out. She worked her butt off when she got to Harvard, writing for the *Law Review,* studying 80 hours a week. Some of the weaker students actually paid her for her outlines because they were legendary. And then, when she got out of law school, she went to work for the prestigious white-shoe firm, where she ended up burning out completely.

She had no idea why Colleen gave her that warning about screwing up. She wasn't a screwup, and she never was.

What was strange was that Colleen was always so kind to her children, especially Samantha, the slacker. Samantha never had her head on straight. She had no ambition to speak of, at least not to Ava's knowledge. Of all her children, Samantha was the one who worried her the most, because Ava just couldn't picture her sweet and free-spirited daughter making anything of herself. Yet, whenever Samantha needed something, she went to Ava or Colleen. Ava usually denied her, but Colleen usually indulged her.

Jackson was higher up on the food chain than Samantha, but only because he did have an ambition in mind, even if his ambition was, in Ava's estimation, pie-in-the-sky. He was trying to break into the dog-eat-dog world of Hollywood. He recently got his first speaking part in a Netflix series set in the 1940s and focused on a detective's life, loves and cases. Jackson's speaking part was minuscule, just a few lines, but he was making his connections like he should. Yet, Colleen only had positive words for Jackson. She never tried to undermine him or tell him he was dreaming. She never tried to give him his odds of making it in that world, let alone staying on top for any period of time, even if he did happen to break through.

As for Charlotte, she was distant from Ava. She lived in Boston, so she was physically the closest to Ava, but she rarely spoke with her mother. Nevertheless, Ava had a bad feeling about Charlotte. There was something off in her marriage, but she just couldn't put a finger on what.

Ava knew that Charlotte had made a big mistake that resulted in her daughter, Siobhan. It was always Ava's understanding that Charlotte and Matthew had decided, before they were married, to not have children. That was one of their iron-clad agreements. But Charlotte was careless and didn't take her birth-control pills correctly. She played Russian Roulette with her pills, month after month because she often forgot to take them. However, she never told Matthew about her mistakes in taking the pill. She managed to not bite the bullet for over a year, and she started to think she was safe, that maybe she couldn't get pregnant at all.

Of course, she never actually asked her doctor about any of this. She just assumed she might be infertile, and she didn't like taking the pill. She gained weight from it, and it gave her migraine headaches. So, she simply stopped taking the pill, again without telling Matthew. As she explained to Samantha, who told all of this to Ava, she really believed she wasn't able to have children.

She was wrong. She got pregnant with Siobhan and then lied to Matthew when he confronted her about whether she was taking the pill as directed. She insisted to him that she'd taken the pill every single day, faithfully, and she apparently was one of the 2% of women who get pregnant while on the pill. Matthew apparently believed her, but Ava got the feeling that all wasn't right with her daughter's marriage.

Again, though, Colleen had a soft spot for Charlotte. Colleen knew about Charlotte's birth control mistake because Charlotte told her, and Colleen didn't have any harsh words about that.

Ava should've been happy that Colleen got along with her children so well, not to mention the fact she seemed to just love Sarah, Ava's sister, and she *was* happy. Yet, at the same time, it just astounded her. Oh, what she wouldn't give for the unconditional love and acceptance that Colleen gave everyone around Ava but denied to Ava herself.

"Mom, when have I ever screwed up anything?" Ava asked.

Colleen just shook her head and rolled her eyes. "You really don't see yourself like others see you, do you? Aren't you the one who let your husband clean out your investment account, just rolling over without a word or fight? Aren't you the one who worked for the same law firm for almost 3 decades, never made partner, and never spoke up for herself about it? You may think that you never screw up, but Ava, I'm here to tell you that you're wrong about that."

Ava swallowed hard. On the one hand, Colleen had a point. Ava did allow people to run right over her. The fact that she had become a victim on more than one occasion probably stemmed from her lack of self-esteem and inability to speak up for herself. Both of which were side effects from her mother's coldness over the years.

On the other hand, Ava noted that Colleen just had to dig in the knife. Instead of noting how hard she had always worked throughout her life for everything she had, how conscientious she always was, and how successful she'd been, especially considering she was a single mother of triplets while she was building her career, her mother had to point out her failures. So typical of Colleen's interactions with her.

"Okay, mother," Ava said with gritted teeth. "You made your point, as you always do. Again, thank you for watching Siobhan on such short notice. I apologize again about your not coming to the party because of it. Now, I'm sure you have someplace to be, so don't let me keep you from whatever it is."

"I get it. I'm going to let the door hit me on the way out. Well, Ava, I'll see you later. Again, if you screw this up, I will kill you in your sleep."

Ava took a deep breath. The sad thing was, she believed that about her mother. Her mother probably would murder her in her sleep if she did something that caused her new business to fail. So, she had to make sure that that didn't happen.

Ever.

CHAPTER 2

QUINN

Quinn Jenkins got home after Ava's big party and went right to sleep. It was 3 in the morning when she, Sarah and Hallie left Ava's house party, and she was exhausted.

At around 8 that morning, her doorbell rang. By then, the light was streaming through her window, and Kona had to be let out, so she didn't mind answering the door.

She walked to the door after letting Kona and Bella, Sarah's dog, out the back door.

There was a tiny girl on her porch. She probably was around 12 or 13, with jet black hair that had a bright blue streak framing her face, pale skin and dark eyeliner. She was around 5'2" and couldn't be 110 pounds, soaking wet.

"Can I help you?" Quinn asked the girl. "Are you selling Girl Scout cookies? If you are, I'll buy whatever you got." Quinn liked to support the Girl Scouts by buying boxes and boxes of cookies, even though she didn't eat the cookies herself. They were handy for her, though, because she handed them out to clients and sometimes took them to the

Nantucket Food Pantry or A Safe Place, which was a battered women's shelter she donated to.

The girl shook her head. "Do I look like a Girl Scout to you?" she asked. "I mean, seriously, dude. I've seen those Girl Scouts, and, let me tell you, they wouldn't let me in the door. No, I'm not selling stupid cookies."

"Oh," Quinn said. "Then maybe you have the wrong house?"

"Your name Quinn Jenkins?" she asked.

"Yes."

"Then I got the right house."

"I don't understand," she said.

"How much time you got?" the girl asked.

"Well, it's Sunday, so I don't have anything going on."

"Good," she said. "Well, you got two choices. You can either invite me in, or you can come out here and talk to me."

Sarah padded down the stairs from her own room. Hallie was around somewhere, Quinn thought, then she remembered that Hallie had planned to go to the new property she found with Willow. She and Willow were going into business, an alternative healing center. They'd found a beautiful house on the waterfront in the Historic District, and Hallie and Willow were working hard to open their unique wellness business.

Hallie was also looking for a cottage to call her own. She was looking around in the same neighborhood where Ava and Quinn lived, 'Sconset Beach, but wasn't having much luck trying to find a house in her price range of $1.5 million. She was looking mid-island at a neighborhood called Sandpiper Place, a newer development with a few houses right around what Hallie was willing to pay.

"Hey," Sarah said. "What's going on?"

"Excuse me," Quinn said to the girl. "I'm not ignoring you, but I have to talk to my roommate."

"Go ahead," the girl said. "But I'm not leaving until you talk to me."

Quinn shut the door and faced Sarah. "There's this girl, this really young girl, who wants to talk to me." All at once, Quinn had a sinking feeling about who that little girl was. "She knows who I am."

"Oh," Sarah said. "And you have no clue who she is and what she wants?"

Quinn bit her bottom lip. Sarah was a new person to her who didn't know her history. She had no idea about the darkest period in Quinn's life. It was a period when she lost her beloved brother, James, and was date-raped one month after she said goodbye to James. Charles was the first guy she'd gone out with since her painful split from Benjamin, her high-school sweetheart and husband.

Quinn blinked, thinking about Benjamin. She'd known him in Helen. Helen, Georgia, population less than 500, was the beautiful little town where she grew up. Nestled in the Blue Ridge Mountains, the place was modeled after German villages. All the downtown shops and restaurants were housed in buildings that looked like they existed in medieval Bavaria.

During the summer, tourists came from all around to go tubing down the river, zip-lining through the mountains, hiking through waterfalls and visiting wineries. During the fall, the town threw an Oktoberfest for the entire month of October, complete with dancers in lederhosen and dirndls, polka music and German food and drink. During the winter, artists organized a massive event to show their work.

Quinn loved her little town. She looked forward to the month-long Oktoberfest celebration every year, and she really adored Christmastime in Helen. The town held an annual lighting of the village, with a parade, music, and appearances by Santa and Mrs. Claus. She tobogganed down steep hills with the kids and never missed the Christkindl-markt with the Christmas gifts, decorations and sweet treats.

She fell in love with Benjamin when she was just 16, and they got married right after high school. Ben was studying to be a sommelier, and he became certified and needed to move to a city where he could ply his trade. He had his sights set on New York, so that's where they moved when the two of them turned 21.

Quinn hated New York right from the start. Everything about the city grated on her. The crowds, the noise, the subway, the smells of curry that permeated her walk-up tenement apartment in Bensonhurst. She hated that Benjamin left her alone much of the time because he was working in a high-end restaurant in Manhattan and never seemed to be home.

Benjamin tried to make her happy, at least at first. Quinn was depressed, perhaps for the first time in her life, so he did things to cheer her up. Such as the time he stood outside the window, on the fire escape, and held a boombox over his head, playing her *In Your Eyes* by Peter Gabriel. After all, Quinn's favorite movie at that time was *Say Anything*. She'd seen it in the theater 15 times when it first came out in 1989, the summer she was 22.

Benjamin saw the movie only once, but he told Quinn she was his very own Diane Court because she was so beautiful and out of his league. He felt like the underachiever Lloyd Dobler next to her.

Quinn thought he was nuts. She never saw herself as being particularly beautiful - her nose was too long, her eyes too close-set, her lips were too thick. She'd been told she resembled Gisele Bundchen, who had similar imperfections, but she always thought those people were crazy, too.

Benjamin always acted like he was over the moon for

THE BEACHFRONT SURPRISES.

Quinn. Always told her how lucky he was to have her in his life. Quinn never imagined they would break up.

At least, she never thought that until she heard about Karen, who was another sommelier the restaurant had hired. Ben and Karen went to wineries on the weekends in upstate New York. Quinn never thought anything of those trips because they were sent to these wineries by the restaurant, which was always interested in purchasing different wines.

Then Ben started to complain to Quinn about her disinterest in wines. She didn't know the difference between a Merlot, a Cabernet or a Zinfandel. She had no idea that these terms referred to grape varietals. When Ben took Quinn to Italy on a business trip, Quinn spent her time sightseeing instead of going to wine country with her husband. She'd always wanted to see the Trevi Fountain, the Vatican and the ruins. They were only in Rome for a weekend, so if she'd gone to wine country with Ben, she wouldn't have seen all the things she'd always wanted to.

That started a huge fight, as Ben screamed at her that he'd taken her on his restaurant's dime, so she needed to act interested in the Italian wines. While he made a point, Quinn resented him for attacking her for wanting to do touristy things in Rome instead of going to boring wineries.

And she'd told him upfront, before he invited her, that she didn't want to spend her time in Italy tasting wines. She wanted to experience Italy and all it had to offer, and, for her, that didn't include spending all her time listening to vintners describe how they pressed their grapes and aged their varietals. Nothing could've been more snooze-inducing for her. She loved to drink wine. She couldn't care less how it was made.

That was how their marriage broke down. She didn't care about the one thing he was passionate about, and Karen did.

The next time Ben went to Italy, Karen went with him. When he returned from that trip, he asked Quinn for a divorce.

Quinn gave up on men after that. She was 23 and divorced and through with dating. She'd given her heart to her high-school sweetheart, and he'd broken it. While men always pursued her, she turned all of them down.

For almost 17 years, she didn't go on a single date. During that time, she'd put her head down and got her degree in interior design from the New York School of Interior Design, and built her business, client by client.

Then her brother, James, died of brain cancer. James was only 11 months younger than her, and she was as close with him as anybody could possibly be. James lectured her on his deathbed about how she didn't any man a chance, and, when he died, Quinn vowed to go out with the next man who asked her. She could fulfill James' last request that way.

So, when Charles Langford, a Goldman Sachs banker, asked her out, she didn't hesitate. For the first time in two decades, she said yes to a date.

That was a huge mistake, as he slipped something into her drink. One moment, she was dancing to live music at the Smoke Jazz and Supper Club, and the next, she was waking up in her bed.

She'd only had one Tequila Sunrise, so Quinn was puzzled about what had happened. But she didn't think anything of it - maybe she drank more than she thought she did. She never imagined anybody would be such a creep as to do something like slipping his date a roofie.

Then came the morning sickness and the missed period. The tender breasts and weight gain. She called Ava and Hallie in a panic, and the three of them went to a CVS and bought seven different pregnancy tests. All of them came back positive.

It was then, and only then, that Quinn figured out what

had happened with Charles. He apparently slipped her something like GHB, which was called the date-rape drug, and had his way with her while she was passed out.

She was going to terminate but thought better of it and went the route of having the baby and putting her up for adoption.

Hallie and Ava were right there through all of it. Through the dark, endless nights after she discovered the rape, to the excruciating visits to the police station to press charges, to the sad decision to put her baby up for adoption. The cops refused to arrest Charles. Apparently, Charles was questioned and told the police the sex was consensual, and the cops believed him.

Quinn struggled with the decision to put her daughter up for adoption, was haunted by it, but she knew it was the right thing to do. It was an open adoption, which meant the kid could find her one day if she wanted to. But Quinn prayed her daughter would never take that option.

Quinn knew the adoption was the right thing because she didn't want the inconvenience of having a child. She was a single woman living in the city and was an extremely successful interior designer. She imagined what it would be like, trying to bring up a child on her own, and she couldn't picture herself doing it. She thought about shlepping her child around in cabs, dropping her off at daycare, feeling guilty for not being around more, cutting back on her work hours, and just changing her lifestyle 180 degrees. She wasn't prepared for it, she'd never wanted it, and she thought she wasn't cut out for it.

Hallie told her she was happy to watch the baby while Quinn worked, much like she watched Ava's triplets when they were young, and Ava was working a ton. At that time, Hallie's own daughter, Morgan, was 18 and going off to college. Hallie was looking at an empty nest with a husband she had nothing in common with and barely spoke to, and she was dying for some responsibility.

But Quinn didn't want to do that. Truth be told, she didn't want children and never did. That made her a bad woman in the eyes of society, she knew, but she didn't care what society had to say about women like her. She was supposed to want children because every woman wanted at least one, right? Wrong. Some women just weren't maternal, and Quinn fell into that category.

Still, putting her baby up for adoption was the hardest decision of her life. She was 41 years old when her daughter was born, and she knew she was giving away her last chance to be a mother. But keeping the baby wouldn't be right, and Quinn knew it.

Now, here was this tiny girl on her porch, and Quinn somehow knew the little girl was her daughter.

"Yes, sugar, I think know who she is and what she wants," Quinn said in answer to Sarah's question.

"The suspense is killing me," Sarah said.

Quinn sighed. "It's a long, long, long story. Listen, go and talk to your sister. She'll tell you the sad story of the child I gave up for adoption. I have a strong feeling the kid on our porch is her."

"Crap," Sarah said and then put her hand on her mouth. "Oh, that came out wrong. I meant to say...I don't really know what I meant to say. I guess I need to know how you feel about your child finding you and showing up like this."

"It depends on what she has to say," Quinn said, feeling her heart start to race. She wasn't going to jump to conclusions. It could be that her kid just wanted to find her and...

What? How could she have gotten here all on her own? Shouldn't her adoptive parents have been with her? Wouldn't they be the ones who would've contacted her to ask her if contact with the child was acceptable?

Quinn had a sinking feeling about all of it.

"Well," Sarah said. "I think you and that young girl need to be alone, so I'll take your advice and talk to my sister. She probably needs more help getting the house together, anyhow, since she's open for business on Monday."

"Thanks, sugar," Quinn said.

"I'll go out the back door," Sarah said, motioning to the door that led from the kitchen into the backyard.

"Good idea."

Sarah left, and Quinn tried to still her pounding heart.

And then she opened the door.

CHAPTER 3

QUINN

"Okay," Quinn said, taking a deep breath. "Come on in."

The young girl walked into the house and took a look around. "Nice," she said. "Cute place."

"Thanks," Quinn said. "Now, uh…"

"Emerson," she said. "My name."

"Emerson. Beautiful name."

"I guess. My adoptive mom thought so, at any rate."

Quinn didn't quite know what to do. What to say.

"Um," Quinn began.

"Not beating around the bush," Emerson said. "You're my mom."

Quinn just stood there. She wasn't shocked by the revelation. She expected it because she had a strong hunch about the young girl when she opened the door and saw her standing there. But she just didn't know what to say.

"Let's go and get brunch," Quinn said. "Shall we?"

"I guess. Weird. I tell you you're my mom, and you want to go get eggs and Mimosas. I didn't know what to expect, so

THE BEACHFRONT SURPRISES.

I'm rolling with it, but I can tell you you're an odd duck, as my adoptive mom would say."

Quinn didn't disagree. It was just that she wasn't expecting, before that morning, that she ever would be face to face with the girl she gave up so many years ago.

But it was strange, in a way. After giving up her daughter, she went to counseling, but she really believed she could never look at her baby and not see that bastard's face.

However, when Quinn looked at Emerson, she didn't see Charles' face at all. The little girl wasn't a painful reminder of the worst period of her life. She was just a pretty little girl who didn't look like her, but who didn't look like Charles, either.

She was just Emerson, a complete stranger, yet was also her daughter. Quinn was having a hard time trying to reconcile these two things.

"Well, odd duck is certainly a good description of me," Quinn said lightly. She wanted to call Ava to meet the two at Black-Eyed Susan's, a popular restaurant in the Historic District that served traditional breakfast food. But, no, she had to deal with her daughter without distractions.

"Let's go, then," Emerson said.

"Okay," Quinn said.

******

About fifteen minutes later, Quinn and Emerson were standing in a huge line, having put their names in for brunch. Quinn had a feeling the place was going to be packed, seeing as it was a Sunday. But she thought it wouldn't be *that* crowded because it wasn't yet Memorial Day. But this place was one of the most popular breakfast/brunch places in town. For good reason, too - their food was amazing.

Quinn loved their tofu scrambles. She'd recently decided to eat much less eggs and cheese, and she'd been off meat for years, except fish, and Black-Eyed Susan's boasted a gorgeous tofu scramble with peppers, spinach, mushrooms and basil that made Quinn's mouth water.

While they stood around, waiting for their names to be called, Quinn stared at her daughter, trying to figure out how to make conversation with her. Emerson wasn't making it easy, though, as she was surfing on her phone the whole time.

Their names were finally called, and mother and daughter were led to a table. The place was packed, and the tables and chairs were close together, so the atmosphere wasn't ideal for Quinn to get to know her daughter. But this was her idea, and she was going to make the best of it.

The waitress came around and took their order.

"Tofu veggie scramble with English Muffin and hash browns," Quinn ordered. "And an orange juice."

"French Toast, corned beef hash and an OJ as big as my head," Emerson ordered.

Quinn looked at the tiny girl and wondered where she put all that food. French Toast *and* corned beef hash? She felt herself gaining weight just thinking about that order.

Oh, to be a tween again!

The waitress took their menus, and Quinn was face-to-face with her biggest fear - her daughter would come and find her and she wouldn't know what to say.

"Okay," Quinn said. "Where are your parents?"

"Dead," Emerson said.

Quinn's heart stopped. Surely, this little girl had somebody to take her in? A relative, maybe? A friend? A grandparent?

"I'm so sorry, sugar," Quinn said. "What happened?"

Emerson shrugged. "My dad went out for a run, dropped dead. My mom found out about my dad, and she dropped dead. Mom was sick, though. She had heart failure and was waiting for a heart transplant. My dad, he just dropped dead out of nowhere. Weird, huh?"

"What a shock it must be," Quinn said. "So, who's taking care of you?"

Emerson folded her hands and stared at Quinn. "Nobody is. Seriously. I mean, I split after I called 911 for my mom. Found an Uber, got on the ferry, and here I am."

"Where were you living with your mom and dad?" Quinn asked.

"Boston. It wasn't easy getting here, let me tell you. Especially when I got a nosy Uber driver asking too many questions. Sometimes you want to get into a car and not talk, you know? But you get a driver who won't shut up, and those plans go out the window."

"But Uber drivers aren't supposed to pick up minors, are they?" Quinn asked.

"Who's a minor? I mean, I am, but I told him I was 18, and he was all like, 'cool, how you doin?' He didn't care."

"How did you get an Uber account?" Quinn asked.

"You're just like my Uber driver, you know that? Asking so many questions. My mom had an Uber account, duh. I used hers. She wasn't using it anymore."

The food came around, and Emerson eagerly dug into her French Toast. "Rad food, by the way," she said.

"Yes," Quinn said. "So, you're a runaway, then?"

"Yeah, I guess I am. Not sure if anybody's looking for me, though."

"Why not?"

"Who would be looking for me? Well, my teachers will be on Monday, but right now, I don't know anybody who'll miss me. My parents had no family alive. They had friends, but I know cops and paramedics and stuff don't call friends when people bite it. No next of kin to be called."

Quinn took a deep breath. No next of kin. That didn't sound good.

"Do you know if your parents made arrangements for your care if they happened to suddenly die?" she asked Emerson.

"Not that I know of," Emerson said. "Their friends all had a bunch of kids of their own. I'm sure if they asked any one of them if they would take me after they died, they were probably all like 'sure, just give me a paper to sign,' then if my parents asked them to sign something, they probably were all like 'well, I didn't think you were serious, bro.' That's how my parents' friends were. Anyhow, I doubt my parents even got that far. My mom, she was sick, and she probably knew she was on her way out the door, but my dad? He ran marathons. He probably was all like 'Imma live forever, yo!'"

Emerson took the syrup off the table, smothered her French Toast and then dumped her corned beef hash into the syrup and dragged it through the sticky sweet liquid.

Quinn smiled as she saw herself at Emerson's age. She did the same damn thing, dragging her meat through syrup and then stuffing her mouth with the salty and sweet combination.

"So, your parents are dead, they had no next of kin, and you don't think any of their friends were given custody, then?"

"You got it," Emerson said. "So, what do you think? You take me in, and I don't have to go into the system."

"Emerson, I can't just take you in," Quinn said.

"Why not? You put me into this shitty world. Wasn't my choice to be born, and it wasn't my choice to be thrown away like an expired coupon. You brought me into this world, so, as I see it, you're responsible for me."

Quinn bit her lower lip, not wanting her young daughter to cuss but not feeling it was her place to stop her from doing so. And, besides, Emerson saying the word "shitty" was really 1,000th on the list of problematic issues in this whole scenario. So, Quinn just didn't say anything about her young daughter's blue language.

"It's a problem," Quinn said. "I'm going to have the call the police and report you running away. That's first."

"Yeah, I figured you'd have to do that," Emerson said. "But I want you to take me in. It's you or the system, and I've heard bad things about the system. I got a friend at school who's been in the system, and her foster parents lock her in a closet when they want to go out and party with their friends." She shook her head. "No, thanks."

"I just can't take you in," Quinn said. "I gave you up for adoption."

"Well, figure it out," Emerson said. "I want to live with you."

Quinn shook her head. It seemed to be an impossible situation on so many levels. Yet, she knew her daughter was right.

Quinn *was* responsible for Emerson being brought into the world. So, she would have to make sure the kid was safe. That was only fair.

CHAPTER 4

QUINN

After her brunch with Emerson, Quinn called an emergency meeting with the ladies. So, that evening, Ava came over and joined her, Sarah and Hallie for drinks and dinner at her house.

"So, what's the emergency?" Ava asked, accepting a glass of wine from Quinn's shaking hands. "I've never known you to be ruffled for any reason at all."

"Sarah told you my daughter showed up, right?" Quinn asked.

"She thought your daughter showed up, yes," Ava said. "Is that what happened?"

"Yes," Quinn said, gulping her glass of wine. "That's what happened." And then Quinn explained about how Emerson's parents had died and that she had nobody else.

"So, what are you going to do?" Hallie asked.

"I'm going to take her in," Quinn said. "I've no choice, sugar. I'm going to find an attorney to figure out how to do it, though." Then she turned to Hallie and Sarah. "We'll be having another person in the house, so-"

"Not a problem," Hallie said quickly. "I can move my stuff

into a storage unit for the time being, and then go and live at The Nantucket Hotel until I find a place to close on. They have extended stay options where the accommodations are more like a house than a hotel."

Quinn nodded her head, relieved. She wasn't quite sure how Emerson was going to fit into her life, and she really didn't know where Emerson was going to sleep, as all her bedrooms were currently occupied.

"Wow," Sarah said. "I'm sorry, but are you just spinning right now? I would be."

"You might say that," Quinn said. "I don't know, sugar, what to think about any of this. I'm kind of in shock, to tell you the truth."

Ava took a sip of her wine and then put her hand on Quinn's. "I guess your life is about to change. But, don't worry, raising a kid is really a rewarding experience. For the most part, that is."

Hallie nodded her head. "I can't imagine my life without my Morgan. I know we went through a long period of time where we were at odds, but we're so good now. I'm so proud of her and her wife. So, yeah, it's probably a shock to you now, but just get through the initial adjustment, and you might find that little girl will be a blessing for you."

Quinn took a sip of her wine and stood up. "You guys want to get a pizza? My treat."

Everybody agreed to order a pizza from the Foggy Nantucket, the ladies' favorite pizza joint. Quinn ordered the chicken bacon ranch, which was Sarah, Ava and Hallie's favorite pizza on that menu, and a small veggie pizza for herself, and then sat back down.

Ava looked at Quinn as if she wanted to ask her a question but didn't quite know how. "Quinn, honey, I hate to bring this up, but –"

"I know what you're going to say, and, surprisingly, it's

not a problem. I really thought if I ever came face-to-face with my daughter, I'd automatically go back to that night. That I just couldn't look at her face without seeing Charles's face. But I look at her, and I see her. She's a tiny little thing, probably isn't 110 pounds when she's soaking wet, she has black hair and beautiful blue eyes. Well, that's not really true. Her hair is blue in the front. But it's supposed to be black. Charles was a redheaded guy with curly hair and freckles, he had some junk in his trunk, and he was about 6'3". No way do I look at Emerson and see him. So that's a good thing. I don't know what I would've done if she would've looked just like him, so good for her she doesn't."

"And what are you going to tell her about her father?" Sarah asked.

"Oh, I don't know. My heart hurts just thinking about that. I'll have to think of something because I don't think I can tell her the truth. If I told her the truth, she might really go into some kind of deep depression. I've heard of that happening, you know. At least I saw it on *Grey's Anatomy*. Jo found out her birth mother was raped, and that's why she gave her up, and Jo spun out into a huge funk. For many episodes."

Quinn heard herself and realized she was going to make a huge decision based upon a television series, and she realized how dumb that sounded. She was just going to have to do her own research on the matter and see what happened when adopted kids found out they were the result of a rape.

The last thing she wanted to do was to cause her young daughter even more mental anguish. The little girl had just lost both of her parents, and it affected her so badly she found her way to Quinn's house from Boston. The girl seemed to have a very hard shell, but Quinn knew that it was just that. A shell. Emerson was only 13 years old, a very tenuous age, and she had enough on her plate as it was.

The pizzas arrived, and everybody helped themselves to a slice. Usually, Quinn was absolutely in love with her veggie pizza. She would marry this pizza if she could. But, at that time, nothing tasted good.

What was she going to do about her business? She worked about 50 hours a week, getting some amazing projects from some high-dollar clients. Aside from her best friends, her business was her life. And that was how she liked it. She loved not having to be responsible for another person, not having to answer to anybody else. Her free time was her own. Now, she was going to have her free time devoted to raising a 13-year-old child whose parents had just died.

To say she was in for adjustment would be an understatement.

And she was going to have to do all of this at the age of 54. She could just imagine herself in the carpool lane with all those thirty-somethings looking at her like, *who is the old lady dropping off that young girl?* Everybody was going to assume she was Emerson's grandmother. After all, she was the right age to be the child's grandmother.

"Oh my heck, what if I don't have the energy for all this? Working full-time, bringing up a child, probably trying to get her therapy because you know she's gonna need it. Hell, I think I'm going to need it. Maybe I can find a therapist who can give us a two-for-one."

Gallows humor. That was the only thing that was going to get her through this.

"Well, Quinn, you know that all of us are going to have your back on this. That kid is going to have one mother and three fairy Godmothers. We'll be like the little mice in the Cinderella cartoon. Or like the three crazy fairy godmothers in the movie *Maleficent*. You're never going to have to walk alone as long as we're around," Ava said.

"I know. And I love you ladies so much for all you're

doing. I'm just nervous because let's face it, none of us are spring chickens. And we all are busy ladies. Well, it is what it is. She was right about one thing – I brought her into this world. I can't just turn my back on her. If it weren't for me, she wouldn't be here. She said I brought her into the world, so I'm responsible for her, and she's right."

CHAPTER 5

AVA

The Monday after her big party, Ava realized she was going to have a wildly successful grand opening of her bed and breakfast. She was doing everything herself, which was extremely stressful, but on the very day she opened her doors, she had a full house. In fact, she had a waiting list. Word got around about her beautiful home, and the busy season was starting, as Memorial Day was just around the corner. All that meant she was going to be extremely busy in running her place.

She knew she could rely upon the ladies to help out in a pinch, but she wasn't going to ask them, because she knew they were just as busy. Quinn continued to get many high dollar projects, and Hallie was immersed in not only studying for her Master's in Integrative Nutrition, but also was completely involved in the day-to-day running of the new spa she'd opened with Willow, called the Willow Tree Spa and Relaxation Center.

As for Sarah, she was working with Ava as a sommelier. Ava had gotten a special license to sell wine on the premises, so she and Sarah had worked together to plan a special wine tasting event on Ava's terrace that faced the beach. Sarah had negotiated contracts with wineries around the country to sell their wine, so when people came to her wine tasting events they could buy a bottle of wine to take home with them. Sarah had stocked Ava's wine cellar spectacularly, with many different blushes, white and red wines, both sparkling and non-sparkling.

Sarah was living with Quinn at the moment, as was Hallie, who was soon going to be getting an extended stay hotel suite to make room for Emerson. Hallie was looking for a home of her own, and was looking to close on a small cottage in the mid-island. Mid-island actually had a few homes in Hallie's price range of $1.5 million, and she was really excited about getting a cottage of her own.

Sarah knew it was going to be a long time before she could afford her own home in the area, but that was okay with Quinn. Quinn told Sarah she could stay with her for as long as she needed to, and Sarah was saving every penny for a down payment on a home of her own. She'd told Ava it was weird she was in her 50s and had a roommate.

"Don't get me wrong, it's been great living with Quinn, but I'm afraid I'm going to get on her nerves. But it's going to be a long time before I can afford a house here on this island."

And that was for sure, considering little tiny homes on the island typically sold for $1.5 million and up. So Ava knew her sister was going to be discouraged by not being able to afford her own place on the island, yet she also knew that Sarah was a survivor, come what may. She never knew that about her sister until recently – on the contrary, Ava always thought Sarah was somebody who wanted things to be handed to her. That was because Sarah always was the girl who was handed everything in life. From her popularity in high school and college, to the billionaire who whisked her out of her architectural career and made her his jet-setting partner, Sarah just glided through life.

Which was why Ava was so impressed with her sister and her ability to bounce back after tragedy. Sarah's billionaire boyfriend Nolan passed away, leaving her penniless and with nothing. And Sarah was still absolutely stunningly beautiful, not to mention brilliant and kind. She really could've finagled her way into being another wealthy man's paramour, but she didn't. She was living life on her terms, even if it meant she was broke, and Ava admired her thoroughly for doing so.

So, while Ava knew she could rely on her best friends to help her, she wasn't going to ask them. This was her baby, the bed-and-breakfast, and even if she was going to be working a hundred hours a week, she would do what she had to do to make the place a roaring success.

What she didn't know was a dark cloud was forming and was about to descend on her like a ton of bricks.

A dark cloud by the name of Colleen Flynn.

CHAPTER 6

COLLEEN

Colleen on Monday had a most unexpected phone call. It was from Judge Allen Jackson, who was the chief judge for the First Circuit Court of Appeals, where Colleen was an associate judge.

"How about you and I go and get dinner tonight?" Judge Jackson asked her over the phone. "There's something I need to talk to you about."

If Colleen had ever heard more ominous words in her life, she couldn't remember what they might've been. The Chief Judge was not strictly her boss – she was appointed to her position by the President of the United States and confirmed by the Senate. Her position was lifetime-appointed, which meant, of course, the Chief Judge didn't have the ability to fire her. Nobody had the ability to fire her.

Yet, she knew she'd been screwing up on the bench and had been since the love of her life, Violet, passed away. The decisions she wrote after Violet died had been overturned by the Supreme Court 80% of the time. Before Violet's death, the Supreme Court only overturned 60% of her written decisions. The percentage was high simply because the Supreme

Court didn't review most circuit court decisions, and when they agreed to take a case, there was a good chance they would overturn. So, her previous percentage, 60%, was actually quite low. But 80% wasn't.

She also had several bar complaints against her for unprofessional conduct. None of these resulted in any kind of discipline against her, but they all were taken seriously by both her and by the Chief Judge. And all of these bar complaints were lodged against her in the past year – in other words, they all occurred after Violet passed away.

She heard in the judge's invitation to have dinner that it was not an invitation or a request so much as it was an order. Either she had dinner with the judge tonight, or she was going to be summoned to his chambers in the morning. Personally, she was much more inclined to have a bomb dropped on her over a nice meal and a dirty martini than in a judge's chambers.

"I'll see you tonight, what time?" Colleen asked Judge Jackson.

"7 at the Capital Grille," he said.

The Capital Grille was an old-school steakhouse where Colleen could get a good gin martini and a juicy steak, cooked just the way she liked. So, the evening might not be so terrible.

****

Colleen got to the Capital Grille right at 7 o'clock to meet Judge Jackson. She always liked this place. It spoke to the traditionalist in her heart. That's what she was in her soul – a traditionalist. Capital Grille was furnished with dark seats and white table cloths, geometrical chandeliers on the ceilings. This was the kind of place that really should have a grand piano in the corner and a cigar lounge in the back.

Judge Jackson was already waiting for her at the bar. He rose from his stool when he saw her coming in. Allen was an imposing African-American man, 6'3" and a former linebacker for the University of Alabama. Colleen always got along very well with the Chief Judge. Whenever they would get together for social outings before, the two would usually end up trading racy courtroom stories, being very careful not to identify the parties in question.

But tonight was not going to be the night for that. Colleen just knew it. Maybe it was the way he called her at home to invite her to this dinner. Maybe it was the somber tone he used when he called her. But it was really just a hunch she had that the dinner was not going to be pleasant, combined with the fact she knew her work had been lacking as of late.

"Colleen!" Judge Jackson boomed to her when she approached him at the bar. "Damn good to see you."

"You too," Colleen said. "But why do I feel like I'm going to my execution?"

Allen started to laugh. "Now, now, Colleen, you know better than that. You know you're on that bench for life. There's nothing I can do about that. So, just relax."

"Which implies you would like to do something about that," Colleen said pointedly. "What gives? You invite me out to dinner in the middle of the week. I know you got something to say. So let's just not beat around the bush."

Allen smiled again. "Easy, easy now. Let's go ahead and get a seat, order a couple of martinis, have some rare steaks and loaded baked potatoes, and then we'll talk. But, your instincts are right. This dinner is only half social."

"Thought so." Colleen suddenly felt her heart start to pound. It was true she could never be fired, but she could be impeached. Not that any of her behavior rose to that level, because she knew it didn't. Yet, it still didn't bode well that she was there with the Chief Judge and he was confirming

THE BEACHFRONT SURPRISES.

her fears that this dinner was going to concern more business than pleasure.

Colleen and Allen got their seats and ordered some martinis – Colleen liked hers extra dirty, more olive juice than anything else, while Allen liked his neat, no Vermouth or chilling - and an appetizer of Tuna Tartare.

The waiter brought their drinks and appetizer, and Colleen ordered a filet mignon, while Allen got a ribeye. After Colleen had a couple sips of her martini – it was smooth, yet briny because of all the olive juice, just like she liked it – she leaned forward.

"Well, out with it. You got me out here, now tell me the bad news."

Allen shook his head and took a drink of his own neat martini. "I like you, Colleen. You're straight up. No BS. So, I'll be just as straight up with you. You need to take a vacation. Now, now, I know what you're thinking. You're thinking I'm being a condescending mansplaining SOB, telling the little lady she needs to take a break. But I'm telling you, if you don't take a break, you might lose your job."

"What are you talking about? I can only be removed by impeachment and conviction in the Senate. There's nothing that can be done to me. Not unless I commit some kind of high crime or misdemeanor."

"That's what you're heading for. I've seen it before – burnout. And burnout can sometimes lead to out-of-character behavior. Which sometimes leads to judges committing the high crime or misdemeanor that gets their butt impeached. At any rate, you're not at the top of your game. And I think that you know it."

"No, I don't know it. I think my work has been stellar, as usual." That was a lie, of course. She knew what he was saying was right. She was not nearly as sharp as she was before Violet died.

Judge Jackson continued as if Colleen hadn't said a word. "Now, I know you've suffered a personal tragedy, and I'm not unsympathetic about that. I also know you not only didn't attend Violet's funeral, but you were back at work the very next day. Now, I know about grieving. I lost my Pearl a couple of years ago. I couldn't think straight for months after she died. But I took time off after her death, because I knew I needed to grieve. I don't think you've acknowledged your very human need to grieve your loss. You haven't acknowledged it, you've buried it, but it's coming out in other ways. And it's hurting your work. Your legacy."

"It's not your business how I grieve," Colleen said. "It just so happens that throwing myself into my work is my way of handling my grief. Maybe you handled your grief by going to Europe or whatever it is you did after your wife died, but that's not my way."

Allen shook his head. "Do you remember why you authorized an autopsy for Violet?" he asked.

Colleen heard that question from him, and she shivered. Damn! Why did she confide in him? Of all the people who she should've talked to after Violet's sudden demise, the Chief Judge probably should've been last on her list. Her poor judgment in talking to him about her feelings after she found her beloved Violet, her partner of 40+ years, motionless on the bathroom floor, was unforgivable to her.

Violet had just had a physical. The doctor didn't find anything wrong with her. There was no way possible she could've suffered a massive heart attack not two weeks after this complete physical gave her a clean bill of health.

Yet, that's exactly what happened. Violet told Colleen she was going to take a nice hot bath. There was nothing out of the ordinary about that evening.

That's what was so hard - everything was so normal that evening. That's what made it all so hard to grasp. The aggressive normalcy of the evening ended when Colleen knocked on the bathroom door after Violet had been in the bathtub for an hour and a half. Colleen wasn't really all that worried. Violet often took long luxurious baths, with candles and sweet-smelling bubbles, reading a book she'd been meaning to get to but never got around to. Colleen was simply knocking on the door to see if she needed anything.

When Violet didn't answer, Colleen opened the door and found her lying naked on the floor. Colleen at first couldn't process what she was seeing. Her brain simply could not take in the enormity of what was happening.When she called 911, she was extremely calm. Her mind was completely clear, her voice measured. When the paramedics came, and worked on her for what seemed like an hour, when it actually was probably less than 10 minutes, all Colleen could think about was her precious Violet would go to the hospital and recover, and she was going to have to hire a nurse to help her in her rehabilitation.

And that's what she was doing when the paramedics were working on Violet. She was on her phone, looking up home health agencies, looking at the reviews and ratings for various ones, making a mental note to herself that she was going to have to call them in the morning after Violet was taken to the hospital and saved.

It seemed like there were hundreds of paramedics in her apartment. Again, however, it was probably less than five. She could hear them talking through their walkie-talkies or whatever it is that paramedics use to communicate. She didn't quite understand anything of what was going on, except for she heard that Violet apparently had gone into cardiac arrest. They'd asked her, of course, how long Violet had been down, and Colleen didn't know. She explained about how Violet took long baths, how she'd been in the bathroom for an hour and a half by the time Colleen had found her, how she didn't know exactly how long it was that Violet had not been breathing.

Even when Violet was loaded into the gurney and taken to the hospital, Colleen was still obsessing on the home health agencies she was going to have to call. She was still fixated on whether or not she was going to have to take some time off the bench to help Violet get better.

The thought that Violet was dead never even crossed her mind.

When she got to the hospital, and a doctor explained to her that there was nothing that could've been done, Colleen still didn't quite understand what was going on. She spotted a water bottle in a trashcan, and thought about how inconsiderate the person was who put the water bottle in the trashcan. Didn't that person know you're supposed to recycle those things? So, after the doctor had explained to Colleen about how Violet apparently had experienced a massive coronary and was gone, Colleen calmly picked up the water bottle out of the trashcan and put it into her purse so she could recycle it later.

The doctor asked Colleen if she would consent to an autopsy. Colleen was considered to be Violet's next of kin, even though the two had never officially married, because Colleen was still a traditionalist in her heart and thought marriage would somehow be wrong. Another contradiction in her psyche. But they each made the other the power of attorney, so Colleen could consent to the autopsy. Which she did.

But she didn't consent to the autopsy in a rational way. She thought that, somehow, the autopsy would save Violet's life. Maybe it was something that could show how Violet could get better. She wasn't rational at all.

Sometimes. Other times, her brain was processing the fact that her Violet was gone. And she became obsessed with asking for a do over. She remembered how Superman in the first movie was able to turn back time, and made it possible for the world to spin backwards. She wanted Superman to do his work, so she could have the last day or so back. If she could just have that chance, she would make sure Violet went into the hospital and she could have all the diagnostic tools necessary to discover she had a clogged artery, and they could give her emergency surgery for it.

She actually believed it was possible to turn back time. And she became obsessed with exactly how to do it. Associated with this were the inevitable what-ifs. What if Colleen didn't wait for an hour and a half to knock on the bathroom door, but knocked on the door after a half-hour? Would she have found a live Violet who would've told her she wasn't feeling well and she needed to go to the hospital? And she could've gotten her to the hospital on time for something to be done to save Violet's life? What if Colleen would've monitored Violet's diet a lot more, encouraging her to eat more fruits and vegetables and less sugar and saturated fats? What if Colleen would've gotten an exercise bike and encouraged Violet to ride it every day?

Why didn't Colleen encourage healthier habits in Violet? Why did she indulge Violet's every whim when it came to diet and exercise? Couldn't she have a complete do-over, go back to when Colleen and Violet met? She would make sure Violet didn't eat quite so many desserts or steaks or drink quite so many martinis or glasses of wine.

These thoughts alternated with thoughts of revenge on Violet's doctors. How dare they miss something as obvious as a clogged artery? And that's what the autopsy showed, that Violet had severe blockages in her arteries, and if a doctor would've caught that, Violet would have had bypass surgery. But the doctor didn't, and he was going to pay.

Colleen tried to use all her influence to find a lawyer who

would sue, but she couldn't find one. During her District Court years, she'd heard enough medical malpractice cases to know why the lawyers thought hers wasn't a good case. For one thing, Violet never showed heart disease symptoms. No chest pains, no shortness of breath. Her cholesterol was fine and so were her lipids.

Violet was just one of those people who didn't have any signs of a clogged artery until she died from it. So the doctor who didn't diagnose it really did nothing wrong, but Colleen wanted him to pay for it anyway. She was enraged she couldn't find a lawyer to take the case.

Unfortunately for Colleen, she confided in the Chief Judge about her thoughts on the autopsy. She told Judge Jackson she believed the autopsy would properly diagnose her Violet, and that once Violet was diagnosed, she could be revived and rehabilitated. She only told Judge Jackson this because she anticipated taking some time off to help Violet get better.

And that was the reason why she didn't go to Violet's funeral. She thought if she went to the funeral, it would all be real. And that, somehow, if she didn't go to the funeral, Violet still had a chance to come home. That was why she refused to take any time off at all after Violet's death – she thought if she changed her schedule, it would be admitting she was grieving. She could never admit to herself she was grieving, because if she did, it would imply she had something to grieve. And she was still hopeful Violet could return to their home they shared for so many years.

Now, a year after her personal tragedy, she realized she had been living through a period of magical thinking. She believed her thoughts could somehow change what had happened, reverse it somehow. That if she took certain actions, like going to Violet's funeral and changing her schedule, she would somehow destroy the idea that Violet

THE BEACHFRONT SURPRISES.

was going to still come home. Her brain was just not thinking rationally, because it could not process what had happened.

Now, here it was, and apparently her grief, that she never acknowledged, had come out in other ways. She knew what Judge Jackson was saying was correct – she was not at the top of her game, not even close. But she didn't quite know exactly how to get her game back. He was telling her she needed to take a vacation. But what exactly was that going to do?

Colleen sighed. "Yes, I remember telling you why I authorized an autopsy. But, you have to understand, I was in shock. I wasn't thinking rationally. You can't hold that period against me now. That wouldn't be fair."

"I know. I understand what grieving can do. I won't tell you I didn't go through a similar period when I lost my Pearl, because I did. Believe it or not, what you went through is something many people go through when they're in the grieving process. It's part of the denial, part of the bargaining. It's not uncommon to think everything could be reversed if only you hoped for it hard enough, for instance. I'm not going to bust your chops about any of that because it wouldn't be right. And if you came through all of that and none of it affected your work, I wouldn't say a word about it. But that's not the case, and you know it."

Colleen took a deep breath. "How long of a vacation do you think I should take?"

"You have six weeks coming to you. I would take the entire six weeks." He looked at Colleen meaningfully. "Now, I'm not going to tell you how to spend those six weeks. You could go on a cruise to Alaska as far as I'm concerned, or maybe you just want to stay home and watch a lot of Netflix series. Whatever you want to do for those weeks, I'm all for it. But I need you to get your head straight. You're an appellate judge. You literally have people's lives in your hands. You hear death penalty appeals, for the love of God. You have to get those right. I hope we're clear."

"Crystal."

"Good. I'm glad to hear the message is getting through to you loud and clear."

The meal was finished, and Colleen considered ordering a dessert. She hadn't really had a dessert since she found Violet, because it didn't seem right. Violet loved her cheesecakes, and she paid the ultimate price for her love of those cheesecakes. Colleen simply could not justify eating something she blamed for her beloved Violet's death.

So, Colleen did order a dessert, but it wasn't a cheesecake. It was the Flourless Espresso Cake, dusted with cocoa powder and served with fresh raspberries. It was delicious, but it wasn't what she wanted, which was the cheesecake.

Maybe someday she'd be able to look at another piece of cheesecake without regret. But that time was not now, and she wondered if that time would ever get there.

****

Colleen took a deep breath as she realized exactly where she wanted to spend her sojourn. She wanted to spend time lounging on a beach. The beach she wanted to spend time on was Siasconset, and the place she wanted to enjoy this beach was her daughter's 'Sconset Inn.

After all, she was a financier of that place.

She might as well enjoy the fruits of her money.

CHAPTER 7

QUINN

That Monday, Quinn made an appointment with an attorney she'd met through a client who owned a huge mansion on the South Shore. Her client's name was Leland Newbury, and he'd hired her to do a redesign on his home.

While working on the redesign, she'd met a man named Asher Martin, a prominent divorce attorney with offices on Nantucket and Boston. He was 55, extremely handsome, and apparently had his own yacht he took out on the weekends. He also had a private Lear jet that he, himself, flew from Nantucket to Boston, where he had his main law office.

Not that he bragged about that, but Leland tipped Quinn off on the existence of the enormous boat when he asked Asher if they were still on for that weekend. Leland also told Quinn about Asher having his pilot's license and owning the Lear jet he piloted between his Nantucket and Boston offices.

Quinn, of course, couldn't care less about the yacht or the mansion or the Lear jet. None of that impressed her, and she still was going to stick to her current man embargo, handsome attorney or not. Still, she was friendly with him, as she was with everybody she met, and he asked her out on a date. Quinn turned him down for two reasons.

One, he was a man.

And two, Quinn knew the man was nothing but a silver-tongued devil, and she had had enough of that kind of guy. He was the kind of guy she thought she left behind in New York City - the balls to the wall jerk attorney. Yet, here he was, living on Nantucket Island, apparently year-round.

After all, to become as wealthy as he was in the field of family law, he had to become essentially a mercenary, taking cases he didn't believe in because they paid the big bucks. There was nothing wrong with that - everybody deserved representation - but she didn't want to have anything to do with somebody who would take noxious cases just because they paid well.

However, when Emerson showed up on her front porch, Quinn knew she needed to talk to an attorney about what she needed to do. And she wanted to do that quickly.

She got online, called around, and found out nobody could see her for at least a month. She really wanted to get this done so Emerson could be underneath her roof at the earliest possible moment. So, she decided to call Asher.

She called him on his cell phone, and he sounded entirely too happy to hear from her.

"Quinn, I knew you would call," he said, his voice a little bit too bouncy for Quinn's taste. Not that she hated bouncy. In fact, it was the opposite – she liked optimistic, sunny people.

However, Quinn was wary of men who were too anxious to talk to her, especially when she knew that the man was hot to get into her pants.

"Listen, I need your guidance. I'll pay you, of course, your going rate, but I need to talk to you about a situation I have here."

And then she told him all about Emerson - about how she gave birth to her at the age of 41, gave her up for adoption and how Emerson's adoptive parents both died.

"And, so you see, I need to adopt her. I need your help."

"Oh, you need my help. And why, exactly, are you coming to me? I mean, there are domestic attorneys everywhere in this area. Why are you calling me?"

Quinn knew what he wanted to hear from her. He wanted her to tell him that she was calling him because she was dying to go out and have dinner and sexy times with him. But Quinn wouldn't tell him any of that because that wasn't what she wanted.

"Let me be honest with you. I'm calling you because everywhere I've called has people lined up out the door to see them, so they don't have any kind of openings on their schedule. I was hoping you'd be able to fit me in."

Asher was quiet for a moment. "Quinn, you do understand that if your average domestic attorney has a month-long waiting list, mine is six months? So, what made you think I could sneak you in? It's not like you can even hope for a cancellation because even my cancellations have waiting lists."

"Okay," Quinn said. "I thought I would take a shot. I guess I should've known you would be busy too."

"I guess. However, we could always meet for dinner and talk about it over a nice rare steak and glass of wine."

Oh, there it was. Quinn knew she'd get sucked into seeing this guy on a social basis. By hook or by crook, she would end up sharing a meal with him in a restaurant.

But what choice did she have? She wanted Emerson under her roof. The sooner, the better.

She finally took a deep breath. "Listen, I'll meet you for

dinner, but I want to make one thing perfectly clear. I'm not meeting you on a social basis, even though it'll be over a meal we two will share. If the only way I'm going to be able to get this show on the road is to see you at a restaurant, then let's do it. Name your place."

"Okay. Let's do it. How about The Straight Wharf at eight tonight?"

"Okay. I'll meet you there at eight. I'll buy my own dinner."

"I have a better idea. Why don't I come and pick you up?"

Quinn had to draw the line at that. That seemed like a date. "No. I'd prefer it if I could just meet you there. So, I'll be there at eight."

* * *

The Straight Wharf was, from the outside, an unassuming place nestled in the heart of the historic district. Housed in a wood-shingled Cape Cod-style home so ubiquitous on Nantucket, Quinn wasn't expecting much. But the interior was elegant, with white tablecloths, high ceilings and a beautiful view of the water.

Somehow, Asher managed to score a window seat, even though the place was packed. She raised an eyebrow, wondering how this guy was able to get such a prime seat in such a short period. Then again, with him being such a wealthy and influential man, he probably knew the right strings to pull to get preferential treatment wherever he went.

Quinn sat down after Asher stood up and pulled her chair out for her. She was impressed that he seemed to have manners. Her mama certainly would be impressed with him.

As she looked at his handsome face – his wavy salt and pepper hair, his piercing blue eyes, his perfectly straight teeth and even straighter nose, his cut jawline - she wondered why he would still be on the market. With his fit, athletic body,

THE BEACHFRONT SURPRISES.

handsome face, and wealth, Quinn figured he could get any woman he chose. So why was he chasing after her so much?

He cocked his head. "I wanted to order for you, but at the same time, I knew you probably wouldn't like that. So I didn't. But why do I think that... Tell you what, let me guess what you'd like to eat on this menu, and you can tell me how close I am. Okay, ready?"

Quinn wondered if he was trying to play a little game, and she had to admit he was just a bit charming. Something about his demeanor made her think of a small boy trying to please a small girl. There was just something about his earnestness that made her think that way.

Two courses were a straight $75, and she would choose the grey lady oysters for her appetizer. The dayboat scallops, served with corn, beans, tomatoes, zucchini and basil, would be her main course. She was also craving sweets, so she had her eye on the apple galette - apples mixed with rosemary, brown butter, and ice cream.

She'd already decided that Asher wasn't going to pay for her meal, so she didn't feel guilty ordering an expensive dessert on top of the meal. Plus, she was going to order a Bloody Mary or two. That was another thing about Quinn – she never wanted anyone to pay her way. She felt guilty if anybody did, so she always tried to get the very cheapest thing on the menu if somebody else was paying.

Asher looked at her with a sly grin on his face. "The scallops, right?"

Quinn was astounded he was able to guess her meal so correctly. And then she wondered if he was secretly a mindreader. In which case, she better watch out - she was having some randy thoughts about this guy, even if she'd never admit that to him. Never in a million years.

She consciously tried to get the lustful thoughts out of her mind.

She crossed her arms in front of her and shook her head. "No." She would never admit he was able to size her up so correctly and so swiftly.

Asher looked confused. "I was sure you'd want the scallops. Okay, then, I guess you're going to have either the salmon, the swordfish, or the catch of the day."

Quinn raised an eyebrow. "And why do you assume I would only get things off the seafood menu?"

Asher leaned back in his chair. "Because I see you as somebody who'd like to be a vegan but doesn't want to go all the way. I think you love animals, and you don't like to see suffering. Yet, at the same time, I don't see you going all the way into veganism. Or even vegetarianism."

Quinn swallowed hard. She was thrown completely off balance on how well this guy could read her and wondered again if he had a mind-reading skill.

"And why did you think that I'd want the scallops, as opposed to the sole or the salmon?"

Asher shrugged his shoulders. "I don't know. I somehow see you as somebody who likes a shellfish better than an actual fish. I think it's because the shellfish doesn't really have a face, and it seems much less like an animal to you than a fish with eyes and a mouth."

Quinn didn't even think about that angle, although he was probably right. She did prefer the shellfish – shrimp, scallops, mussels, oysters. And she *did* feel that these particular creatures were not as much of a life as the ones with a face. However irrational that was, that was how she felt.

She took a deep breath. What should she do? Admit this guy had a read on her already? That would make her vulnerable to his charms.

She was determined that wasn't going to happen.

At the same time, she couldn't order anything that involved meat. She hadn't had meat in at least 20 years.

"Actually, I was going to order the Moroccan-spiced eggplant parmesan." That sounded good to her, now that she thought about it. It was eggplant served with a red sauce, spinach, fresh mozzarella, roasted peppers, honeyed onions, mint, feta, and sesame-spiced chickpeas.

Asher seemed crestfallen, but then his face brightened. "How about we go double or nothing on the appetizer."

"Okay, you're on." Quinn *was* going to order the oysters, but not if this guy figured it out before she ever said a word.

He smiled. "This is really easy. The oysters."

Quinn tried to keep her face as impassive as possible, but it was difficult. "Why do you think I want the oysters?"

"Because I still think you won't eat meat because you have a heart for animals. So, that leaves out everything on the menu but the salmon, the oysters and the island lettuces. I don't think you want the lettuces. That's just a glorified salad. And with the salmon, again, it has a face. That leaves the oysters."

Quinn felt shocked, although she really shouldn't have been.

"How good are you in front of juries?" she asked.

While she knew Asher never actually practiced in front of juries at the moment, he used to, having once been a personal injury attorney. And, with his intuition, he probably was excellent at choosing a jury. Having gut instincts goes a long way in finding the right panel.

"I'm one of the best there is. In fact, even though I'm not doing jury trials anymore, I still consult for trial attorneys. Why do you ask?"

"Just had a feeling, that's all. I will say this, though. If I ever get hit by a bus, I want you to try the case. Anyhow, let's get down to business. How much are you going to charge me to have my adoption set aside?"

The waitress came around and took their orders. Quinn

decided to bite the bullet and order the oysters, even though she was proving him right. She also ordered the eggplant parmesan because she didn't want to prove him *that* right, along with a Bloody Mary. Asher ordered the Scottish salmon appetizer, the swordfish for dinner and a Tanqueray and Tonic for his drink.

Asher took a deep breath. "You have dinner with me again, and I'll do it for you for free."

Quinn was ready to get up and walk away from this entire scenario.

"Nope, not doing that. I talked to your assistant, and I understand it's $1,000 an hour for people like me. All you need to do is tell me how many hours it will take you to have the adoption set aside, and I'll figure it out for myself. But there's no way I'm going to just let you do this case for me for free."

Quinn glared at him and his presumptuousness. Who did he think he was, trying to sneak in more social outings with her? She'd made it clear she was all business, but he evidently wasn't getting the hint.

"Okay, you got me. Let's just call it 10 hours. That's probably how long it's going to take. However, before the adoption is finalized, you're going to have to go through foster care training and have a home study done. That will take several months, but after you complete all that, you can have her under your roof. That's where I'm going to come in to have your adoption finalized."

Quinn cocked her head. She'd done research on her own about the foster care thing, and she'd hoped she could somehow bypass that since she was the biological mother. "Is there any way possible I can get her under my roof before I complete all that foster care business? Can't you just have the adoption set aside or reversed?"

"It doesn't work like that, at least not in the state of Massachusetts. There are some states where you could have the adoption reversed, but generally, once you sign the adoption papers, your parental rights are severed. But I'm going to investigate on your behalf and make sure all the i's are dotted and the t's are crossed. I'll take a look at your adoption paperwork, and I'm going to investigate to see if anybody was designated as a guardian. Obviously, if there was a designated guardian, it'll be much more complicated for you to adopt her. Not impossible, but complicated. I would have to get the new guardian's permission and so forth, but it would be doable."

"Thank you."

Quinn was happy this guy would be so thorough, even if he wasn't sure she'd actually get Emerson. And, although she didn't want to admit it, she found him extremely attractive. And he was. Objectively. He also impressed her with his amazing instincts, even though that also unnerved her.

"You're welcome." The bread basket arrived, and Asher put some butter on his bread and popped some into his mouth. "Listen, I'm doing this because I really like you. I don't even know why I have a great feeling about you, but I do. I also think I know how you feel about having your daughter in the system. I grew up in the system myself, and I wouldn't wish that on anybody."

Really? This guy wasn't always a handsome, wealthy attorney with a multimillion-dollar house in a very exclusive area of Nantucket?

Quinn was intrigued, but she didn't want to pry.

"That must've been rough."

"It was. I never knew my mother. She died giving birth to me. She had eclampsia or something like that. She was only 15, and she lived in the slums of Dorchester, which is one of the roughest areas of Boston. She never named my father on the birth certificate, and I don't think she knew who he was.

Her parents were still alive when I was born, but they didn't want to raise a kid. So, I went into the foster system."

"But, you were adopted, right?" Quinn couldn't imagine a guy like Asher being in the foster system and not being adopted by somebody. She knew there were scores of parents lined up to adopt a kid like Asher.

"Well, I was, eventually. Because I went into the system, families took me on a trial basis. It was like leasing a car to buy it later on. However, one foster family after another decided I wasn't quite right. Something would always come up, and they wouldn't be able to adopt me, so I was shuffled from one family to another."

Quinn leaned forward. She was interested in his story, despite herself. "That sounds like a nightmare," she said.

He shrugged. "It wasn't that big of a deal, except for some of the families clearly were just after the money they would get from the state and didn't want to raise a child. And I couldn't read at seven years old. My teachers didn't know why. The family I was living with thought I was a special needs kid, so they didn't want to deal with me."

Quinn was impressed this guy had to overcome so many obstacles in his life. He didn't strike her as somebody who would've had a learning disability.

"How did you overcome your learning disability?" she asked.

"It turned out I just had a severe case of dyslexia. I didn't know that, and neither did that family. They thought I was a kid who couldn't learn, and they wanted somebody who was more ready-made, I guess you could say."

The guy was talking about his troubles so matter-of-factly that Quinn cynically thought maybe he wasn't telling the truth. He was a lawyer. And, as such, he was undoubtedly good at spinning tall tales into gold. He'd already shown he was a silver-tongued devil.

Yet, there was something in his eyes that made Quinn think maybe he was telling the truth.

"So, how did that work out? How did you figure out your problem was dyslexia, not that you were a slow learner?"

"Well, you have to understand, for my first seven or eight years, I was shuffled around to families who didn't have a lot of money. So the school districts that I went to were piss-poor, and that's the technical term for it. Those schools barely had enough money for special education classes. So I fell through the cracks."

The first course came around, along with Quinn's Bloody Mary and Asher's Tanqueray and Tonic. Quinn took one bite of the oysters and knew she'd made the right choice. They were served with a fresh cucumber granita and a kumquat vinaigrette that lent sweetness to the dish.

Asher silently cut off a piece of his appetizer and put it on Quinn's plate. Quinn did the same for him, giving him one of her oysters.

Was she relaxing? Maybe. Asher's hard-luck background and overcoming it impressed her, and she knew there was more to him than what met the eye.

But he was still a guy, Quinn reminded herself. And men hadn't interested her in all these years. For good reason. It would take a lot more than a hard-luck story to turn her head at this point.

"So, what happened? How did you get help?" Quinn asked while she silently moaned with pleasure about the delicious food and equally tasty Bloody Mary. The drink was just as Quinn loved it - spicy, salty, tangy and strong.

"Well, my next family was a suburban family, and I went to a much better school district. The teachers understood my problem, and I got the help I needed. I quickly caught up to all my peers. I ended up graduating valedictorian. That's the reason I'm so passionate about education reform."

Quinn cocked her head. He certainly was different than she thought. Maybe she didn't really give him a chance.

"What do you do for education reform?"

"I'm on the board for the Cape and Islands chapter of the United Way. I also give millions to nationwide educational reform charities. I think these poor schools don't give our kids a chance to succeed. How can you learn when there are 35 kids in your class? I also know special education is really underfunded. We don't need to give all schools more money, just the poor ones. The schools in the rich areas do just fine for themselves."

The waiter came back around, and the dinners were presented to them after the appetizer plates were bussed.

Quinn dug into her food, looking up at Asher every once in a while, still trying to figure out if she could trust this guy. Yes, he seemed like a sincere do-gooder. Quinn loved nothing more than a man who had integrity and heart. But Charles seemed that way too. He knew how to speak all the words Quinn wanted to hear. He was the last man who managed to pierce her defenses, and she swore he would indeed be the last, period.

Quinn finally just nodded her head. "And that's the reason why you got into domestic law?"

"Yeah. To tell the truth, that is the reason why. I mean, I was making millions a year when I was a personal injury attorney, and that was a very satisfying job. There's nothing more satisfying than getting a really big settlement for a client who deserves it and sticking it to The Man in the process. But, I also knew that my heart lay with custody cases."

"What drew you into family law and custody cases?"

"The children are so innocent, and they need an advocate. Otherwise, they're voiceless. So I started getting into custody cases after making my money in personal injury, and I really

THE BEACHFRONT SURPRISES.

liked it. Yes, yes, the high-dollar divorces pay for my yearly month-long jaunts to Switzerland to ski, it pays for the chalet I have there in Zürich, it pays for the beachside house here, the yacht and the jet. I'll admit it. But those high-dollar divorces really don't get my juices flowing."

"What does get your juices flowing?" Quinn asked. She was digging into her eggplant, and she really loved it. The fresh mozzarella combined well with the feta and mint, and the chickpea side had just enough heat to make it interesting.

Once again, Asher put some of his salmon on her plate. It was slow-poached and served with a vinaigrette and a sauce gribiche, which was apparently a French sauce made by emulsifying egg yolks, tarragon, olive oil, mustard and capers. Quinn took a bite of his salmon and rolled her eyes with pleasure.

She should've ordered the salmon. Her eggplant was delicious, but this salmon was out of this world.

Asher nodded his head as he took a sip of his drink and continued to eat the salmon. "The things that get my juices flowing are the looks in the children's eyes when I go to bat for them and get them what they want out of their parent's divorce. And, by far, the best part of my practice is the court-appointed work I do in my Boston office, and trust me, I get paid diddly squat for that. But that's the most rewarding work. Because in that kind of work, you're purely advocating for the child."

"What is your court-appointed work?"

"I get appointed by the court to become the child's counsel. You get warring parents or some kind of allegations of abuse or neglect, and the minor's counsel gets to the bottom of it and makes recommendations to the court about what should happen. You talk to everybody who knows the kid, and talk to the kid and see what they want to do. I know when I do that work, I'm really helping somebody. That was the reason I got into law in the first place. So, everybody wins, except for an abusive parent who wants custody of a child. They don't win, not when I'm the counsel for the minor."

Quinn took a deep breath. She had to be very careful. If she wasn't, she would fall for this guy, hook, line, and sinker. That was the last thing she wanted.

"Well, at any rate, I'm really happy you're going to be working on my case. And trust me, your bills are going to be paid promptly. No problem there. In fact, I'd like to pay you extra since you're going out of your way to do this for me."

The two sat in the restaurant for the next couple of hours, chatting easily like friends. Quinn even admitted to him how Emerson was conceived. She was still loathe to tell that story to anybody except her two best friends, who were there for all of it. Yet, she found herself telling him about it, and she saw in his eyes two pools of sympathy.

To his credit, he didn't try any macho "I'd like to ring that guy's neck" nonsense because that would just turn her off if he did. He just quietly put his hands on hers and squeezed.

By the time Quinn arrived home, she was feeling out of sorts. The dinner with Asher didn't go the way she thought it would. She really thought before the dinner that he was a cocky rich dude, and he was. There was no disputing that. He was cocky, and he was definitely rich. But he was also so much more than that.

That's what confused her.

And the food was divine.

****

Two days later, Quinn got some amazing news.

"You're never going to believe this, but Emerson's parents designated you as her guardian in their will. So, now we just have to go to court and apply for custody. As long as the judge decides it's in the child's best interest to honor Emerson's late parents' wishes, Emerson should be under your roof within a week. I'll get the case fast-tracked."

Quinn was confused. "I don't understand. They designated me as her guardian if they passed away? I thought I had to consent to that."

"Well, generally, it's a good idea that the pending guardian consents to the arrangement. But it's not necessary. It's a risk because sometimes the designated guardian refuses the guardianship, but in this case, you want it. Everybody wants it. So, I don't see a problem."

Quinn took a deep breath. This was going to happen. It was really going to happen.

She was going to finally be a mother.

Her life was about to change.

CHAPTER 8

AVA

Ava was working at her bed-and-breakfast - cleaning every surface until they gleamed, scrubbing the toilets and the bathtubs, lighting candles, vacuuming, dusting, mopping, doing laundry and making beds, in between greeting guests and taking reservations.

Right when she was in the middle of doing all of that, her mother appeared.

"Hi, mom," Ava said hurriedly. It was a Tuesday, the middle of the day. Why was her mother here? Why wasn't she on the bench?

"Hey," Colleen said. "I need a room. I'm gonna be staying with you for the next six weeks. Hope that's not a problem."

"Hang on," Ava said to her mother, who apparently had lost her frigging mind. "I need to register these guests." And then Ava turned to the young couple who apparently were on their honeymoon - at least, Ava deduced that by the way they pawed at one another while they stood in front of her and her computer.

"Where's a good place to eat?" the woman asked. "And I just can't wait to get to the beach. It's been so long since I've

THE BEACHFRONT SURPRISES.

been to a beach. You just can't imagine. I've been so excited to visit this island. I've heard so much about it. And I just love all the old architecture, how quaint everything is. Don't you?"

Ava shook her head. The woman's stream of consciousness started with a question, but she couldn't, for the life of her, remember what the question was. Her mother was distracting her.

It seemed like her mother said something about needing a room for the next six weeks, but surely Colleen didn't say that. Ava must've been hearing things.

If Ava actually heard her mother tell her she'd be staying with her for six weeks, Ava would lose her mind right then and there.

"What kind of food are you looking for?" Colleen asked the couple. "If you're looking for high-dollar fancy stuff, I'd direct you to the Straight Wharf in the historic district. Or maybe Toppers, in the Wauwinet Hotel. Great seafood, great steaks, great everything. But high dollar. For burgers, I'd try Lola's. Pizza, Foggy Nantucket. You want some brunch, Black-Eyed Susan's. I also hear the menu right here in this place is pretty damn good. You got some nice choices."

The woman smiled and nodded at Colleen. "Thank you. You know what, I think I might try the food here today. I hear this place has awesome balconies attached to the rooms, and there's a killer terrace with tables and loungers and hot tubs. Maybe we'll just eat in."

Ava gave the woman the key card for her room, and the woman and her guy walked up the stairs, arm in arm. And then Ava faced her mother. "Mom, I know I didn't hear you tell me you're going to be staying here for six weeks. I know I must've been hearing things. Some kind of auditory hallucination. And if I did hear those words coming out of your mouth, I know you were joking, and I can tell you it's not funny."

"You see me laughing? Listen, the chief judge told me I needed to take a vacation. So, here I am. Gonna spend the next six weeks lounging by the beach and having you wait on me hand and foot. After all, this place wouldn't exist without me and my money. So, as I see it, I have a free room coming to me at the very minimum. And, I'd like one facing the beach."

Ava closed her eyes and counted to 10. This *was not* happening. Her mother *did not* tell her she would take one of her prime rooms for six weeks during her busy season. Colleen *did not* just say she would deprive Ava of $400 a night x six weeks, which would come to about $17,000 of lost income. Not to mention, Ava and her mother were like oil and water. Her mother always caused her a great deal of stress just by being around.

Colleen would be following her around everywhere, criticizing everything she did, for six whole weeks?

No. This could not be happening.

"Mom, be reasonable. I can't just give you a beach-facing room for six whole weeks. That'll cost me around $17,000 in lost income."

Her mother rolled her eyes. "Really? Are you really going to play that card on me? When I gave you hundreds of thousands of dollars to renovate this place from stem to stern? Seriously? Why don't I just call my note in right now, and then sue your ass if you can't pay it? I can do that, you know, according to the agreement we made when I gave you that money."

"Mom, be reasonable. You're getting 10% of the profits." The acceleration clause made Ava hesitant to sign that note, but she had no other choice. She hated knowing that Colleen could call in the note at any time. Ava worried that Colleen

THE BEACHFRONT SURPRISES.

could pull some kind of shenanigans, and, lo and behold, here was her mother pulling just that.

"Yes. You're right. I *am* getting 10% of the profits," Colleen said. "But I also have a note, and you know it. You know I can call in that note at any time, and I will if you don't let me stay here for six weeks. If I got a judgment against you, I could attach that judgment to your house. From what you tell me, that would be a violation of the terms of the bequeathment. You would lose this house and be out on your rear."

Ava knew she was over a barrel. Her mother was going to be staying with her, and nothing could be done about it.

She felt like crying. It was stressful enough trying to run this place on her own. Now she had to worry about her mother coming in behind her and bitching about every little issue possible? Colleen was impossible to please. Plus, she and her mother just didn't like each other. Ava did love her mother, but she didn't like her. What was there to like? She never got a kind word from her mother, ever. Her mother made her feel like she was completely incompetent and unable to do anything right.

"Okay, you win. But all those rooms are occupied now, and I have a reservation for all of them as well. I guess I'm just going to have to cancel one of the reservations. You can have the room on the west side of the house. The couple in there now has to check out at 2 o'clock today. As soon as they check out, I'll clean it up, and you can stay there."

Colleen nodded her head. "That would be fine. I'm not so unreasonable that I would make you toss somebody out of their room before their time. I'll go down to the beach and come back up at three. That should give you enough time to make my new room white-glove clean." Then she smiled sweetly. "So, I'll see you in a few hours. For now, I'm going to the beach."

Ava watched her mother walking out the door and felt

her blood pressure rise. What was she going to do now? Just when she thought her life was getting together - she'd come through the stress of getting the house in order and everything was going great for herself, her children, and her friends - here was her mother, like a dark cloud about to burst into rain.

She was going to have to think about that later. She typically had breathing room in the evening – after everybody was checked in for the day, she would typically spend some time on her terrace, just like before, drinking wine and staring at the surf. She knew what she was going to be contemplating that evening. Her mother.

****

That evening, after Ava scrubbed the room where Colleen would be staying, and Colleen was resting comfortably in that room, Ava called an emergency meeting with her girls. That was a signal it was time to drop everything and come together. She only liked to call these emergency meetings when it truly was an emergency.

And, in her eyes, nothing could be more of an emergency than this.

CHAPTER 9

AVA

"Now, tell me what's going on," Quinn asked Ava that evening. Quinn, Ava, Sarah, Hallie and Willow were gathered together at Quinn's home. Bottles of wine were opened, pizzas were on the way, and everybody was ready and eager to hear Ava's news.

Willow didn't always join the ladies, but Ava asked that she be there. Willow struck her as somebody who not only was amazingly intuitive, but was actually psychic. There was no getting around that fact – Willow knew things she had no business knowing. At any rate, she knew Willow would have some insight that maybe the other ladies wouldn't necessarily have, just because that was the kind of person she was.

"My mom. She's come to stay for the next six weeks. And to say this is stressing me out would be understating the matter."

Willow nodded her head. "Your mom. There's something she's keeping from you. A couple of things, actually. I don't know what they are, but that's just the feeling I get. And, dude, they're major things. I wonder if these huge secrets are why your mother dropped in on you like this."

Ava snorted. She couldn't help herself. Her mother, and keeping secrets? Yeah, right. Her mother was blunt, honest. Too honest. She was a woman who didn't mince words, and you never had to wonder what she thought because she always told you exactly what was on her mind. Even if what was on her mind was hurtful and devastating, her mother would verbalize it without even batting an eyelash.

Ava sometimes wondered if her mother was on the spectrum. Maybe she had Asperger's Syndrome. One of the hallmarks of that particular syndrome was that the person who suffered from it simply didn't take social cues when speaking. But Ava decided her mother probably didn't have an undiagnosed case of Asperger's Syndrome, because she didn't display any signs of it other than how she blurted out whatever she was thinking. No, her mother was just a cold, mean person.

There was no medical diagnosis for Colleen unless being a jerk was considered a medical condition.

"Listen, Ava, think of this as an opportunity," Sarah said. "You and mom have never seen eye to eye. To say the least. But I've always gotten along with her. I've always wanted you to also get along with her. Maybe this is a chance for the two of you to finally make nice."

Ava closed her eyes, feeling her blood pressure rise. "You've always gotten along with our mother because she's always been nice to you. I've tried to please her, but there's just no pleasing her when it comes to me. I don't know what I'm supposed to do to make my relationship with our mother better somehow. It takes two people to make a good relationship, and if she's not going to do her part, then we can't get along."

"I'm just saying, maybe our mother is reaching out in her way. You can't discount that possibility. You'd be so much happier if you had a good relationship with our mother. You could stop being jealous of my relationship with her, which always has been a thorn in your side, I know."

Ava looked over at Hallie, who was sipping her wine and looking at Ava meaningfully. "Ava, why don't you send your mother over to our spa? She could certainly use some relaxation. After all, she's been working as a Circuit Court judge for quite a few years without much of a break. I couldn't imagine anything more stressful than your mother's life. Send her over. Willow will do some acupuncture and maybe crystal therapy if your mom's game for that. I can tell you that Willow works miracles, just from my own experience."

Willow nodded at Ava. "That's a good idea. I'd love to meet your mother. As I said, I feel there's something your mother isn't telling you. There's some reason why your mother has always been mean to you. Some reason that has absolutely nothing to do with you."

"Okay," Ava said. "I'll send my mother your way. Maybe you can work your magic, Willow, and turn my mother into a kind person."

Willow smiled. "I can work magic, but I can't make your mother be nicer to you. Free will and all that. That's all down to you. But I think if I met her, I probably could get some kind of read on her issues. Once I can figure that out, maybe you can do something about it."

"Well, it couldn't hurt," Ava said, taking a sip of her wine. "Now where is that pizza?"

As if by magic, Quinn's doorbell rang. She came back in with two pizzas – one which was all veggie, which was what she and Sarah usually ate, and the other one was a chicken bacon ranch, the pizza that everybody else loved.

"I come bearing gifts," Quinn announced. "Now, let's dig in. And Ava, you're burying the lede. What's going on with you and Deacon?"

Ava felt her heart start to race just at the thought of her handsome contractor crush. "Nothing. Why?"

"I was thinking about it," Quinn said. "The man can play the piano, that's for sure. I know you thought you wouldn't see him anymore now that the house is done. What if you hire him to play piano for your guests once a week or something like that?"

Ava took a bite of her pizza, her all-time favorite flavor. The smoked chicken blended so well with the cheese, bacon, jalapeño ranch dressing and buttery crust. "You know, I never even thought of that angle. It would be a way to still see him. Even if I can't have a relationship with him."

"And why couldn't you have a relationship with him?" Hallie asked. "He's so good and kind and intelligent."

"Not to mention, he's *really* easy on the eyes," Quinn added as she mock-fanned herself.

Ava smiled at the ladies. "He is all those things. He's also 19 years younger than me."

"So?" Sarah asked. "What does that have to do with the price of tea in China? Who cares that he's a lot younger than you? If you're into him and he's into you, you should go for it. I love you, sis, but you're always so cautious about romantic relationships."

Ava was tempted to throw in Sarah's face that maybe she, Sarah, should've been a bit more cautious about romantic relationships. Because if Sarah were more cautious, she wouldn't have gotten into the situation she was in, that of giving up her life and career to follow a man who wasn't worth the wax in Willow's candles. But, Ava bit her tongue, not wanting to reopen an old wound.

"Well, we'll just have to see how things go," Ava said. "Now, let's eat. I'm starving. That's always a problem with me, you know. Stress makes me just want to chow down. If I gain 20 pounds in the next six weeks because I'm stress

THE BEACHFRONT SURPRISES.

eating, and I have to go to Weight Watchers or Jenny Craig or something like that after mom leaves, I'm sending her the bill."

Ava was only partly joking about that.

"I've always been the exact opposite," Sarah said, taking a piece of pizza. "Whenever I'm under stress, I can't even look at food."

"Which is why I've always had a problem with my weight, and you've always been thin as a rail," Ava said pointedly. "Apparently, neither of us handles stress very well."

Hallie was chowing down on a piece of vegetable pizza. She'd already eaten a piece of the chicken bacon ranch, which tended to be a very heavy pie. So, she always liked to chase the chicken bacon ranch pizza with the lighter vegetable one. "I, for one, like the idea of Deacon coming to play the piano at your inn. He seemed to really get into it when he played at your party. I think you should make the offer to him. See if he bites. By the way, how are things going over there?"

"Well, it's tough trying to manage everything on my own. But I think I've got it down to a science. I check people in between nine in the morning and two in the afternoon. I check people out between two in the afternoon and three. Then I clean the vacated rooms like a demon between 3 o'clock and 5 o'clock. Then I check more people in between five and six, and after that, my work is done."

Ava knew she would have to put strict timing on her check-ins and checkouts. It was the only way things were going to work. So, when people called to make a reservation, Ava explained they had to be checked in between nine and two, or between five and six. That hadn't been a problem, at least so far.

The most stressful part of her day was between three and five o'clock, because that was when all the spit polishing was done. She had to change the bedding, vacuum, mop, dust and scrub the toilets and bathtubs down to where everything was spic-and-span. And sometimes she had to do that for every room in the house, because, on occasion, everybody left at the same time. That was a lot of work to get done in two hours. Yet, it was invigorating. It was hard physical work doing all that on her own, but it was gratifying all the same, because she prided herself on providing the best experience possible.

She knew when she finally was able to take a break in the evening that it was a break well-earned. Still, she was working nine-hour days, and it would have to be seven days a week. She hoped she didn't get burned out the way she did with her law practice. Keeping that kind of schedule, the possibility of burning out was definitely on her mind.

She knew she should probably hire somebody, but she didn't know where to start looking for help. She was also hesitant to take on help, at least until she was sure the place was going to be a success and she would have enough money to get her through the lean season, which was going to be after Labor Day.

It didn't help that her mother was threatening to call in the note and intimating she would get a lien against the house. A lien would destroy Ava's bequeathment, which would, in turn, lead Ava to lose the house altogether. So, Ava was nervous. She hated having her mother's note hanging above her head. She knew her mother wouldn't hesitate to use that note to manipulate her, much like she already did when she finagled her way into staying at Ava's inn for free for six weeks.

Because of all this, Ava was extremely hesitant to hire somebody to help her out at the inn. She was going to keep doing everything herself, at least for the time being. Maybe in a few years, when she had her mother paid off, she could breathe easy. But, for now, it was what it was. Ava would have to work long hours to keep her guests happy and the word-of-mouth going.

Ava munched on some pizza as she contemplated the possibility of bringing Deacon in as a draw. She started offering dinner on the weekends and found that it was a popular idea. Many of her guests enjoyed having an early dinner on the terrace with a glass of Sarah-recommended wine to go perfectly with their meal. And then they would either head out to the nightlife or go down to the beach and build a bonfire.

It would be fun to have some musical accompaniment to their meals, and Deacon would be just the guy to provide this, Ava thought. And it wouldn't cost too much for her to take him on because he'd be playing for only a few hours a week. It wouldn't be like trying to hire somebody full-time, so she'd be able to swing his salary.

"I'll definitely think about bringing him in," Ava said. "I'll give him a call tonight."
****

After Ava had a few glasses of wine, she called Deacon.

"Hiya," Deacon said in his friendly manner. "Ava. I was just going to call you. How've you been? How's the bed-and-breakfast so far?"

Ava felt her heart pounding. "It's great. I mean, it's only been a week, but it's been one hell of a week. The place has been full every day, thanks to your beautiful handiwork in making the house look spectacular. Anyhow, the reason I'm calling is because I think you're an amazing piano player. And I have that baby grand that can be moved into the dining room. But I don't have anybody to play it."

"Say no more. When would you like me to come in and play for your guests?"

"How about Saturday night? And maybe you could play

every Saturday night? I mean, assuming you don't have a date or something like that. I mean, I know you have a life, and I respect that. So, if you ever need to not play on a Saturday night, I'll understand."

He laughed lightly. "Saturday nights will be great," he said. "I'll be looking forward to it. I love to play for people. I love the feedback, and, I'll admit it, I love the applause. I've even been writing some original music I'm anxious to put out into the world. Your guests can be my guinea pigs."

"Great," Ava said.

"Ava, there is something I needed to talk to about." He paused. "That kiss the other night. I've not been able to get it out of my mind. I'd like for that to happen more often."

Ava drew a breath. Was this really happening? Was her dream crush from the past nine months or so actually telling her he wanted to be with her? Or at least, kiss her again? She closed her eyes. And then she blurted out the words her brain was screaming, but her heart was contradicting just as loudly.

"Deacon, I'm so sorry. I mean, that kiss meant everything to me as well. And I'll confess, I haven't been able to get the kiss off my mind either. But, you're just too young."

Ava never wanted to get involved with anybody unless she saw a future. She could just picture herself falling head over heels for the guy, only to find him taking up with a woman his age because he probably wanted kids of his own. Just like Ashton Kutcher and Demi Moore. Ashton married Demi knowing that Demi could no longer have children because she was past childbearing age. Then they divorced, and Ashton had children of his own, which was probably his plan all along. Even Demi admitted their age gap was probably why they ended up breaking up.

Why get started when the odds were so against the two of

THE BEACHFRONT SURPRISES.

them making it work? Why head into something she knew would end with her broken heart?

Perhaps she was overthinking it. Perhaps not. But she wasn't going to give herself a chance to find out.

"I see. So, that's it? I'm 35 and you're 54, and that means that we're just not even going to see where this goes?" Deacon asked.

Ava nodded her head, knowing that Deacon couldn't see that nonverbal cue. "Yes," she said with great reluctance. "I'm sorry. But I know you're going to find somebody your own age. Even if you and I took this journey to see where it went, I just think you would end up with someone who's a bit more Occam's Razor, if you will. The most logical scenario is the one that's going to be fact. And the most logical scenario here is that some young woman will turn your head, and I'll be forgotten. So, I think it's best we remain friends."

Deacon was quiet. He finally spoke, after about a minute of radio silence. "So, am I still going to play piano?"

"I was hoping you would. You're a lovely player, and I think you would be an amazing draw for the guests. You could provide the extra value-added that'll keep the word-of-mouth going for my place. So, I hope I don't discourage you from playing for my guests and me."

Ava didn't tell him the real reason why she wanted him to play. The truth was, she wanted to keep him close to her. Even if she couldn't have him, she wanted to see him. To be near him. To keep his friendship close. Because, if Ava were honest with herself, she would admit the possibility of not seeing him anymore would be devastating. So, in the end, she wanted him for her own selfish reasons.

"Okay, then, mate. I guess I'll be seeing you on Saturday evening. What time do you want me to come over and play?"

"How about six? That's about when the guests like to start dinner. They like to eat early a lot of times so they can go out and see the town or head out to the beach for some fun bonfires. And then, of course, I get some guests who like to eat a bit later. So I typically see shifts of people between 6 o'clock and, say, 9 o'clock. So, that would be the times I'd want you to play. Would that be okay?"

"Sure, mate. That would be great. I'll see you then."

"See you then."

As Ava hung up, her gut was screaming at her that she was doing the absolutely wrong thing. There was a part of her that thought Deacon was right for her. The ladies were right about him. He was kind and intelligent and so easy on the eyes.

But, the part that controlled her, her brain, was telling her Deacon was exactly wrong for her. And Ava always let her brain rule over her heart.

Maybe that was the reason why she was alone.

CHAPTER 10

COLLEEN

*A*va had encouraged Colleen to go to a place called The Willow Tree Spa and Relaxation Center, and Colleen had booked an appointment. It sounded like this place was what she was looking for, as far as relaxation went. She'd always believed in acupuncture, even if she never actually went in for the procedure. The other services that the place offered – herbalism, Crystal therapy and Reiki, not to mention tarot reading and astrological charts – seemed ridiculous to her. But, that wasn't a problem because she wouldn't indulge herself in those services.

She found the place easily enough. After all, this was a very small island, so it was difficult to get lost. She was amazed so many people could pack themselves into such a small space, and traffic was terrible because the island didn't have stoplights. Colleen thought that was really dumb – how are 50,000 people on a small island supposed to navigate traffic without stoplights? Yet, that was exactly what she was faced with on Nantucket. She did like the architecture because nothing was run down, and there were no ugly strip malls and homely and boring midcentury architecture to mar the landscape.

The Willow Tree Spa was housed in a large Cape Cod home right in the heart of the historic district. She walked in, smelled the incense, and smiled. It reminded her of her Vassar days, when she used to burn incense in her dorm room when she wasn't burning her bras. Her hair was long and straight back then, and her legs were nice, so she wore a lot of miniskirts and high boots, which was always the fashion. She was always into causes – agitating against the war, protesting oil drilling, saving the whales, protesting the male-dominated hierarchy, marching for civil rights and women's rights, protesting pesticides, protesting the death penalty - Colleen did it all.

Nowadays, she wondered what all that protesting, sit-ins and marching did. Men, especially white men, still ruled. Women still got paid a lot less for doing the same job as a man. The country was still dependent upon oil. We still got into stupid wars. The use of pesticides had only gotten worse. Civil rights were still an issue, as was the backlash against these rights. The whales were no longer in as much danger as they were when Colleen was in college, so that was one thing.

Yet, when Colleen was in college, she was still a fresh-faced idealist who somehow believed her voice, in concert with millions of other young voices, would change the world. She was not yet the cynical 78-year-old woman who had seen too much, both in her personal life and on the bench, to ever believe the utopian society she once thought possible could ever happen.

But the smell of the incense brought her back to those days when she thought all was possible if you just believed and acted on those beliefs. So, she immediately felt relaxed and cheerful when she walked into the beautiful spa.

THE BEACHFRONT SURPRISES.

Hallie was already there and came up and gave her a hug. Colleen hugged her back. She'd always liked the girl. She'd known Hallie since her days of banging the gavel for the District Court of Kansas City. Ava used to bring Hallie home to stay with them whenever they had a break from college. And, sometimes, Ava went to stay with Hallie in St. Louis, where Hallie's family lived.

There was another girl there at the spa. Somebody Colleen didn't know. She had dark hair and green eyes and had the most beautiful skin Colleen had ever seen. She was almost luminous, as many women were at her age, which seemed to be about 25. Colleen herself was a hottie at that age. Maybe not quite as much of a hottie as this girl was, but she held her own, and she knew it.

"Colleen, welcome," Hallie said enthusiastically. "This is my healing partner – Willow Killeen."

Willow studied Colleen. That was the only word that came to Colleen's mind when she saw the beautiful young woman looking at her – and that was she was studying her. She had narrowed eyes and pursed lips, and, at some point, she raised an eyebrow and shook her head.

Colleen felt uncomfortable. Like she was under a microscope. It was as if she were made of glass, and the girl was looking right through her.

After a few minutes, Willow just nodded her head slightly. "Come on back. Have you ever done acupuncture before?"

"No, I haven't."

"Well, you're in for a good experience," Willow said. "But, you know, you've had a major loss sometime in the past year. You have all this stuck energy that's concentrated in your chest. The energy from this loss is so palpable I can see it. Like an aura. I don't usually see auras around people, but, every so once in a while, I can, in people who are suffering major unacknowledged grief."

Hallie looked over at Colleen, then turned to Willow. "Willow, I don't usually say this, but I don't think you're correct. Colleen hasn't suffered a close death, not since her husband died when Ava was only five. So, you must be sensing something else."

Willow raised an eyebrow. "No, Hallie, you're the one who's wrong. You're not sensitive like I am, but if you were, you would understand this is a woman who's like the walking wounded."

Colleen should've been offended by Willow's blunt talk to her, not to mention she was openly talking about her in front of her face, but she wasn't. She was too busy feeling intrigued that Willow was able to uncover her secret so quickly. Back in the day, when she was at Vassar, she knew young girls like Willow. Sensitive, gifted, psychic.

She followed Willow into the back of the spa. She somewhat knew the procedure for acupuncture. Stick a bunch of needles in her head and palms and the soles of her feet. She was never exactly clear what these needles were supposed to accomplish, but she knew the procedure had been around for thousands of years. As she figured, if it didn't work, like some Dr. Oz BS cure, the practice would've died out long ago.

She lay down on a table and looked at Willow. She knew she had to ask her some questions before it was time to drift off into la la land.

"How did you know?" she asked her.

Willow shrugged her shoulders. "It's a gift. But I'm trying to figure out why you always felt the need to hide. Do you think your daughters would really be offended by your loving a woman?"

Colleen felt a chill when Willow said those words. It was a contradiction in her psyche, and she had so many of them.

Her close friends, including the Chief Judge, knew about her relationship with Violet. She'd met her friends for dinner and drinks with Violet by her side. Nobody cared.

And the strange thing was, she knew if she told her daughters, they wouldn't care either. Neither Sarah nor Ava would ever shun her like her own parents would've if they'd ever known about Violet.

Yet, there was still a big part of her that was ashamed of who she was. And she always wanted her daughters to see her in a certain light. That meant she wanted Ava and Sarah to not be privy to the parts of her soul she hadn't come to terms with, even after all these years.

Colleen sighed at Willow's question about why she always hid such a huge part of herself from her daughters. "It's complicated. My brain, it's just so whacked out, I just don't think rationally all the time. My parents, they drilled into my head that homosexuality was wrong. A sin. And there's a part of me that still believes it. So I guess I'm ashamed. And I've never wanted my daughters to see the parts of me I hate."

Willow nodded her head. "Well, maybe my treatment can help you. Part of what I do is release negative energy from your body and mind. And you've had a lifetime of negative energy. All those thoughts, all those cruel words from your parents, and from society, all those lessons about how you're somehow wrong for who you love. It's all gotten trapped inside of you."

Colleen was skeptical that somehow she could just release the shame she had always pushed down about her relationship with Violet. But it was worth a try.

"Can I ask you another personal question?" Willow asked.

"Shoot."

"Does Ava know the truth about her father?"

Colleen's blood immediately got cold.

"What do you mean?"

"I don't really know what I mean," Willow admitted. "It's just a feeling I have that there's something major you're not telling her."

"Just stick those needles in and mind your own business," Colleen ordered.

"Okay," Willow said. "Not going there, I guess."

And then Willow stuck tiny needles into Colleen's forehead, hands, abdomen, chest, and the soles of her feet. Colleen closed her eyes and drifted off and tried not to think about the bombshell that was just dropped on her head.

CHAPTER 11

QUINN

Asher was as good as his word as he filed an emergency motion and fast-tracked a temporary custody hearing. "You simply have to show the court there's an emergency situation, that a delay by the court would result in substantial harm for the kiddo, and that nobody else has the authority to act on Emerson's behalf," Asher explained. "I'll file the motion, along with an affidavit that details why Emerson needs to be under your roof without a hearing, the judge signs the order, and Emerson will be legally under your roof. I'll do all this immediately."

All those steps were taken, and Quinn would soon be getting Emerson under her roof. She'd already met with a family therapist to ask how to help Emerson transition and with the social worker assigned to Emerson's case.

The child was temporarily staying with a foster family in Boston, and Quinn went to pick her up.

The foster family, the Newberrys, consisted of a mousy woman and a strapping, and rather large, man.

The woman, Leona Newberry, spoke so softly that Quinn could hardly hear her, and her body language told Quinn she was very much an introvert and quite shy. Her shoulders slumped, she could barely make eye contact with Quinn, and she had a peculiar habit of wringing her hands. The man, Ralph Newberry, looked like he'd played college football, and was the opposite of his wife. When Quinn appeared on the doorstep, Ralph grinned broadly and extended a meaty hand for Quinn to shake.

"Quinn Jenkins, Ralph Newberry," he said in a booming voice. "This is my wife, Leona, and we're damned glad to meet you." He nodded his head. "Emerson tells us you're her natural mother. I don't mind saying this is probably the weirdest situation we've ever been involved in. Right, Leona?"

Leona just nodded her bowed head and continued to wring her hands. She looked like she wanted to cry, and maybe she did. Emerson had been staying with them for just under a week, and perhaps the poor woman had gotten attached to the young girl. Quinn imagined that the bonding process between a foster mother and foster kid probably happened pretty quickly sometimes.

"Oh, trust me, I know how weird all this is," Quinn said. "It's not every day that a natural mother has to adopt her own kiddo, but here we are. And thanks for looking after her."

Leona nodded her head again. "I'll go and get Emerson," she said, her eyes still not meeting Quinn's.

Leona walked up the stairs and, less than a minute later, reappeared with Emerson in tow. The young girl came down the stairs with a suitcase on wheels and on her back was teddy bear backpack. Quinn raised her eyebrow and Emerson rolled her eyes at Quinn. She was wearing a t-shirt that said *Yeah, you're right, let's do it the dumbest way possible because it's easier for you.*

"Don't ask," she said, her eyes moving towards the teddy bear backpack. "I'll tell you about it when we get in the car."

Quinn just smiled and shook Ralph's hand another time and then shook Leona's hand. "Thanks again to both of you for fostering my Emerson. Well, we'll be on our way."

Ralph smiled again and put his hand on Quinn's shoulder. "Good luck with her," he said. "That one there, she's a pistol, I'll tell ya. A real pistol."

At that, Emerson rolled her eyes, shook her head and said, under her breath, "who uses words like 'pistol' anymore?"

Quinn and Emerson headed to Quinn's SUV, and Quinn made sure Emerson buckled up. "So, how was it, staying with the Newberrys?" Quinn asked her young daughter.

Emerson shrugged her shoulders. "The mom was okay. She really tried to make me feel at home, but she's really lame. I mean, she gave me this teddy bear backpack, like I'm some baby. My mom bought me one of those backpacks when I was three years old. I used to take it to slumber parties with all my clothes and hairbrushes and everything."

"It does seem a little strange that she would buy that for you."

"Oh, she didn't buy it for me. She had it in the house already."

"What do you mean?"

"She had a little daughter who was hit by a car when she was only three, and I guess the backpack belonged to that little girl," Emerson explained. "I really felt sorry for Leona, actually. She's so sad. There's an entire room in that house that's been untouched for years. It belonged to the little girl who died. That's the only reason why I took that backpack without saying anything. I didn't want to hurt her feelings."

Quinn saw a little glimmer of sadness in Emerson's eyes when she talked about the little girl who died. Quinn knew Emerson was struggling with the sudden death of her own parents.

"Honey, I've set up a counseling appointment for you. I think you need somebody to talk to."

"Whatever," Emerson said. "I know, I know, you think I'm just nuts in the head because my parents died so quickly. And, here I am, coming to live with you in this tiny lame town where there's nothing to do. I've already had one counseling thing with a shrink. It was okay. She kept trying to get me to talk about my mom and dad, and I kept telling her I didn't want to. That's what I'm going to tell your counselor, too. I don't want to talk about it, and I'm not gonna."

"You don't have to talk about it, but you do need to go and see this doctor. I don't think you're nuts in the head, but you should still see the counselor. You're only 13 years old. It's hard for people of any age to lose their parents, let alone both of them at the same time."

Quinn didn't really know what else to say to Emerson. What could she say to a 13-year-old girl who'd lost everything she'd ever known in one fell swoop? And now Emerson would have to completely uproot her life and start over with a woman she didn't know. Quinn couldn't imagine a more stressful situation than what Emerson was about to go through.

But Emerson didn't say another word on the way home. She just looked out the window, and then, when the two of them arrived to board the plane to go to Nantucket, she didn't say much except to talk about how tiny the plane was.

"Oh, we're going on a puddle jumper," Emerson said when she saw the small plane on the tarmac. "Great. A flying sardine can. I feel so safe." The sarcasm in her voice left nothing to Quinn's imagination.

"You're not afraid to fly, are you sugar?"

"No." But the look on Emerson's face told Quinn otherwise. "I've never flown before, but how bad can it be? Of

THE BEACHFRONT SURPRISES.

course, I'd feel a lot better if it was one of those jumbo jets, but I can't be picky, can I?"

Quinn smiled, thinking back to her first time on an airplane. It was in the late 80s, and she'd won a trip to Chicago to spend New Year's Eve there. She was upgraded to first class, just because the first-class section had room, and she'd tried lox for the first time. That was back when airlines actually served things like lox, not just peanuts and cookies. It was a large plane, not the "flying sardine can" they were about to fly in.

Truth be told, Quinn never felt comfortable in the small planes either.

"Well, honey, the only planes that go from Boston to Nantucket are these little puddle jumpers. Don't worry, it's safe."

"I know. They always say it's much safer to fly than to drive. But have you ever seen a movie where the plane crashes for real? I have. There was this movie where they show the plane crash in graphic detail, and it doesn't look fun. People screaming and burning to death and stuff like that. Maybe it's safer to fly than to drive, but, trust me, I'd rather die in a car accident than in a plane crash. I mean, think about it, when the plane is going down, you have all this time knowing you're going to bite it in the worst way possible once the plane hits the ground. In a car accident, it just happens like that." Emerson snapped her fingers.

Quinn took a deep breath. "Honey, this plane isn't going to crash."

"And how do you know that? You got some kind of a crystal ball?"

"I just know. I can't remember the last plane crash I've heard about."

"Oh. So you're just playing the odds, then, is that it? Well tell me, Quinn, what are the odds that a health nut freak who's only 44 would go out for a run and drop dead in the street? Probably the same odds this plane will crash, yet that happened with my dad. Sorry, Quinn, you'll have to do better than just tell me it ain't gonna happen."

Quinn had to acknowledge that Emerson had a point. "Well, Emerson, what would you like to do? It's either the plane or we Uber it to Hyannis and take the ferry over."

Emerson cocked her head. "That's how I got to your house in the first place, remember? So I know that way." She raised an eyebrow.

Quinn knew she was already being tested, even if Emerson wasn't necessarily trying to test her, *per se*. But she knew she had to step up and make a decision, and persuade her daughter it was the right one. She couldn't let Emerson lead her around by the nose.

"The plane's going to be fine," Quinn said. "It's going to be a little bit squished, because planes always are, but, trust me, it's not going to crash."

"Okay, but if we do crash, Imma be the first to tell you I told you so."

****

About an hour later, Emerson and Quinn arrived at Quinn's home. Sarah wasn't around, because she was working at the inn.

Emerson came into the house and looked around. "What you got to eat?" These were the first words she said when she came in the door. Kona and Bella barked their heads off at the girl but soon were sniffing her, after which they settled down. Emerson really liked the dogs, which was a plus, as they were soon licking her face.

Quinn nodded her head. "I have all kinds of things to eat. I know you're hungry, so I made some homemade coconut yogurt in the instant pot. I also have some organic raspberries I got at the Farmer's market. I think that's a healthy snack I can give you right now."

Emerson gave her a look. "Out of the frying pan, into the fire." Then she shook her head. "What is it with you people? My dad, he was a health nut too. He never brought in Ding Dongs or Doritos or donuts or ice cream. You know, the basic food groups. He ran every day of his life and ate nothing but rabbit food. Correction, he ate nothing but rabbit food he grew in his garden. Dude dropped dead out of nowhere. I'll bet he wished he would've eaten that ice cream after all."

Quinn shook her head. "I don't buy that junk, and you're not going to eat that junk, either."

"What's wrong with ice cream? Calcium. I'm a growing girl, and I think I need it. And Doritos, those are made with corn. Corn's a vegetable, last time I checked."

Quinn couldn't argue with this kid's logic. "Okay. I'll go and buy some organic ice cream if I can find some. And I think Sun Chips aren't too bad."

Emerson crossed her arms. "What did you eat when you were growing up?"

Quinn didn't want to admit what she ate when she was young. That was back in the day when she used to eat meat and put any old junk into her growing body.

Her mother's Southern cooking was legendary, but it involved a lot of grease, breading and saturated fats. And then, when she and Andy first moved to Brooklyn, and they didn't have a pot to piss in or a window to throw it out of, they lived on what was known as "shit on a shingle." It was made of melted margarine, milk, and flour made into a gravy and poured over Buddig chipped beef and served on toast. It was delicious, satisfying, and oh so bad.

When she wasn't eating this delicious concoction, she

sometimes made Rotel dip, which consisted of Velveeta cheese, Rotel tomatoes, and hamburger. She served all that with a healthy helping of regular Doritos. Her freezer also was stacked during those days with frozen burritos, tamales, Ore-Ida French fries, Mrs. Paul's fish sticks and frozen pizzas of every type. Her favorite food of all time was called Cajun Poutine, which was a creamy cheese sauce with mushrooms and fresh fish served over a bed of French fries. She also was addicted to McDonald's quarter pounders with cheese, which she usually got with a large French fry and an apple pie.

That was then, when she didn't know any better. Now, she really tried hard to take care of herself, which meant she watched her diet closely. Her fruits and vegetables were organic, as were her eggs, potatoes and coffee. Her fish was wild-caught. She also learned how bad processed food was for her body. She kept in shape with Pilates, yoga, and spin classes, so why should she undo all that hard work with a crappy diet?

Emerson went into Quinn's kitchen and marched right back into the living room with three bottles of wine in her hand. "So, I looked in your fridge, and besides the lame yogurt and raspberries, there's nothing but almond milk, fruits and vegetables, and Kombucha. Even your cheese and butter are made out of grass-fed milk. Yet you got a wine cellar in your pantry. What's up with that?"

Of course, Emerson found her Achilles heel. "Never mind about that stuff. Now, as I said, I'll be happy to get you some organic ice cream if you like. I'm very sorry you don't approve of my food choices, but since you're going to be living under my roof, you're going to have to put up with it."

"I don't have to put up with it. I'll call the social worker and tell her you're starving me."

Quinn rolled her eyes. "Oh, yeah, making you eat organic raspberries is the very definition of child abuse." She took a deep breath, closed her eyes, and counted to 10. "Listen, this is going to be an adjustment for you. It's going to be an adjustment for me, too."

That was the wrong thing to say. "It's going to be an adjustment for you? Oh, because you didn't want any kids, is that what you're trying to say? That's why you gave me away, wasn't it?"

Quinn understood at that moment what Emerson's attitude was about. "Sugar," Quinn said to her daughter. "I hope you understand that when I gave you up for adoption, it wasn't because I didn't love you. I did, darlin'. To the moon and back. But I just –"

At that point, she didn't know what to say. She couldn't make the excuse that she was young and didn't have the resources to take care of a kid. After all, she was 41 when she gave birth to Emerson and was a sought-after interior decorator. Truth be told, she just didn't have the inclination to take care of a child at the time. But how could she explain that to Emerson?

Emerson cocked her head at Quinn. "You loved me to the moon and back, but what?"

"It just wasn't the right time for me to take care of a child. I'm so sorry."

Emerson shrugged her shoulders. "Yeah. Whatever. Anyhow, I guess you're telling me I'll just have to get used to eating rabbit food."

"Well, aren't you used to that? You just told me that your father was a health-food nut."

"My dad was. My mom wasn't. My mom would serve up Hamburger Helper, frozen Eggo waffles, and cold cereal for dinner. Loved it. My dad didn't really eat with us. He was always making weird shakes with whey protein and calf livers and things like that, and he would eat that with a salad with spinach and tomatoes and peppers and stuff like that."

Emerson scrunched up her nose and made a face. "I tried one of those shakes. It was rank."

Quinn smiled. "Well, if it's any consolation, sugar, I won't be making you eat calf liver." Liver was one of the things Quinn couldn't stand. She hated the texture, the smell, and the taste. Besides, it was meat, and she was off that.

Emerson was going to try a different tact. "Listen, I know you met with my social worker. I know my social worker told you it's best not to change my routine much. I mean, I'm going to a different school and all, that can't be helped. But isn't diet part of my routine? Maybe you shouldn't be messing around with that, either. Maybe I'll adjust better if you give me things I'm used to."

Oh, this kid was good. Quinn was catching on fast that Emerson would try anything she could to manipulate her. Yes, the social worker told her that Emerson's routine should be disturbed as little as possible. Quinn just figured that meant she enroll Emerson in a chess club and sign her up for violin lessons. And she also would allow Emerson to play at least an hour of video games every day, which she played online and apparently was a part of a large and growing Fortnite community.

Quinn wasn't aware that ensuring that Emerson's routine wasn't interrupted also included indulging her daughter with as many Eggo waffles as possible.

Emerson narrowed her eyes. "You know, if you'd just kept me around, I wouldn't have gone through the trauma of losing both my parents at the tender age of 13. Who's my sperm donor, anyway?"

Quinn felt her heart crash into her stomach. "Your father was..." She paused, looking into the bright blue eyes of Emerson. Those eyes were penetrating her, and Quinn knew she could just not give her an easy answer. Should she try to make up some story? That was the dilemma she'd thought

THE BEACHFRONT SURPRISES.

about before Emerson ever came in. Her original idea was to tell the girl her father was dead.

However, after spending time with this girl, Quinn doubted she could get away with a lie. Emerson was just too intelligent.

So, what should she tell her?

Emerson raised her eyebrow. "My father, was what? An alien? A cyborg? A Vulcan? A Jedi? A Klingon? A wizard? A vampire? A turkey baster?" She shook her head. "Nah, no way was my father a turkey baster. Women just do that when they want a kid, and you obviously didn't want me. So I think he was just a rando. How close am I?"

Quinn's heart hurt because the last thing she wanted her daughter to think was she simply had a one-night stand and got pregnant. At the age of 40. That certainly wouldn't look very responsible of her. And what kind of example would that set for her young daughter?

"Your father slipped something into my drink and took advantage of me when was I passed out," Quinn blurted out before she could think about what she was saying.

"Oh. So he gave you a Cosby. Cool." She shrugged her shoulders. "Well, I guess I'm glad you didn't decide to do away with me after that. I probably would've, to be honest with you. So, I guess it's probably not a good idea I try to find this dude, huh?"

Quinn couldn't believe she'd actually told her daughter the truth. She hadn't intended to. She'd spoken about the whole situation with her family therapist she had hired when she found out about Emerson's existence. She had had only one session with him, and he advised her not to tell Emerson about the circumstances of her conception, at least not right at first. He warned her that sometimes children felt dirty and depressed after discovering they came about in such a situation. But Emerson seemed to be taking it all in stride, so Quinn was relieved.

"Sugar, if you want to find your father, you can. I can certainly give you his last known address. Well, not his last known home address, but I can give you his last known work address if you want it."

"The dude's name?"

"Charles Langford. He worked for Goldman Sachs as an investment banker at the time."

"So, he's a rich dude. Figures."

"What do you mean?"

"Nothing."

"Do you want to try to find him?" Quinn asked anxiously.

"Hard pass. Won't be looking for my rapist father anytime soon." She nodded her head. "But at least I know now why you would've given me up. Don't blame you there. Like I said, I guess I'm lucky to be alive at this point. Lucky to be alive."

"Well, maybe you want to know about your heritage, or at least about any possible genetic health problems you might have."

"It's safe to say that probably one of the genetic health problems that my dad would pass onto me would be some kind of a mental illness. Because who does things like that? Messed-up freaks, that's who. I guess if I turn out to be some kind of crazy serial killer, I'll know who to blame. So thanks for that."

Quinn blinked, not quite knowing what to think of her child casually predicting she would become a crazed serial killer. She guessed it was dark humor. At least, that was what she was dearly hoping for.

"Anyhow," Emerson said. "You going to show me to my room?"

At that, Quinn led her up to her bedroom. "Obviously, I'm going to customize it just for you. I'd like to look at bedroom furniture with you, bedspreads, curtains, pictures to hang on your wall. You know, when I was a kid, my mom bought me this amazing light that projected onto the ceiling and spun around with different colors at night. I loved it. Maybe you'd like something like that?"

Emerson nodded her head and lay down on the bed. "Sure. Let's talk about that later. For now, I'm really tired."

It was only 6 o'clock, but maybe the kid *was* tired. Quinn was hoping to have a little more time with Emerson on the first day, but she wouldn't push it.

"Well, go ahead and get some rest. I'll have dinner waiting for you when you wake up."

Emerson rolled her eyes. "Oh, joy. Brussels sprouts and liver paté awaits. Looking forward to that."

"Sugar, I won't be serving you Brussels sprouts and liver paté."

" Okay, then, seaweed salad and chicken livers," Emerson said.

"Actually, I have a nice salmon steak, a salad and a baked sweet potato ready for dinner."

Emerson just nodded her head and rolled her eyes. "Can't wait. I'll be in my room dreaming about that food all day. Anyhow, I'll be good to to go in an hour or so."

After Emerson went upstairs to take her little nap, Quinn sat down and put her head in her hands. All at once, she realized exactly what she was taking on, and it was scary as hell.

She was a mother. She was a mother. She.was.a.mother.

What was she getting herself into?

CHAPTER 12

AVA

That Saturday night, Deacon showed up at the 'Sconset Inn, ready to play the piano for the dinner guests. Ava had already gotten a headcount for the people who were to show up for dinner that night. She had 30 guests in her seven rooms, as each room had two queens plus the option of a trundle, and several of the rooms had 5 people or more in them. 25 of those guests were going to be eating dinner in-house. All of them were excited about the possibility of having live music to dine by.

Deacon was apparently just as excited to be playing for them. He looked a little nervous. "Mate, what do you want me to do tonight? I mean, I know all the classics, a little jazz, lots of contemporary, and some great big-band standards. But I've also written quite a few pieces on my own. I'm really keen on trying out at least a few of my new compositions, but sometimes the audience just wants to go with what they know."

Ava put her hand on his shoulder and squeezed. "Just go with your gut. Read the room, decide what you think they want to hear and go with it. Personally, I'd love to hear some of your original pieces."

Ava was so impressed that Deacon not only was a musician but was also a songwriter. It showed a level of creativity she never knew he had, not to mention a great degree of talent. She still remembered when she discovered he was an amazing piano player. He came to play for her open house soirée and blew her socks off. Until that time, she'd only known him to be a very talented contractor and carpenter. But the piano playing was another level that really impressed her.

While Ava was standing there next to Deacon and squeezing his shoulder, Colleen came into the dining room. She looked at Ava, and then at Deacon, and back to Ava again. And then she crossed her arms in front of her and narrowed her eyes.

"Hello, mom." Her mother had been staying with her for a little under a week, and, thus far, there weren't any fireworks. Which meant that Ava tried to avoid her mother as much as possible.

She made sure she cleaned Colleen's room especially well. God forbid there was even a single dust bunny under her bed. If there were, Ava would never hear the end of it. So, every day, when Colleen would go to hang out on the beach, or go into town, or go to her appointments over at Hallie and Willow's spa, Ava would go into Colleen's room and scrub everything down like mad.

So far, so good. She'd not heard a single complaint yet from Colleen. Still, she knew it was just a matter of time before her mother cut her down right where she stood.

Her mom nodded her head. "Ava." And that's all she said.

Then Colleen sat down at one of the tables. "Find me my other daughter. I'd like a glass of wine to go with the pasta I'm going to order."

Ava drew a breath. This would be the first dinner Colleen would be eating at the inn. So far, Colleen would either go to a restaurant on her own, or invite Sarah to join her, but she'd always eaten her meals out on the town ever since she came to stay with Ava.

Ava turned to Deacon. "Well, go ahead and warm up. My guests will be joining us shortly. For now, I guess you're going to have my mother as your audience."

Ava went to find Sarah and found her in the kitchen. Sarah had offered to wait tables that night. She was also consulting with Riley, the new chef Ava had hired, about the best wine to use for a menu dish. Ava liked to give all her guests a choice between three different dishes. One would be a meat dish, one a fish or seafood, and one a pasta. On that evening, Riley was cooking *coq au vin* for the meat dish. Sarah was recommending a particular burgundy Shiraz, and Riley was nodding his head.

"Yeah, I think that wine probably hits the right notes," he said. "I really like a cherry finish for this dish, and that wine really provides that extra hint of sweetness." He took a few sips of the wine Sarah had recommended and nodded his head. "Star Anise and peppercorn notes, too," he said. "This is the perfect wine for what I want to do with this dish."

Sarah looked at Ava. "What's up?" she asked.

"Mom will be eating dinner with us this evening," Ava said. "And she wants to see you because she wants you to recommend a wine for her meal. I think she's getting the pasta dish if that tells you anything."

Sarah just smiled. "Oh, good. I've been trying to talk her into having dinner here. I'm glad she chose tonight. After all, Deacon will be playing the piano, and you know how mom likes a good live performance."

Ava rolled her eyes. "No, I didn't know mom liked live music. What kind of music does she like?" Ava realized she

THE BEACHFRONT SURPRISES.

didn't know the basics about her mother and was irrationally angry that Sarah apparently did.

"Well, she really likes piano music, so she goes for the classical composers that create piano-heavy pieces. Rachmaninoff, Chopin, Mozart, any composer that writes a lot of piano concertos. She likes a lot of jazz pianists, too. Chick Corea, Bill Evans, Thelonious Monk, Jelly Roll Morton, Dave Brubeck, Alice Coltrane. I've hung out with her at piano bars a time or two when she'd come to visit. You'd be surprised about how knowledgeable she is about jazz and classical pianists."

Ava closed her eyes and counted to 10. She loved Sarah, and she was so, so, so happy that Sarah was back in her life. But Sarah was stabbing her in the heart without even realizing it. For all those years when she wasn't speaking to Sarah, she could tell herself her mother hated both of them. Misery loves company, and just the thought that maybe Sarah was on the outs with their mother, too, made Ava feel her mother's indifference and cruelty to her wasn't personal.

But Sarah obviously had a great relationship with Colleen, even more of a relationship than Ava had realized. Colleen and Sarah just casually hung out at piano bars, and Colleen waxed poetic about the composers she loved? What else did Sarah know about their mother that she didn't know? Well, considering she knew next to nothing about Colleen, it stood to reason that anything that Sarah knew about their mother would be something Ava didn't.

Sarah had a look on her face that told Ava she knew she'd hurt her sister's feelings. "I found her record collection and looked through it. That's how I knew about the piano composers she enjoys. And we only went out to piano bars a couple of times. It's no big deal."

Ava swallowed hard and loved her sister all the more for trying to soothe her hurt feelings. She knew Sarah was lying

– to her knowledge, Colleen didn't have a record collection. And she knew Sarah probably socialized with her mother more than she let on. She imagined Sarah and Colleen having a ball at a piano bar, drinking dirty martinis and laughing like girlfriends.

Sarah left the kitchen to go and talk to their mother, who was sitting at a table alone. Ava's heart pinged a little as she saw her mother sitting alone. She wondered if Colleen was lonely. Ava always thought it was strange her mother never remarried after her father, Kenny Flynn, died so young. She was an attractive woman, always had been, and very accomplished. Ava was sure she came across a man or two over the years who might've turned her head. Yet, to Ava's knowledge, Colleen never even dated a man after her father Kenny's death.

Then she shook her head. Why was she feeling bad about her mother? If her mother was lonely, that was because she chose to be. She probably drove off every man who tried to get close to her.

After Sarah talked to their mother and then left to get a bottle of wine, Colleen motioned Ava to her table.

Ava sat down.

"Sarah's getting a bottle of Malbec, my favorite varietal of wine. Maybe you can join me?"

Ava squinted her eyes. "What's the catch?"

"No catch. I'm getting some wine, I can't drink the whole bottle on my own, and I know you want to hang out in the dining room tonight. You got eyes for that Deacon, and don't try to tell me differently."

Ava had to admit her mother had a point. She *did* want to hang out in the dining room. She wanted to hear Deacon play, and she wanted to stare at him a little.

"Are you sure there's not a catch?" Ava asked her mother.

"Why do I have to have a reason to spend time with my daughter?" Colleen demanded.

"I guess because I've never felt you thought I was your daughter."

"And just what's that supposed to mean?" Colleen asked.

"Nothing."

"No, really. What did you mean by that? Of course, you're my daughter. You came out of my body, after 20 hours of hard labor, screeching and screaming and carrying on like a scared banshee. That makes you my daughter."

Ava took a deep breath. "Is that what makes me your daughter? The fact that I just happened to come out of your body?"

Colleen rolled her eyes. "Yes. What else makes you my daughter?"

"Oh, I don't know. Usually a mother at least likes her daughter. Preferably a mother loves her daughter. At any rate, a true mother would not take one daughter out to piano bars and have a ball, while ignoring another daughter and having nothing but insulting words for her."

Ava felt tears coming to her eyes. Good, God, she was 54 years old, and she still was letting her mother crush her. She heard herself talking and thought she sounded like a teenager who was stomping her foot and screaming about how her mother was being so unfair.

To Ava's surprise, Colleen's face softened. "Just sit down, and quit being such a drama queen about it all. You can either join me for a bottle of wine, or you can sit in the corner and pout. What I know is, you're not going to storm off. You want to sit here and listen to your man-crush."

Her mother was right. She *had* planned to listen to Deacon playing. However, she had *not* planned to listen to Deacon while sitting with her mother. Yet, that seemed to be the plan for the evening. She was going to enjoy Deacon's piano playing while actively trying to avoid her mother at the same table. This was going to be tricky.

She sat down next to Colleen.

Her mother nodded her head. "I thought so. Now, tell me about the boy."

Was her mother really asking? Her mother never asked about any boy - not when she was growing up and having boy problems, not when she was in college having her heart broken, not when she was married, and not when she was newly widowed. Her mother never asked a single question about any of these boys and men, nor did she ever provide Ava a soft shoulder to cry on when some member of the opposite sex devastated her.

"Number one, Deacon is not a boy. He's a 35-year-old man who owns his own contracting business and is a very talented piano player and songwriter. Number two, there's nothing to tell. He and I are not dating, nor will we ever be dating."

"Why not? He's hot. He seems into you. I see how he looks at you. And how you look at him like a puppy dog looking for a treat. What gives, Ava? Why aren't the two of you making the beast with two backs together?"

Ava blinked. Her mother was such a strange duck. She was almost 80 years old, she was a respected federal judge, and she used words like "hot" and "beast with two backs." Just the incongruity of those two things made Ava want to crack up in spite of herself.

"Mom, as I said, he's too young and wrong for me. Just drop it. Let it go."

Colleen put her hand on Ava's shoulder and squeezed hard. "Now, you listen to me. You don't let anybody tell you who you should and shouldn't be with. Do you hear me? So, society will look down on you. People will look at you like you're some kind of a silly cougar. 'What are you doing with a young guy like that?' Big whoop. You just go with what's in your heart and don't let anybody steer you away from it. Trust me, you'll be happier if you do that."

Ava was struck by the ferocity in her mother's voice. At the same time, she was confused. Why was Colleen so adamant about not letting society dictate who she would be with?

"Mom, with all due respect, you don't know what you're talking about. Dad died when I was five years old. That was, what, 49 years ago? And you haven't been on even a single date since then. So, I'm sorry, I'm not going to be taking relationship advice from you."

At that, Ava could swear she saw a look on her mother's face she'd never seen before. A look of devastation, hurt, anger. Ava struck a nerve, but she had no idea how or why. What did she say to get such a reaction?

"Ava, you have no idea what you're talking about. And let's just leave it at that."

Whatever, Ava thought. It wasn't the first time she was confused by the enigma that was her mother. And it wouldn't be the last.

Ava took a sip of the wine. "This is a nice wine. Sarah has some good taste."

"Your sister doesn't only have good taste. You're insulting her when you say she recommends wine based on her taste. The girl has been studying wines for years. It's not just a hobby for her. It's a passion. And after what happened with her and that ridiculous Lauren, not to mention that loser Nolan, I'm thrilled she was able to have a second act. You should be, too."

"Excuse me for breathing. I wasn't trying to insult Sarah. I admit, I don't know that much about wine myself, so I admire Sarah for learning all she can about it. I wish I had the same kind of passion in my life as she has for learning about wines. But I don't. I've never felt that calling, that thing in my heart that makes me want to get up in the morning and face the day."

"Yes, you do. Running this inn. That's your passion. That's your calling. And you're doing a good job of it. I'm proud of you." She patted Ava's back to emphasize the point.

Ava wondered if her mother had been taken over by a body snatcher. Colleen was not only complimenting her, but she was saying she was proud of her? What was getting into her?

"Thank you," Ava said.

"Ava, do you know why I'm here?"

"Yes. You wanted a free vacation. At my expense, by the way."

Colleen rolled her eyes. "A free vacation. Really. Don't you know I could've been taken a vacation anywhere with my kind of money? Trust me, I'd much rather be sitting on a beach by the Riviera or Jamaica or taking a river cruise down the Seine. But I chose none of those things. No, I chose this two-horse town with no stoplights and no real luxury accommodations because I wanted to spend time with you."

"With me. Really. I don't believe you."

Colleen took a deep breath. "Ava, life is short. You never know when your number might be up. You might feel fine one moment, and the next, you're lying dead on the bathroom floor. Just out of nowhere - lights out."

"Mom, I don't understand. Dad died many years ago, and he had lung cancer for a year before he died. His death wasn't sudden. So, what's all this talk about lying on the bathroom floor?" Her mother's scenario that she'd just spelled out was oddly specific.

Colleen just shrugged. "That's what happened to Elvis, you know. He went out on the toilet. So did a lot of people.

Lenny Bruce and Judy Garland, both of them also went out while using the toilet. It happens."

Ava had a chuckle. She couldn't help herself. "Well, mom, you're quite the aficionado about people who die on the toilet. I have to hand it to you. I knew Elvis died on the toilet. I didn't know about the other two."

"It's true. It just shows you can buy the farm at any time. Since life is so short, I figure it's about time I try to put my affairs in order before I end up in a pine box."

All of a sudden, Ava felt a chill. "Mom, you're not sick, are you?" As much as Ava and her mother had never gotten along, that didn't mean Ava wanted her mother to die.

Colleen shook her head. "No, unfortunately for you, I'm in perfect health. I still walk four miles every day, I watch what I eat, and I get checkups every year. Mammograms and colonoscopies when I'm supposed to. Everything has checked out under the hood of this classic car. Assuming there's not some silent time bomb inside my chest that's not detected, I'll probably be around to torment you for another 20 years. 10 years at a minimum."

"That's good to hear." Ava meant that because she did love her mother. She didn't really like her that much, but she always loved her. And there was a very big part of her that always hoped she and Colleen could make nice at some point in their lives.

"I had a friend," Colleen said. "She and her mother would go round and round. Love each other, hate each other, love each other, hate each other. They got into a big fight, and they weren't speaking for months. The mother died just out of nowhere. My friend can't forgive herself because she wasn't speaking to her mother when she died. I don't want you to have any regrets if I get hit by a bus tomorrow. So, that's why I'm here. To spend some time with you. And, Sarah, too. But, mainly with you."

Ava took a sip of her wine. She didn't trust her mother. It was difficult to trust her after a lifetime of disappointments.

She still could remember the mother who hung up on her when she called to tell her about Daniel's death. Daniel was the great love of Ava's life, a talented photographer and the kindest man she'd ever known. He made a mistake when he got into a car with a very drunk man. A mistake he paid for with his life. Ava was 5 months pregnant at the time.

When she called Colleen to tell her about the accident, her mother didn't want to hear about it. "Serves him right," Colleen had said about Daniel. "What kind of an idiot would get into a car with a guy who was that blotto?"

And then her mother hung up on her. No sympathy card. No offers to help her with her upcoming birth. No visit to the hospital when she gave birth to the kids. In fact, Colleen might've said something about how dumb Ava was for having kids with Daniel because now she was trapped. Trapped. That was the word Colleen had used for Ava's decision to have children with her beloved husband.

Now her mother wanted to be friends. It was going to be difficult for Ava to meet Colleen even halfway.

Yet, if her mother was sincere, maybe that was what she should do. Meet her halfway.

"Okay," Ava said warily. "If you really want to have a relationship, let's do it. Let's just look at the past 54 years as water under the bridge. Where do you want to start?"

Colleen motioned to the bottle of wine. "With this bottle of wine. And your hunk of a boyfriend-to-be playing piano. These are two really good places to start."

Ava smiled. "I guess it's as good a place to start as any."

So, the two ladies listened to Deacon play for the rest of the evening. Colleen made several requests, and Ava was able to glean some of Colleen's favorite musicians from those requests. For instance, Colleen requested several jazz numbers by Chic Corea and Alice Coltrane. She also requested some George Gershwin and Rachmaninoff. Being a very versatile pianist, Deacon was able to accommodate her every request. In fact, he did it with a smile that lit up the entire room.

Colleen kept looking over at Ava. Ava knew her every emotion was on her face. There was no hiding how she felt about Deacon, so she didn't even try. Besides, her mother had already called her on it earlier.

After the two ladies had dinner and wine and Deacon had stopped playing, Colleen suggested that Ava come to her room and sit on her balcony. "I'd say we should go to the terrace on the roof, but I have a feeling there's a bunch of people up there. I'm kind of in the mood to just have a one-on-one. Hope that's okay."

"Sure, that's more than okay." Ava still wasn't ready to trust her mother, but, at the same time, if her mother was going to keep trying, Ava was going to let her. At the very minimum.

So, Ava went to Colleen's room. The two ladies sat on the loungers on Colleen's balcony with another bottle of wine opened and poured. Colleen asked questions about Ava's life, and Ava answered them. Ava did the same, and she found out a few things about her mother she didn't know earlier. Such as the fact the Chief Judge was her best friend.

And that her mother's oldest friend, Violet, had died.

"Oh, mom, I'm so sorry. I know how much she meant to you." Violet and her mother were such good friends that Ava had always referred to Violet as "Aunt Violet" when she was growing up.

Colleen just nodded. "Violet was good people. I don't think there has ever been a more pure soul than that woman. But she could tell a dirty joke with the best of them, I'll tell you that."

"Yes, I remember," Ava said. "I guess you guys kept in touch over the years after moving away from Kansas City?"

"Yes. We kept in touch. You know, phone calls and emails and that kind of thing. Even though we didn't live in the same city, Violet was the best friend a woman could have."

"That must've been quite a loss," Ava said. "And I'm really so sorry. I wish I could've been there for you, but you didn't tell Sarah or me about it. Does Sarah even know about it now?"

"No. Only you. I mean, I'll tell her later. It's not that big of a deal, really."

"How did she die?"

Colleen just shrugged. "Not sure. It was one of those things, I guess."

"Well, I'm sorry."

"Thank you." And then Colleen took a deep breath and another sip of her wine. "Well, it's getting late. And I know you have a lot of work to do tomorrow and every day of your life. I'll let you go. But, you know, I didn't have too bad of a time hanging around with you tonight."

"I didn't have too bad of a time either," Ava said.

And the weird thing was, Ava really meant that.

CHAPTER 13

QUINN

Sarah and Quinn were sitting on the back porch one day, enjoying mimosas and the day. It was a beautiful June day, and Quinn had worked hard on her garden in her spare time. Her cottage was covered in roses that were just starting to bloom, and, since Quinn loved roses anyhow, she planted them in her backyard as well. She loved different colors of roses, and she especially loved the ones that were multiple colors. White ones with pink tips, lavender with hot pink edges, a rare blue one with purple leaves, and a dark red rose with orange highlights were in Quinn's garden.

Quinn seemed to have a green thumb, which Sarah admired greatly. Sarah told Quinn she never seemed to be able to grow anything successfully. Quinn explained that growing flowers and plants was a science, because every plant and flower had different needs and required different nutrients, and the trick was always to experiment and try to be as precise as possible when adding things to the soil.

"I've got the advantage though," Quinn said. "My momma raised prized roses. She used to enter them in the annual rose show in downtown Thomasville, a city south of Atlanta and five hours away from where we lived. She traveled 300 miles away, as the crow flies, that's how much my momma wanted people to admire her beautiful roses." Quinn took a deep breath and smelled the fragrance of her blooms.

Sarah nodded her head. "I love sitting out here amongst all this color. It's very relaxing."

Quinn agreed, and it was important she had some relaxation. She had her first counseling appointment with Emerson the next day, and she was extremely nervous.

Sarah looked over at Quinn. "What's wrong?"

Quinn took a sip of her mimosa and shook her head. "I just don't know what to do with Emerson. I'm not prepared to be her mother. I don't know what I'm doing with her."

Quinn had been trying to talk to Emerson for the past few days about how she wanted to decorate her bedroom. She thought if she personalized Emerson's bedroom that the little girl would feel at home.

"Paint the walls black," Emerson had said with a raise of her eyebrows. "Other than that, I really don't care."

Quinn just nodded her head and showed black color swatches to Emerson. She waved them all away. "Not black, purple. Dark purple. The darker the better."

Quinn knew there were many bedrooms with black or dark purple walls that were beautiful, and she had done quite a few of them herself. So, she brought some color swatches that were dark purple and dark red and midnight green and blue. "Here are a lot of darker color ideas for your walls," Quinn said. "Why don't you look at these and tell me if you like any of these colors."

Emerson was laying on her bed, her tablet above her head, earbuds in her ears. "Quinn, I really don't care what you do with my walls. This isn't home, and all your fancy decorating ain't gonna make it home."

THE BEACHFRONT SURPRISES.

Quinn was stung by her daughter's words. "Sugar, I took you in because you asked me to. You wanted to come here."

"Like I had a choice? You made sure about that. You really set it up, didn't you?" she demanded.

"I don't understand?" She had no idea what Emerson was talking about.

"You're the one who threw me out like an expired coupon. If you didn't do that, I would've been living with you all along, and I wouldn't have both my parents die at the same time. If my life is in the toilet, it's because of you."

Quinn focused on the conversation with her daughter while she sat there with Sarah. She didn't tell Sarah the hurtful words her daughter had flung at her. She felt that was a private conversation, and she didn't want to betray Emerson's confidence.

Sarah put her hand on Quinn's hand and squeezed. "You got this. I wish I had some kind of parenting advice, but of course, I don't. But Ava does."

That was true. Ava was going to come over that evening, along with Hallie. The ladies got together at least once a week, but, when there was a lot going on, as there was with both Quinn and Ava, they got together more often.

"Yes. I'm going to have to pick Ava's brain, but she doesn't have experience in this exact situation. Very few people will have experience in this situation. If anybody." Quinn shook her head. "Emerson hates me, and I don't know what to do."

****

That evening, Ava came over with a bottle of wine, and Hallie did as well. Quinn decided to cook dinner for everybody, which consisted of a veggie cassoulet, which was a stew made with white beans, carrots, artichoke hearts, onions, kale, garlic, sherry, stock and lots of fresh herbs from the garden. She put all of this into a Dutch oven and baked it.

Hallie brought over a loaf of crusty bread, and Sarah made the salad.

"It's just going to be veggies all the way tonight, y'all," Quinn said with a smile.

" Nothing wrong with that," Ava said. "I think I could speak for everybody when I say you can never have too many vegetables."

"I agree," Hallie said.

Emerson, who was going to eat dinner with the ladies, disagreed. "It's veggie this veggie that," she said. "I don't think I've ever seen anybody who knows every single way to cook every single vegetable in the world. And that's not a good thing."

Quinn laughed lightly. "Emerson would be happy if I brought home Kentucky fried chicken every night."

"Ha, ha," Emerson said. "Where you going to get the Kentucky fried chicken, in Boston? This stupid island doesn't have any fast food restaurants I've seen."

"There's Stubby's," Hallie said, referring to the restaurant in the historic district that served burgers and fries along with a large array of sandwiches, soups, salads, paninis and Jamaican dishes.

"Dude, Stubby's don't count," Emerson said. "That place has Paninis, clam chowder and Jamaican jerk chicken. A real fast food restaurant is not that fancy. Try again."

"Walter's Deli?" Ava ventured.

Emerson rolled her eyes. "Walter's Deli is known for their lobster rolls. No self-respecting fast food restaurant is going to have lobster rolls on their menu. You don't see lobster rolls on the McDonald's menu, now do you?"

"Lola's?" Hallie asked.

"Come on. Their burger is $16, and they have a falafel sandwich, also a lamb burger, a kale salad and a Wagyu beef hot dog that's also $16. Sorry, anyplace that has that fancy of a menu and the hamburgers and hot dogs start at $16 isn't considered to be fast food."

The ladies got quiet, and Emerson nodded her head. "Yup. This island is my idea of hell. No fast food restaurants, no stoplights, and no fun. But this place is perfect for Quinn, who thinks Big Macs are the product of the devil. Apparently this entire island agrees with her on this."

Quinn got the dinner on the table, and the ladies ate the rich and delectable stew that was heavy on the aromatics, yet tasted light, like a perfect summer meal. Emerson, for her part, picked at the stew and didn't touch the salad. Quinn felt a little sorry for Emerson, because she didn't know how she would've reacted if she was 13 years old and was forced to eat nothing but healthy food. She probably wouldn't have been very happy, to say the very least.

After dinner, Emerson helped clear the table and wash the dishes, which she always did after dinner even though she rarely actually ate the dinner. She did this because she wanted to be able to play Fortnite with her online buddies. Quinn didn't mind letting her daughter play this, because Emerson was a part of a close-knit gaming community, and it kept her busy.

After dinner, everybody gathered on Quinn's back patio.

"So, how are things going with your daughter?" Ava asked.

Quinn shook her head. "I don't know what to do. I don't think she's eaten much since she's been here, and she seems to hate me. I've uprooted her completely, and she really seems to not like this island. I mean, she came from Boston, a city that has everything, including all her friends. And now, here she is. She doesn't know anybody on the island and she doesn't like the small town feel of the place. To say the least. I'm just afraid she's going to wither away to nothing because she won't eat."

"What advice can I give you?" Ava asked. " I've raised three kids, not exactly successful, but they're all doing okay. Well, except for Samantha. I still don't know what she's going to do with her life."

"I don't know what I'm looking for," Quinn said to Ava. "I just need to talk to her therapist and see if I can break through to her somehow. I just feel crazier than an outhouse rat because I never thought I was going to be a mother. And I really didn't think I was going to be getting a grieving child under my roof. There are just so many issues here. I don't even know where to start with this girl."

"So, when is your therapist meeting?" Hallie asked her.

"I managed to get one this Wednesday. I was really lucky to get in. My lawyer, Asher, he helped me with getting this appointment. The doctor is married to one of his golfing buddies."

Quinn didn't tell the ladies that Asher was helping her quite a lot, and that she wasn't exactly turning down his help. She didn't quite know how she felt about the handsome lawyer, and, until she could figure it out, she wasn't going to say anything about him.

"Well, Quinn you know if you ever need anything, we're here for you," Sarah said.

Quinn knew Sarah was right about that. The ladies had her back, no matter what. But she just didn't know how to lean on them. They were all so busy, and she knew Emerson's issues were deep. It wasn't just that Emerson was starting over with her. It was also that her daughter resented her for putting her up for adoption.

"I don't know what to say about Emerson right now. I'm just trying to get a feel for her and how I'm supposed to be with her and help her. I'm hoping the therapist will guide me in the right direction. But, Ava, I really want to know what's happening with your mom."

The ladies talked about Ava's mom and Ava's relationship with her at length. Quinn was happy she was able to take her mind off of her own problems so she could help her friend with hers.

It was a small blessing, but a blessing nonetheless.

CHAPTER 14

COLLEEN

Colleen went to her appointment with Willow that Monday. After her first acupuncture treatment, she felt so good that she wanted to make it a regular thing during the six weeks she would be staying on Nantucket. She didn't think it was changing her fundamentally, but she did find it relaxing. And, after the year she had, anything that made her feel less depressed and more relaxed was something she was going to pursue.

Willow looked at Colleen when Colleen came in the door. "You still didn't tell her, did you?"

"About what? About her father, or about my relationship with Violet?"

"You didn't tell her about either one, did you?"

Colleen shook her head. "You know, I came close to telling her about Violet. But something stopped me." She knew what stopped her. It was her parent's attitude still ringing in her ears. Her father made ridiculous homophobic jokes. Her mother took her aside when she suspected Colleen was into girls and tearfully told her she would never speak to her again if she ever brought home a girlfriend.

THE BEACHFRONT SURPRISES.

Plus, society, in general, told her in a thousand different ways she was wrong, mentally ill, was sinning against God, and was breaking the law.

"Colleen, I know it's not my business because I just met you. But, let me tell you what secrets do to your energy. They turn all the free-flowing energy, that should be white and pure, into balls of blackness. When you speak your truth, no matter how painful that truth is, all that blackness gets released. You'd just feel this sense of lightness. Trust me, taking back your power is the healthiest thing you could do. Right now, you've given that power away to other people."

"Well, I know what you're saying. And maybe I'll tell my daughters about Violet. But I'm not making any guarantees. I always thought I'd take that secret to my grave. I don't know why it's their business what I do in my private life."

Colleen lay down on the table, and Willow put the needles in her forehead, upper chest, palms, and the soles of her feet. "You say it doesn't matter if your daughters know the truth about your relationship with Violet, but you have to understand, it's a barrier between you and your daughters. It's like a wall you've put up. How can they possibly get to know the real you when you won't admit to them something as important as the fact you've been in love with a woman for many years?"

"They can know me just fine. I've always shown them what I wanted to, and, so far, it's worked." Colleen, of course, was lying to herself and to Willow. She knew hiding her true nature put her at arm's length with her two children.

Willow was right – they couldn't know the real her if she wasn't willing to show them the real her.

"Okay. It's your life, obviously. Your decision. But I still think you should tell Ava the truth about her father."

"What, pray tell, good would that do at this point? It's

going to make her hate me more than ever. No, that's not a good idea. I can't see any good coming of that."

Willow raised an eyebrow. "A lot of the reason why you have a problem with your daughter is because of what you're hiding about her father. Clearing the air would knock down the resentment between you two. You should at least acknowledge how many barriers and problems have sprung up from that secret."

"Thanks, but it's really none of your business." At that, Colleen closed her eyes and concentrated on the soothing sounds of rain, birds, and ocean waves, all set to the soothing sounds of a harp.

The next thing she knew, Willow was taking the needles out of her skin. Colleen got up, paid for her session, and left.

Willow is getting too nosy, Colleen thought. At the same time, deep down, Colleen believed Willow was right. Speaking her truth to her daughters and being brave would go a long way towards helping her to repair her relationship with Ava.

Why was it so hard to do?

CHAPTER 15

QUINN

Quinn took Emerson to her therapist appointment that following Wednesday. Dr. Woodley was a 35-year-old woman with dark hair and warm brown eyes. She smiled when she saw Emerson and Quinn in the waiting room.

"Hey," she said in a very friendly manner. "I'm Caroline Woodley. You must be Quinn and this must be Emerson."

Emerson looked at Quinn. "She knows our names. And she knows I'm the daughter and you're the mother. I'm so impressed." The tone of voice Emerson used showed that she was anything but impressed, however.

Dr. Woodley just smiled. "Emerson, let's go back and have a chat."

"You mean let's go back and have a head-shrinking sesh, don't you?" Emerson said. "I'll go back and talk to you, but you'll get nothing from me. I don't know why Quinn is bothering with even bringing me here."

*****

An hour later, Emerson came out of the room. "Your turn," she said to Quinn. "She's going to tell you all about everything I told her, which wasn't a lot. She wasn't going to get anything out of me. So I don't know what she's going to tell you about me, but have at it."

Quinn just nodded her head and, when Dr. Woodley came out of the office to usher her in, Quinn followed her. She felt as nervous as a cat in a room full of rocking chairs as she sat down across from the therapist.

"So, what did Emerson tell you?"

"She didn't tell me much, but she blames herself for her mother's death. And she blames you for her mother's death as well."

"Me? Why would she blame me for her mother's death?"

"It's unclear. She simply told me that if she was never put up for adoption, her mother would still be alive. So, she told me she resents you because you quote killed her mother unquote. And that she was the direct cause of her mother's death. So, she feels you're indirectly responsible for her mother's death and she directly."

Quinn shook her head. "That makes no sense. Her mother died of heart failure. Why does she blame herself for that? Why does she blame me for that?"

"Again, it's unclear. I asked follow-up questions about why she felt she was responsible for her mother's death and that you were, but she shut down when I tried to get to the bottom of it. She also told me she wasn't going to talk about it anymore with me. But she did say her mother was too young to die, was a good person, and didn't deserve what happened to her."

Quinn took a deep breath. "What else did she talk about?"

"She talked a lot about how bored she was. She said she had five close friends in Boston, and they all gathered at each other's houses all the time. She's having a hard time with her new situation. She misses her friends, she misses living in a city, and she misses her parents."

THE BEACHFRONT SURPRISES.

Quinn started to wring her hands, and Dr. Woodley silently gave her a stress ball to squeeze. "Thank you," Quinn said to the doctor as she took the stress ball and squeezed hard. "What am I supposed to do with this kiddo? How can I help her?"

"You just need to give her space to grieve. If she can talk about it to you, you need to listen and not interject. But I don't believe Emerson is the type of girl who will verbalize her feelings. If she does, really listen to what she's saying to you. She might be telling you exactly what she needs in her own way."

Quinn just nodded her head. She still had the stress ball in her hand and was squeezing the life out of it. "Space to grieve," Quinn said. "What does that mean in English?" Quinn hated, more than anything, vague pieces of advice like "give Emerson space to grieve." Those words meant nothing to her, and they sounded like psychobabble. She wanted something more than a trite piece of advice she might get from the Dr. Phil show.

"Just be understanding. Don't judge her behavior, and don't take it personally. She also mentioned she really enjoyed playing the violin. I'd encourage that from her because that might be an artistic way to express her feelings."

Quinn had encouraged Emerson to play her violin every evening, and Emerson obliged. She was very impressed with her young daughter because she seemed to be quite a virtuoso on the instrument.

"Okay. I can certainly encourage the violin. But what am I going to do about her eating? I'm not going to bring junk into the house. I refuse to do that. But she doesn't want to eat the healthy things I cook for her. She's wasting away, and I don't know what to do about that. I know she wants me to bring home a lot of potato chips, cookies, donuts, sugary cereal, frozen waffles, and things like that. But I'm not going to do it. How do I get her to eat the food I fix?"

Dr. Woodley raised an eyebrow. "Well, here is one thing I can help you with. I can give you something concrete on this. Get a book called *The Sneaky Chef*. That whole book is all about sneaking puréed vegetables into things. Like making brownies with puréed black beans and carrots, chocolate pudding made out of avocados, zucchini bread that tastes like cake, things like that. If you have a daughter who wants to eat nothing but cake and sweets and things like that, you can use that to your advantage."

Quinn cocked her head. That sounded way too easy. But, sometimes, things that originally sounded easy turned out to be the way to go. "Making chocolate pudding out of avocado and brownies out of veggies and beans. Why didn't I think of that?"

Dr. Woodley just winked. "You'll get there, Quinn. You're new to the game, and yes, sometimes it is all a game. I have three kids at home, and the book I told you about has saved my sanity."

"I'll see if that works," Quinn said. "If it does, there's one less thing to worry about. Which leaves 86 million other things to worry about with this kid."

Dr. Woodley smiled. "Welcome to motherhood. Whoever said 'they gave you life and in return you gave them hell' was a real poet in my book."

Quinn laughed. "Tears for Fears. *Shout.*" In her head, she heard the opening strains of the cowbells or whatever instrument played the opening notes of that song. "And, now, I have a song in my head, and it won't ever leave. Thanks for that," Quinn said with a smile.

"Not a bad song to have as an earworm," Dr. Woodley said. "Try having *Tiptoe Through the Tulips* in your head all

THE BEACHFRONT SURPRISES.

day. That would drive you crazy. Tears for Fears, you can't go wrong with them."

"True," Quinn said. "You can't go wrong with any of those 80s bands." She swallowed hard. She was still curious about why Emerson told Dr. Woodley she killed her mother. What could that possibly mean? "Is there any other kind of advice you can give me?"

"Just make sure she keeps coming to these counseling appointments. Even though it'll be like pulling teeth to get information out of her, you'll still be helping her by bringing her in. She might be a tough nut to crack, but it'll still help her to talk to me."

Quinn left Dr. Woodley's office feeling unsettled. She gathered Emerson together and the two of them headed to her car. On the way home, she tried to ask her about what she meant when she said she killed her mother.

Emerson just shrugged her shoulders. "Figure of speech, Quinn. I was just trying to throw the old shrink a curveball and see if she hit it."

"That's it? You were just messing with her?"

"It's what I do. It's kind of fun trying to get a rise out of adults. Fun, and like shooting fish in a barrel, to use a phrase my mom used to always say to me. But it's never made much sense. Just how easy is it to shoot fish in a barrel?"

Quinn recognized Emerson was trying to change the subject, but she didn't really know why. There was something about Emerson's demeanor that made her believe her daughter was serious when she told Dr. Woodley she killed her mom. Emerson was trying to make light of it, was trying to imply she was just joking, but Quinn sensed there was something more to it.

She tried to ask Emerson several more times on the way home, but Emerson refused to speak about it. She was hitting a brick wall, so she decided to let that go.

****

They got home at 3 o'clock, and Emerson announced she was tired. "I'm a teenager. I need a lot of sleep," she explained. "Look it up."

Quinn knew that what Emerson was saying was correct. Teenagers did need a lot of sleep. Yet, Quinn worried that Emerson might be coming down with something. "You're not feeling sick, are you?" Quinn put her hand on Emerson's forehead.

"No. I'm just tired, that's all. Can't I be tired without being sick?" Emerson asked.

"Of course. Go to bed if you're not feeling right."

Emerson just nodded and headed into her bedroom and shut the door.

Two hours later, Quinn cracked the door open to Emerson's room. "Emerson, honey, I baked some brownies for you." She'd just ordered the book Dr. Woodley had recommended to her about sneaking vegetables into sweet things. In the meantime, she found a recipe online for black bean brownies. They were made of black beans, oatmeal, applesauce, maple syrup, and chocolate chips. She tried one of them, and, to her surprise, she couldn't tell there were black beans in the mix. Amazing.

Emerson didn't respond, which concerned Quinn. She supposed the child was in such a deep sleep she couldn't hear her, yet a rising sense of panic started to form in Quinn's gut.

She walked over to the bed and turned on the light. There were lumps underneath the covers, and when Quinn put her hand on one of the lumps, she felt only pillows.

Quinn initially breathed a sigh of relief. Emerson didn't just somehow die in her bed.

Then, the rising sense of panic was back. Emerson was nowhere to be found.

What was found was an open bedroom window.

CHAPTER 16

QUINN

Quinn shook her head. She was alone in the house because Sarah was working over at the inn, and Hallie wasn't around because she was staying at the extended-stay place. She was going to call Hallie, but she wanted to handle this crisis on her own. So, she got in the car and drove everywhere around the island. She went to all the beaches, drove downtown, and went everywhere she could think of where Emerson might be.

She also called the police, but the 911 operator said he couldn't help her because Emerson wasn't missing for long enough.

She got home, and made herself a glass of wine and sat on the back patio. She had a feeling she knew exactly what had happened to her daughter. But she wasn't sure. She then realized how little she knew about Emerson. Of course. Emerson hadn't been with her for long enough for her to get to know her. However, she knew that one person probably knew a little bit about Emerson, and that was Asher.

It was Saturday night. She had a feeling Asher was probably busy, but, nonetheless, she was going to have to call him. So, she dialed him, and he immediately picked up.

"Quinn. I was just going to call you. How are things going with Emerson?"

"Not good. She's already left the house without my knowledge. I went to her bedroom, and she wasn't there. I've been on a wild goose chase for the past couple of hours. Anyhow, I needed to call you to see if you could give me any insight on her. You've done some background checks on her family, and you've talked to her teachers and school counselors, right? I think I need a copy of your file to see for myself what I'm getting into here."

Asher was quiet for just a few seconds. "Listen, I actually was going to take a woman out on a date. I'm not going to lie. But I'm going to cancel that because I need to meet you to brainstorm this one. You're right. I probably do have some insight into where she might have gone. I'd like to help you look for her."

Quinn wasn't too keen on the idea. She didn't want to mess this guy's plans up, and she never wanted to think of herself as a damsel in distress. At the same time, she knew she would appreciate his support right now. "I don't want to intrude like that," she said weakly, so weakly that she knew he would rightfully call BS on her.

"Give me your address. I'll be there in less than half an hour," Asher said confidently. "We'll figure it out."

Quinn found herself giving him her address.

He was at her house in 20 minutes. Which was impressive, but not that much, considering his house was probably about 10 minutes away from hers. So it wasn't like he flew to get to her.

"Okay," Asher said. They were sitting on Quinn's back patio, around the bonfire she had lit for the two of them. Quinn had ordered a pizza because she didn't want to cook for this guy, and they were both hungry. "Now, tell me what happened."

Quinn told him about the counseling appointment, leaving out the part about how Emerson allegedly thought she'd killed her mom. She also explained the little fight they had about what Emerson would be eating there at the house. "I probably shouldn't have been so strict with her. I probably should've given her some kind of leeway on this. After all, I'm eating pizza tonight with you, so –"

At that, Asher chuckled. "So, you're a heathen who really doesn't care about your health. Come on, Quinn, the pizza we're getting has a cauliflower crust, and the toppings are mushrooms and olives. It's not like we're ordering a deep dish Pizza Hut meat lovers."

"That's what I'm trying to say. Obviously, this girl was raised on junk food, and I'm trying to force a completely different lifestyle on her. But I'm doing it because I know it's best for her. She's 13. She doesn't need to live on Eggo waffles and cold cereal." What was unsaid was what Quinn ate when she was her age. She was a trash compactor herself, and she turned out fine. Why couldn't she think the same thing about Emerson? "And, anyhow, I think I might've found a solution, thanks to Dr. Woodley." She then explained about *The Sneaky Chef* and about the brownies she baked.

"Okay. What else did you and your daughter discuss?"

Quinn took a deep breath. "Her father. Her birth dad."

Asher raised an eyebrow. "I see. And did you tell her how she was conceived?"

"Yes. I did. But she didn't seem to really care about that."

"Don't be so sure. Listen, you understand you're not living with an ordinary child?"

"What do you mean?"

"I mean, the girl is scary smart. Her IQ is off the charts. She was also diagnosed with ADHD way back in the second grade. She's going to be restless, easily distracted, and will test all the rules. That's what her file said about her, and now, you're seeing it all for yourself."

Quinn leaned back on her lounger. She had a feeling she was going to have a lot of trouble with this kid. She just didn't know what kind of trouble it would be.

"So, what? What does this mean for trying to find her?"

"I don't know. I'm just telling you this bit of information. You need to be careful with Emerson. She's smarter than both of us."

Just then, Quinn and Asher heard somebody coming in the gate. It was Emerson sneaking back into the backyard. She looked at Quinn and Asher and raised her eyebrows. "I saw a dude outside, delivering a pizza to this very house. I told him he had the wrong house because no way are you going to be ordering a pizza. So, he left."

Quinn didn't know how to react. She was relieved and quite angry, but she didn't know what to say to her daughter. "Where did you go?"

Emerson shrugged her shoulders. "You don't have a computer for me right now, so I went down the street to a guy I know. His name is Joe, I'm not gonna give you his last name, and he's the only friend I know who lives in this neighborhood. I had to use his computer. But, once you find out what I did with his computer, you'll be happy."

"I can assure you, I'm not going to be happy." Quinn wondered just how Emerson met the guy and who he was. "How do you know this Joe, and who is he?"

"He's a guy, obviously. Not telling you more than that." Emerson looked over at Asher. "So what are you doing here? Quinn decided she had to have reinforcement?"

Asher just smiled. "Something like that."

"Cool. In case you're wondering, Joe's not my boyfriend.

THE BEACHFRONT SURPRISES.

I'm not into that. No way will I subjugate myself to patriarchy by allowing myself to be bossed around by a dude."

"Go, Gloria Steinem. A woman needs a man like a fish needs a bicycle," Asher said with a smile.

To that, Quinn nudged him. She would have a rough enough time raising this kid without Asher undermining her by making Emerson's antics seem cute.

"Tell me why you had to go to your friend's computer?"

"I wanted to find out all I could about my sperm donor. I don't want to meet him, but I wanted to see if I could find info on him. Turns out, dude's in jail. Had his hand in the Goldman Sachs cookie jar, defrauded a bunch of investors, now serving 10 to 20 years at Club Fed. From what you tell me, couldn't happen to a nicer guy."

Quinn smiled in spite of herself. She knew she was supposed to scold her and threaten her with some kind of restriction or another kind of punishment, although she had no clue what that punishment might be. Yet, she just couldn't bring herself to do it.

"How do you know about this?"

"Public information, Quinn, public information. It's been in the news. A simple Google search was all I needed to find out what happened to him. Have to admit, it was too easy. I was hoping I'd have a tougher job of trying to find what happened to him, but it was all right there. Anyhow, you're welcome."

Quinn was at a loss for words. On the one hand, she was grateful Emerson cared enough to find out this information about Charles. On the other, she didn't want to encourage her. It wasn't okay for her to be sneaking out the window. It was dangerous, and it scared the crap out of her.

"Emerson, you can't be sneaking around like that. If you want to go visit a friend, just ask me."

"K," Emerson said nonchalantly.

Quinn felt incredibly impotent. She thought about Asher's words about her daughter. About how she was not only scary smart but also extremely restless. And now, she was sneaking out the window.

"Did you really send the pizza guy away?" Asher asked.

"No. I intercepted it. It's on the dining room table inside. At first, I thought Quinn was being hypocritical, sentencing me to Brussels sprouts and calf livers while you eat pizza. Then I took a look at the pizza, saw it was cauliflower crust with mushrooms and olives, and knew it was totally on-brand."

"Well, I had a special treat made for you. Brownies. But you disappeared, so it all went out the window. It's in the fridge if you want it."

"Hard pass. Me and Joe, we got a burger at Lola's. Joe's mom brought it to us. With fries. Later."

Lola's was a place that was close to the bay that served all different kinds of burgers and sandwiches. Quinn had never been there, but she'd always heard it served delicious food.

At that, Emerson went into the house, came right back out with the pizza, and flopped it down on the table in front of Quinn and Asher. "I was just kidding when I said I turned the pizza dude away. Enjoy."

"What am I going to do about her?" Quinn asked Asher after Emerson disappeared again. "I'm not going to be able to keep her in the house. Not unless I want to handcuff her to the bed."

"Don't have any advice for you, but you have my sympathies. You know, a lot of parents would think that they would be eager to trade their kid for yours. After all, your kid is brilliant and talented. A lot of kids struggle, or they're merely average. Emerson is decidedly not average. I hate to say it, but you're probably going to have a lot more trouble with Emerson than all those parents who are raising average children. I wish I knew what to tell you about that, but I just don't."

They dug into the cauliflower crust pizza, and Quinn made a face. "This sounded so good. But you know what really sounds good?"

"Lola's?"

"Oh, yeah," Quinn said. "They have a Beyond Burger on their menu that sounds divine."

The Beyond Burger was actually one of her favorite things. It tasted like a hamburger, and the fixins were the same as the burgers. And a side of greasy fries sounded like they would hit the spot.

So, Quinn told Emerson where she was going, and the two of them headed out to Lola's.

CHAPTER 17

AVA

It was Saturday night, and the 'Sconset Inn was hopping. Word got around about the food served at the inn, so more and more of her guests opted to eat dinner in-house. Ava knew part of the draw was Deacon's piano playing, because word also got around about that. Ava had a feeling the food served at the inn, along with Deacon's playing, actually brought in more people to stay with her.

Ava was busy pitching in with the kitchen help. She was chopping the vegetables, bussing the tables, bringing people drinks and food. She was a waitress in her earlier years, both in college and right after. She hated it so much that she promised herself she would never do it again. That could be because one of the places where she waited tables was Red Lobster, a job straight from the ninth circle of hell. However, she didn't mind doing this waitressing job because she was doing it for her own place.

That made all the difference.

What she didn't like was the way all the single ladies looked at Deacon. It was as if word had spread about a handsome guy playing the piano and women were coming from far and wide to check it out. Women constantly came up to him, giggling and tossing their hair and putting $20 into his tip jar as they leaned over to show him their cleavage. What was worse, Deacon seemed to be eating it all up.

"I just love a guy in touch with his sensitive side," one lady said straight to Deacon's face. "Let's hear you play *Endless Love*. Do you know that one?"

More than one woman offered to sit on top of the piano and sing along to the music. It reminded Ava of Dorothy on the *Golden Girls* in the episode where she crashed Blanche's bar and wowed some sailors with her amazing tenor. But Bea Arthur, who played Dorothy, had an excellent voice. Not so the woman currently at the helm, a microphone in her hand. She was probably around 35 years old, her stunning curves poured into a too-tight satin dress, her hair big and blonde, her face caked with makeup. She sat on top of the piano, obviously fancying herself to be a world-class chanteuse, but Ava thought she couldn't hit a note. She'd obviously had a few too many, for she started giggling in the middle of her song as her girlfriends laughed along.

She was like a dime-store-poor-man's version of Michelle Pfeiffer in the movie *The Fabulous Baker Boys*. A VERY poor man's version at that.

Ava would've stopped all of it, except she didn't want to do anything to hurt her business. It seemed this whole fake-chanteuse-at-the-piano-with-Deacon thing was a popular entertainment hub. She looked around at the people who were eating and drinking. They all seemed to be getting into it. It was as if Saturday tonight had become karaoke night, without Ava's knowledge.

And so it went for the entire night. Along with various women, and the occasional guy or two, who got up to sing along to Deacon's piano playing, Ava noticed more than one woman slipping Deacon her phone number.

Ava didn't have a chance to think too hard about the women flirting with Deacon that night. She was too busy waiting on tables, bussing them, checking the kitchen to see what needed to be done and pitching in there, playing bartender, and just basically running her tail off.

10 o'clock finally got there, and Ava was able to take a breath. Ava stayed behind to clean up with Riley and, after everything was done, she went upstairs to the deck to relax.

When she got to the deck, she saw Deacon. He was talking to the blonde who had been singing on the piano, who no longer seemed drunk.

The two of them were sitting side-by-side on the loungers. The blonde was wrapped up in a blanket, and she kept offering Deacon to get under the blanket with her.

What was she doing? Ava thought. She thought it was a good idea for Deacon to come and play piano for her patrons, and it was, because it seemed to be very good for business. It certainly did bring in the lady folk. But she wasn't prepared for the emotions she felt when she saw Deacon with that blonde.

She'd grasped at happiness and had thrown it away. All because of her insecurities. She didn't feel she was worthy of a guy like Deacon.

The past couple of weeks, with all the women throwing themselves at him, just heightened her insecurities more.

She walked into the kitchen and made sure that everything was clean and tidy and put away. Riley had already left, as had the prep cooks. That left her to walk around the deserted kitchen, which she saw as a metaphor for her life. Darkness had descended upon the kitchen, and upon the dining room as well. There was nobody around anymore except for Deacon, who was still apparently upstairs with the blonde.

She just quietly went up to her room and went to bed.

CHAPTER 18

QUINN

*A*fter Emerson pulled her stunt with climbing out the window, Quinn attempted to punish her by putting her on restriction and grounding her, but soon discovered how pointless those two things were.

Quinn bought Emerson a new computer. She wanted that to be a carrot because she wanted something to reward her daughter for good behavior. She didn't want Emerson to use the lack of computer as an excuse to sneak out. If Emerson did certain things, like complete chores Quinn assigned to her – doing dishes, vacuuming, feeding the dogs and picking up the poop in the yard - Quinn not only gave her an allowance but let her play Fortnite for two hours every evening.

Quinn also wanted the computer to be a stick. She wanted something to take away from Emerson when she caught her sneaking out the window. So, the second time Emerson sneaked out the window, Quinn took the computer out of Emerson's room and put it into the den. "If you want that computer back, then you need to live by my rules."

Unfortunately, that didn't work. Emerson just sneaked out the window more, to use her friends' computers.

******

"I don't know what I'm going to do with that girl," Quinn said to Asher. She'd just tried to force Emerson to come back home with her after the third time she found her on the beach with a group of new friends who were all around 15 or 16 years old. Emerson basically told her she would come home when she wanted to, and there was nothing she could do to bring her home.

"You're not even my mom yet," Emerson pointedly said to Quinn. "I mean, I know you gave birth to me and all, but you gave me up all those years ago, so you're basically a stranger."

It was true that Quinn was not officially Emerson's mom, as the adoption had not yet gone through. The hearing for the adoption was set at the end of the year, so, in the meantime, Quinn was considered to be Emerson's guardian.

Quinn felt she was a failure even at being a guardian, much less a mother. She had no idea what she was doing. And the only thing she wanted to do when she was at her wits' end was get a glass of wine and sit on her back patio. She knew that this ritual wasn't constructive, but at same time, she didn't know what else to do. Emerson was not yet enrolled in school because she came to Quinn's house in late May, right after her school was let out for the summer.

The upshot was that Quinn was left with a bored child who was left alone for eight hours a day because Quinn was still working her job, and Hallie was gone, as she was staying at her extended stay place while she looked for a new home. Sarah still lived with Quinn and Emerson, but she, too, was gone most of the day, helping Ava. Besides, she couldn't ask Sarah or anybody else to be Emerson's babysitter. That just wouldn't be right. It was Quinn's responsibility, and she felt overwhelmed.

THE BEACHFRONT SURPRISES.

However, she was finding Asher was more than willing to help. Quinn didn't call him about Emerson leaving the house on a regular basis, but he always seemed to show up right when Quinn needed him. He would help her look for the girl, and they usually couldn't find her anywhere, but one time they found her on the beach with a group of friends around a bonfire. Quinn smelled the telltale scent of pot when she busted her daughter in this group, and she tried to ground her for that, but grounding her was proving useless.

Most of the time, when Emerson went missing, Quinn had to wait until her daughter showed up back at the house.

Quinn also wasn't used to being a role model. She knew she would have to mind her P's and Q's with a young daughter under her roof, which meant she would have to not drink a glass of wine every night. Emerson had pointed out that pot was no worse than alcohol, and there were many medical reasons to smoke pot and no medical reasons to indulge in white wine.

"Wine has antioxidants that protect your heart," Quinn had said.

"Red wine, Quinn, red wine. You drink white," Emerson said, her arms crossed in front of her chest. "And do you know how many medical problems are helped by cannabis? We're talking everything from helping migraine headaches to helping chemo patients. Doctors use it to treat depression, pain, diabetes, seizures and ADHD. And, guess what I was diagnosed with at the age of 7?"

"ADHD," Quinn said. Asher told her this about Emerson. It wasn't surprising because Emerson was wired and had a short attention span.

"Right," Emerson said. "If I were 21, I could get a doctor to prescribe that stuff to me."

"But you're not 21," Quinn said. "That's the whole point.

Your brain and body are still developing. That's why you can't legally drink or smoke pot."

Emerson rolled her eyes. "Whatever. Anyhow, I wasn't smoking pot with those kids on the beach. I wasn't drinking, either."

"Then what were you doing out there with them?" Quinn asked.

"Hanging out, Quinn, hanging out. You can't expect me to hang around here all the time, do you?"

"How did you meet that group?" Quinn asked.

"Joe."

"Joe, your non-boyfriend?" Quinn asked.

Emerson rolled her eyes. "What's with all the labels? Boyfriend, non-boyfriend, blah, blah, blah. We're hanging out."

Quinn shut her eyes. "How old is this Joe?" she asked between gritted teeth.

"He's 15. Why?"

Quinn opened her eyes. "15? 15? What are you doing hanging around a boy that age?" Oh, that couldn't be good. It was bad enough when she thought Joe was 13 or 14. But 15? The boy would be a sophomore in high school in the coming semester while Emerson was going into the eighth grade.

To Quinn, there was a world of difference between the ages of 15 and 13, and the biggest one was that the boy probably was pressuring her daughter for sex. If Emerson was 16, Quinn would be lecturing her about contraception and probably dragging her to the family planning clinic on Vesper.

Quinn wouldn't be thrilled if Emerson was having sex at the age of 16, but she also would be realistic and know it would probably happen. After all, she was 16 when she lost her virginity to her loser ex-husband Benjamin.

But Emerson was 13, not 16. And her having sex was not

THE BEACHFRONT SURPRISES.

something Quinn could tolerate. So, Emerson hanging out with a boy at an age when the hormones were raging made her want to hit the roof.

"He's cool. That's all," Emerson said.

"How did you meet this boy?" Quinn asked.

"Online."

Quinn was ready to blow a gasket at that one. "Online? Online? What do you mean, you met him online?" Quinn had always heard bad things about young girls who meet men and boys online. There was usually a pervert on the other side just waiting to pounce on a fresh young girl like Emerson.

"Yeah. Online. And, don't worry, it's not what you're thinking. I've seen those 'Catch a Pervert' shows. Don't worry, I'm not meeting Pervy Pervuson from Pervert-town." Emerson scrunched up her nose. "Give me some credit, Quinn."

"Listen, Emerson, pedophiles use the Internet to lure young girls into their homes. Just because you're extremely intelligent doesn't mean you're not going to fall for a catfish."

Emerson rolled her eyes. "You gonna start giving me a lecture about 'good touch bad touch' now? You think I haven't heard about catfishing dangers? Trust me, I've heard all about it. Teachers, my mom, my friends, the Internet itself, everyone's always talking to girls my age about that kind of thing. I'm surprised perverts find anybody to fall for their BS anymore because we've all had it drilled into our heads from birth not to meet a strange dude in person after only talking to him online."

"Regardless, I don't want you meeting men or boys online," Quinn said.

"Again, you need to give me some credit. You ever see that movie *Hard Candy*?" Emerson asked.

Unfortunately, Quinn had seen that movie, and it was

scary as hell. *Hard Candy* was a movie where a very young girl lures a pedophile into a trap where she proceeded to torture him, and, after getting him to confess he'd killed a young girl, made him commit suicide.

"Yes, what about it?" Quinn asked.

"Let's just say that anything Haley did to the perv in that movie would pale against what I would do to any dude who'd try to get with me like that."

"No meeting men online," Quinn said.

"Quinn, Joe's a member of the Fortnite group," Emerson said. "So, he's cool. Everyone in the group knows him. We've been playing together for the past six months."

That made Quinn feel a little bit better. She felt meeting people in the Fortnite group was safer than meeting people off of Tinder or something of the sort.

"Okay. But, I'm warning you, if I find out you're on Tinder or Bumble or anything like that, I'll take away the computer and you'll never get it back."

To that, Emerson rolled her eyes. "Quinn, again, give me a little bit of credit here. You don't think I know to stay away from those apps? Sorry, Quinn, but I'm not trying to get sucked into some sicko psycho's web."

"And Joe, does he smoke pot with that group?" Quinn asked.

Emerson shrugged her shoulders. "No, Quinn, he doesn't. And neither do I. Some of the kids do it, some of them don't. Joe's one who doesn't."

"You better not be lying."

"I'm not. Listen, I tried pot once, and I hated it. Made me paranoid. Joe's the same way. That stuff makes both of us feel terrible, so we just don't do it."

"But you still shouldn't be sneaking around with an older boy."

"Oh? Listen, your friend, Ava, totally has the hots for a

dude who's like a zygote compared to her. I don't hear you giving her the big lecture about age differences."

"How do you know about Ava and Deacon?" Quinn asked.

"I got eyes."

"But when did you see Ava and Deacon together?"

Emerson shrugged her shoulders again, a gesture that was really starting to grate on Quinn's last nerve. "I snuck over to Ava's bed and breakfast one night when I was with the kids. Dude was playing the piano. Ava was all googly eyes and gave the stink eye to the women drooling over him. I don't think anybody noticed me hanging around that night, so if you ask Ava about it, she probably won't know what you're talking about."

Quinn shook her head. "Ava and Deacon are not your business, and their age difference is not the same as being 15 and 13. Emerson, you just hit puberty. And you aren't ready for sex."

"Sex? Quinn, that's gross." Emerson screwed up her nose. "No, thank you. Sorry, Quinn, but I'm not about to get knocked up by some loser. And I'm not trying to get an STD, either. If Joe tried anything with me, I'd just kick him where it counts." Emerson made some karate-chopping moves with her hands and kicked her foot in the air to illustrate what she would do to Joe if he tried to have sex with her. "Maybe you should've tried that with my sperm donor, and I wouldn't be here right now."

"Emerson, I told you—"

"Yeah, yeah, he Cosbyed you. I get that. But don't you know you never leave your drink alone when you're with a dude you don't know? Man, that's life 101 stuff right there, Quinn. I'd never be that dumb."

Quinn had no idea if she could trust Emerson with this Joe and didn't know what she could do even if she didn't trust them together. She supposed that it was a good thing if

Emerson wasn't having sex with the guy, and she seemed to be adamant that sex wouldn't happen. But she couldn't trust Emerson not to drink or smoke pot with Joe and his friends.

And, worst of all, she had no clue how to stop Emerson from sneaking around. She could hire a nanny to watch her while she was working, but Emerson was such a slippery one she probably would be sneaking around on the nanny, too.

What was she going to do? She could certainly take away Emerson's computer. But she didn't know a way to keep Emerson in the house.

CHAPTER 19

AVA

Something was nagging Ava, and had been ever since the evening she shared with her mother. She didn't think their evening was entirely successful, because, even though she knew her mother slightly more than she did before, she still felt there was an unspoken barrier between them.

The thing nagging her was Violet. Her mother and her best friend Violet apparently met when Colleen was a District Court judge in Kansas City. Ava was 10 years old, and, all of a sudden, there was Violet in the house. Violet babysat her when her mother would work late. The lady was a school teacher, so she would typically be off of work around 3:30, and there were many, many times that Colleen would be working late.

Ava was always so happy whenever Violet would watch her and Sarah. The lady was a lot of fun, much more fun than her own mother was. Violet would play card games and board games with her, would read her stories, and tell her silly jokes and riddles. And because she was a schoolteacher, she was very good about helping her with her homework. Ava learned a lot from Violet. So did Sarah.

Once Ava went to college and law school, she lost track of her mother's friend. By that time, Ava was barely speaking with her mother. She'd hoped that Violet would be almost like a surrogate mother for her, but, when she got into the rhythm of college, met Hallie, started going to parties and just enjoying college life, she forgot about her mother's friend. Much to her shame.

Violet wasn't somebody she'd even thought about for the past thirty-plus years. She wasn't close with her mother, so Ava wouldn't have known if her mother had kept in touch with Violet over the years. Ever since she went to college and no longer lived under the same roof as her mother, she barely spoke to Colleen.

Still, it broke her heart to discover Violet had passed away. She did love her when she knew her, and Violet was very good to her during her formative years.

Her curiosity led her to the internet, because she wanted to find Violet's obituary. She typed in the name Violet Boville, and she immediately found what she was looking for. She pulled up the obit and read about Violet's love of animals, her work at the Humane Society, and that she'd been a schoolteacher until she retired at 70.

The one thing that interested her was that Violet apparently died in the city of Boston. And, apparently, she'd been working in the school district of Los Angeles County. The dates she worked in the Los Angeles County school district coincided with the dates her mother was judging in the Los Angeles District Court. Same for Violet's stint in the Boston school district.

Why did her mother lie about that? She explicitly told Ava she'd kept in touch with Violet through the years through emails and phone calls, and that they didn't live in the same city after Colleen started moving around the country. Yet, according to this obituary, Violet followed her mother around through the years.

Ava raised an eyebrow. She wasn't going to jump to conclusions, but it seemed odd.

Suddenly, it didn't seem weird that her mother hadn't dated since her father died. Maybe she was dating, but maybe she wanted to keep it on the down-low.

For a reason.

CHAPTER 20

QUINN

One evening, around the first of June, Quinn invited Ava and Hallie over for a glass of wine. Quinn made sure she was positioned to where she could see if Emerson tried to sneak out her window. She wanted to brainstorm with Ava and Hallie. Sarah was on a trip to the West Coast to secure some wine contracts, so she didn't partake in the festivities that evening.

The three women talked about the options Quinn had with Emerson. "I've been taking her to counseling, but I don't know what good it's doing. The only thing I've found out is she somehow blames herself for her mother's death, and she also blames me. Other than that, Dr. Woodley hasn't gotten much out of her."

"That's so strange," Ava said. "What do you mean, she blames herself for her mother dying? Didn't her mother die of heart failure?"

"Yeah," Quinn said. "I don't know what she means by that, and she sure ain't telling me. Asher has told me a bit more about the girl, but I still feel like I'm flying blind. I really have no clue on how I'm supposed to keep her in the house."

THE BEACHFRONT SURPRISES.

"Is she eating?" Ava asked.

"Yeah. I finally figured that one out, with Dr. Woodley's help. I've been sneaking beans and veggies into cakes, muffins, brownies and stuff like that, and she's been eating them up. I've also learned to make her precious chicken nuggets with ground almonds and pecans, and I've made mac and cheese with butternut squash. She has no clue on what's in there, so that cookbook has been a lifesaver."

Quinn told the ladies she was seriously thinking about putting bars on the window, as if she was living in her Brooklyn apartment again. "It's going to look like a prison, ya'll, but I don't know what else to do," Quinn said.

Just then, the beautiful lilting sounds of a violin wafted through Emerson's window. Ava heard the music, and smiled. "Well, at least your young daughter has good taste in music. I recognize that Mozart piece anywhere. And it's so loud, it almost sounds like it's live."

Quinn had to laugh. "That's actually Emerson playing. Yes, having her under my roof has been a bonus, because I get treated to a classical music concert just about every evening she's here and hasn't sneaked out to the beach."

Hallie raised an eyebrow. "Oh my God, she's good. I've never heard her play."

"I have an idea," Ava said hurriedly. "You say she's bored, right?"

"Yes. So bored."

"Have her come over to my house. I can set up a place for her to play for my patrons. I've a feeling she's going to like an audience. Anyhow, it'll give her something to do, if nothing else. Tomorrow is Friday night, and she can come and play. And also on Saturday night when Deacon comes to play - she can play the violin while he plays the piano. What do you say?"

"Well, I suppose it's worth a shot. I'll go up and ask her."

To Quinn's surprise, Emerson actually jumped at the chance. "Oh, God yes. No offense, Quinn, but I'm going stir crazy being kept in this house. Climbing the walls."

"Really?"

"Yeah. What time does she need me over there?"

"5 o'clock?"

"I'll be there." She seemed really excited. "Finally, I have something to look forward to here. Quinn, I was thinking about talking to you about this anyhow. You've got to give me something to do. My parents, my adoptive parents, they found that out when I was two years old. You have to keep me occupied. I have to have something to look forward to. I think I'll not want to climb out the window as often when school starts because I'll have things to do."

Quinn went to tell Ava the news. "Oh my goddess, that worked. You should've seen her little face light up when I went to tell her she was going to have a job every Friday and Saturday night." Quinn shook her head. "I'm still holding my breath because I don't trust her. I hope the solution is something as simple as giving her an outlet for her energies and talents."

"Yeah. And it's a bonus for me, because it means that maybe the bimbos will stop laying all over the piano and singing if there's a young girl playing the violin next to him," Ava said.

They all raised her glass to that.

"I have to admit, so far, having Emerson here has been a stress, but also a joy," Quinn said. "She's been challenging, to say the least, but she's funny and brilliant and has brought a breath of fresh air to my life. Now, if I can only channel her energies towards something constructive, I'll have it made. Well, not have it made, exactly, but I'll at least feel I've taken back some control."

THE BEACHFRONT SURPRISES.

Quinn hoped that the violin-playing idea would help her get a handle on her restless daughter.

Because something had to change.

Otherwise, she would go insane.

CHAPTER 21

AVA

That Friday night, Ava was excited she'd be able to have young Emerson play for her patrons. She was looking forward to getting to know the little girl better. The plan was for Emerson and Deacon to play together on Saturday nights and for Emerson to play for the guests alone on Friday nights.

Ava found that Emerson wasn't only a virtuoso but could play pieces by ear. She was also an amazing ad libber with her violin, which meant she could listen to Deacon's original music and accompany him even though she'd never heard the piece before.

Ava was a bit blown away by the child. She seemed to be such an old soul, and not just because of all the tragedy she'd endured in her young life, but also because she was so wickedly intelligent and talented. At the same time, Ava knew Quinn would have her hands full with Emerson just because she was so advanced and would be bored when she went to school. Quinn also told Ava that Emerson had been diagnosed with ADHD, which complicated matters a lot.

Sarah was back from her West Coast trip. She was at the

'Sconset Inn the following Saturday afternoon after Emerson played for the first time at the inn and, as with Deacon, was an immediate hit with the dinner guests.

At that time, Emerson and Deacon were practicing for their evening show.

"Hey," she said. "What's going on? Why is Emerson here?"

Ava explained about Emerson's boredom and her desire to do something constructive.

Sarah cocked her head as she listened to the duet. "Yeah, I'd say she's doing something constructive. She's only 13? Damn. That girl could end up playing Carnegie Hall when she gets a little bit older. You ever see those sexy, edgy women violinists with big hair and skimpy costumes on stage, playing the hell out of their instrument? I could see Emerson doing that in about 10 more years. Is Quinn going to look into putting her into some kind of performing arts college? Like Juilliard or something of the like?"

"I think that that's a little premature, but maybe not. It'll be up to Quinn on what she wants to do with her daughter to make sure she lives up to her potential."

"Well, I tell you, this duet will pack them in. I also think you'll have fewer bimbos on the piano singing. Who wants to writhe all over the place like Michelle Pfeiffer in *The Fabulous Baker Boys* when there's a young girl right there?"

"Yep. That's what I was thinking too." Ava was staring at Deacon and feeling like she wanted to do more than stare.

Sarah sighed. "Sis, have I told you how dumb you are? It's obvious to anybody with eyes that you and Deacon are meant to be together. You're letting a hot guy like that slip through your fingers because why? I don't get it."

"No, you wouldn't get it," Ava said to her gorgeous sister. "You've always been the one to snap your fingers and 100 guys would fall out of the sky and land at your feet. You have the confidence that comes with being born stunning. I don't know, Sarah. I'm still scarred from our high school days when guys like Deacon would've run right over me to get to you."

Sarah rolled her eyes. "Ava, at some point, you have to leave high school behind. Yes, high school Ava would've thought high school Deacon was way out of her league. And he wouldn't have been, by the way, but you would've assumed he was, so you wouldn't have even tried. But Ava, you're 54 years old, you graduated from Harvard, and you're running a successful bed-and-breakfast. You have a lot to bring to the table now, you had a lot to bring to the table back then too, and you need to go for it."

"He's too young."

Sarah put her hands together in a motion that said *I'm going to strangle you right now.* "Ava, life is too short to not try to get what you want. I'm walking proof of that. Don't forget, I spent 20 years trapped and fearful. If I'd gone for what I wanted, damn the torpedoes, my life would've taken a much better turn all those years ago. There's something to be said for living your truth, whatever that truth is. It's all about living without regret."

"How did you get to be so smart?" Ava asked her sister.

Sarah shrugged. "You know, I go to hot yoga three times a week with Willow and Hallie. I've gotten to know those girls pretty well. I've also started meditating every single day. Digging down deep into that part of me I've hidden from the world for so very long. That part of me I've hidden from *myself* for so very long. I'm starting to understand what my inner self wants out of life. I'm starting to understand what part of me was shaped by what was expected of me, what part was shaped by what other people wanted from me, and what part of me is me. Ava, you always thought I had it all in high school. You didn't see the pressure on me to conform. I couldn't be like other people back then – I always had to be on. The entire school had this image of me I had to live up to. You were lucky. You didn't have any pressure on you at all."

"So Hallie and Willow have made you so introspective?" Ava was fascinated by her sister's insights. She realized that, like Sarah, she didn't exactly know what her truth was. She knew what her role was, that of a mother and a business owner. But she'd never just sat in the silence and really thought about who she was and what she wanted. Let alone sit in the silence and discover why she was so insecure. She really wished she could let go of high school Ava, the bullied, picked-on girl who wanted more than anything to fit in but never quite did.

"Yeah. Pretty much. You should really get to know Willow, by the way. Talk about a woman who lives life on her terms and is completely comfortable in her own skin. The great thing about her is if she wants something, she's going to go for it. She really knows what's important to her, and, trust me, she's not going to let society or any individual tell her the sky is green. There's no gaslighting that girl. I really admire her. She wouldn't let Deacon slip through her fingers. You shouldn't either."

Ava thought about the changes she'd seen in her friend Hallie ever since she was taken under Willow's wing. Hallie went from a mousy woman who drank too much and was controlled by her husband to a total bad-ass who kicked that same husband to the curb and enrolled in a Master's program in nutrition while she worked with Willow at their wellness spa. Hallie was now a woman who was brave enough to tell the world what she wanted and didn't let anything stand in her way.

She admired her friend Hallie thoroughly, even if she didn't feel she could be as brave to just go for what she wanted. She wished she could, though.

Oh, she wished she could.

****

That night, Emerson and Deacon, as a duo, completely blew everyone away. Emerson was a true prodigy, Ava realized as she watched the two. No matter what Deacon played, Emerson was able to accompany him. There were many songs Deacon played that Emerson also knew, but when she didn't know the song, it wasn't a problem for her. She ad-libbed to the songs she didn't know, and it sounded perfect.

Sarah was right - Emerson had a real talent, and she had the potential to become famous one day. Quinn would have to find a way to harness Emerson's potential because, with Emerson showing her wild side, the little girl could go either way. Emerson could either stay on the straight and narrow and hone her gift and excel in school, or end up with a bad crowd and completely spiral down.

She prayed that Quinn had the strength to steer little Emerson in the right direction.

CHAPTER 22

AVA

The next evening, Ava and Sarah were sitting on the beach, which was crowded that evening with groups of people sitting around bonfires and chatting loudly. The moon was full and the waves were relentless and calming. Fog was starting to roll in but had not yet reached the shore. Everywhere in the air were smells of burning cedar, sounds of laughter, and the distinct odor of pot.

Sarah's dog, Bella, a beautiful pit bull mix, was sitting in between them. Sarah had her arm around the dog and was squeezing her neck. Sarah and Bella had such a tight bond. Ava knew Sarah was probably lonely, so she was happy her sister was kept company by her beautiful canine friend.

"So, how are things going with mom?" Sarah asked Ava. "I guess the two of you spent some time together a few weeks ago. When I saw you guys hanging out, I thought, before you know it, dogs and cats would be living together because it was going to be the end of the world. But I was really glad that you guys spent time together, just the two of you. I think you guys needed that."

Ava nodded her head. "Yeah, it was okay. I felt more like

she was trying instead of just going with the flow. It's almost like she had a box to tick off, and she was doing it. I don't know. There are still a lot of walls between the two of us."

"What do you think would bring those walls down?"

Ava sighed. "It would start with our mother being honest."

Sarah chuckled. "Isn't that the problem with our mother? She's a little too honest? I mean, how many times did she tell both of us 'you look like hell' or 'yes, those pants do make your butt look fat?'"

Ava laughed. "Oh, yes. Not to mention all those times we would give her a gift, and she would tell us to our face how much she hated it. But, I have to hand it to her. I learned exactly which gifts would be despised. And, to my credit and yours, we were able to give her what she wanted a time or two."

"Yeah," Sarah said. "In a way, it's better to know if a gift is well received. We never had to wonder. Still, a few white lies along the way probably wouldn't have been so horrible."

"Unfortunately, our mother just didn't have it in her to have a filter on what she would say," Ava said. "And, just think, if she would've been a normal person and had a filter, I wouldn't have gotten to know my therapist so well."

"Touché."

Ava looked at the surf and smelled the air. She was debating whether or not she should discuss her suspicions about Violet with Sarah. She thought that it was probably a good idea. Maybe Sarah would be able to offer an alternative explanation for Violet's inexplicable decision to traipse around the country following their mother. More importantly, if Sarah thought the same thing about Violet as Ava did, maybe Sarah could give some ideas on why their mother would keep all of it secret.

"Do you remember Violet?" Ava asked Sarah.

"Of course. She was like a fixture around the house for

quite a few years when we were growing up. Why do you ask?"

"She died. Apparently, a little over a year ago."

Sarah put her hand to her heart and shook her head. "Oh. No. No. Oh, that hurts my heart. She was such a kind person and so much fun. She was really the only person our mother was close to over the years."

"Yes. But there was something odd about her obituary. I guess she worked in the Los Angeles school district and in the Boston school district. The years she worked in those two school districts coincided with the years that our mother was on the bench in Los Angeles and in Boston. I guess Violet spent her life following our mother around. Do you think that's odd?"

Sarah nodded her head. "Yeah, that's a little weird. But then again, Hallie and Quinn followed you out here. Maybe when two people are such good friends that they're attached at the hip, they just want to stay in each other's lives."

"Well, it was a little bit different with Quinn and Hallie. I mean, Quinn was sick of the city, and she already had her eye on buying a beach house in Georgia when I invited her to come out here with me. Not only that, there are so many opportunities for her to expand her business out here, what with all the mansions and rich people living out here who can afford to pay her fees. As for Hallie, she wasn't originally going to move out here. She just decided to stay after leaving her husband and snatching up the opportunity to become Willow's business partner. So, both women had their reasons for coming out here. It wasn't just that they were coming out here for me."

"Hmmmm," Sara said. "On the one hand, I can almost understand Violet following our mother around. Violet wasn't attached to any one city or location, and, as a schoolteacher, she could get a job anywhere she wanted to go. And, you have to admit, both Los Angeles and Boston have their own lure. In Los Angeles, you can live close to the beach. And Boston has that historic charm and distinct vibe."

"On the other hand, mom hasn't dated in all these years, since dad died. Do you think that's kind of odd?"

Sarah shrugged her shoulders. "No. I'm inclined to think it's smart at this point. Mom had her career, a very respected career, I might add. She probably just decided it was better to live life on her terms, without anybody around to control her. You know, I've kind of come to that same conclusion. My whole relationship with Nolan has just disillusioned me so much. If mom chooses to live her life alone, that's her choice. It's not for you or me to question it."

"I guess." Ava was starting to come around to Sarah's point of view because Sarah was correct – there was a logical explanation for all of her questions.

"Why? What were you thinking?" Sarah asked.

Ava cocked her head. "I thought maybe our mother did have a relationship all these years with Violet. The puzzle pieces do seem to fit."

Sarah seemed to think about the possibility but then shook her head. "I see what you're saying, but, at the same time, why would she lie about something like that? What motivation would she possibly have to keep something like that from us?"

Ava shrugged. "That's what I'm stuck on. I mean, if mom was in a same-sex relationship, who cares? I think I can speak for both of us when I say we would be nothing but happy for our mother to find happiness with somebody to love. Surely she knows that too, right?"

"Maybe. You have to understand, our mother was born at a different time. You know, she was born just before the war ended."

"Yes, but she came of age during the 60s," Ava said. "She

was at Vassar and Harvard during the period when everything was changing – civil rights, women's rights, and gay rights."

"I know that, but she also came of age at a time when homosexuality was considered to be a mental defect," Sarah countered. "Did you know the DSM classified homosexuality as a mental disorder until 1973? And even after the DSM took homosexuality out of its manual, it still had something called sexual orientation disturbance that was considered a mental disorder? That was only removed in 1982. Not to mention, people are still weird about gays. We've come a long way, I won't dispute that, but there are still plenty of people who would consider mom to be defective somehow if she had a relationship with a woman."

Ava nodded. "Mom would hate it if anybody thought she had a mental disorder or thought she was different."

"At any rate, she probably wouldn't want her daughters to think she was less than perfect."

Ava rolled her eyes. "Oh, the irony. I think our mother is FAR from perfect. You've always had a better experience with her, but, in my eyes, she's about as far from perfection as you can get."

"True. But I think she's always wanted us to see her as being together. Competent. A superwoman. And, I, for one, do see her as all those things. Maybe she thought if we knew she was gay, we'd see her as less than a superwoman. Like maybe she thought being gay was like her kryptonite or something. Who knows? That's even assuming she was in a relationship with Violet. I don't know if we can necessarily jump to conclusions about that."

"So, do we ask her directly about it? Or do we just not bring it up?" Ava asked. "On the one hand, it's her business. On the other, I think I'd like to know her a bit more. The real her. And there's no way that I, or you, can ever know what she's really about unless we knock down her walls and see what's there."

Sarah hugged Bella tighter and stared at the surf. "That's a tough one. But one thing's for sure - our mother isn't getting any younger. Do you think we might have some regrets if she gets an aneurysm and suddenly dies? Do you think we couldn't get close to her because she hid who she was? I, personally, think that if we could get her to come clean about something like that, it would bring us closer. Then again, if she doesn't want to talk about it, she might get defensive and push us further away. It could go either way, to be honest with you. I'm not sure if we want to explode that bomb."

Ava weighed the options in her mind.

She concluded it was best to let sleeping dogs lie. If their mother was gay, there were reasons why she didn't want to tell her daughters. Ava just had to respect those reasons.

She would still try to get to know her mother superficially. Ava wanted to get past the superficiality with her mother, but she didn't think it was possible. If her mother was struck down by a brain aneurysm tomorrow, Ava would have to live with the regret she couldn't get closer to Colleen.

That would be a shame, but Ava saw no other alternative.

CHAPTER 23

COLLEEN

Colleen was going back and forth on what she would talk to her daughters about. She thought the acupuncture, combined with Willow's counsel, was getting her closer to where she could be open and free with her daughters about Violet. Ever since she started the acupuncture with Willow, she felt lighter. The dark cloud hovering over her head for the past year was starting to lift and she was beginning to see through the fog.

But something was still stopping her.

One of the things she brought on her trip were the letters she and Violet had written back and forth over the years.

It was Violet's idea to write the letters. She said their life together would be one big blur at some point, and the letters would be like signposts to document the special moments.

"After all, life is just a series of moments," Violet had said. "I think it's good for us to document them. It'll be fun to read the letters years from now – we can go back and relive a certain period. It'll make everything we do somehow meaningful, knowing it'll be captured for posterity."

Colleen thought it was silly. Violet was always much

more romantic than her, much more ethereal. Violet taught classic English literature to AP students. She was always reading about love and romance in such books as *Dr. Zhivago* and *Anna Karenina*. Not to mention the works of Jane Austen and the Brontë sisters. Colleen thought all the romantic notions in those classic literary books, and all the poems Violet taught to her students, warped her brain just a bit. But in a good way.

Colleen was definitely much more pragmatic in her thinking. Not for her a romance to read - she liked her fiction without gooey great-love prose. Give her the works of Stephen King, Tom Clancy, or a good psychological thriller over Jane Austen, any day of the week. She would much rather read a book like *Gone Girl,* with its plot about two horrible people stabbing each other in the back at every turn, then read a Harlequin romance or something of the sort.

Violet balanced out Colleen's inherently cynical nature, just like Colleen anchored Violet, a woman who had her head in the clouds. Violet liked to shoe shop and get dressed up like a girly girl, she loved the color pink, rom-coms, Sandra Bullock, and her favorite channel was the Hallmark Channel. Especially during Christmastime – Violet would watch all those corny Christmas romance shows while Colleen would roll her eyes at those movies.

Meanwhile, Colleen preferred CNN and the History Channel. She didn't care about her shoes, not the way Violet did, and she only wore a dress for social functions, such as a fundraiser.

Violet was always highlighting her hair – usually, she just chose honey blonde highlights, but one time she went a little crazy and got some pink streaks in her light ash-blonde hair. Colleen thought it was beautiful on her and wished she had the guts to do the same.

Then again, it probably wasn't so great for a federal judge to have pink hair.

Colleen didn't go in for fancy highlights. She let herself go grey when the time came because she didn't want to mess with it.

Violet had a warmth about her that attracted people to her side. She made friends wherever she went, and she was always ready with a helping hand whenever anybody called on her. Colleen was much colder, much more introverted, and rarely got close with anybody.

No doubt about it, the two women were different as night and day. Yet their striking dissimilarities were what bonded them together for all those years. Colleen knew she couldn't be with another person who was like her. It would be two misanthropes together, which would be a deadly combination.

There was a part of her that always wanted to be more like Violet – free-spirited, thoughtful and kind, with a romantic soul. But, at the same time, she knew if she were more like Violet, she wouldn't be in the position she was.

Colleen could never imagine Violet making hardheaded judicial decisions that impacted people's lives, often for the worse. Violet would've been too sympathetic, and she would never have wanted to make a decision that would hurt somebody's feelings. And, if there was one thing that Colleen knew about litigants, it was that somebody's feelings would get hurt by the end of any trial.

Even in her appellate judge position, it was the same – in every single one of her written decisions, somebody was hurt.

Violet wouldn't have been able to take the responsibility of making the kinds of decisions Colleen had to make every day.

Now, Colleen found herself in a strange position. She was

feeling nostalgic, a little soft, and all she wanted was to read through the letters Violet had written to her over the years.

So, for the next few hours, she found herself laughing and crying and ruminating over Violet's words. And, again and again, Colleen was faced with the truth in these letters. It was a truth constantly at the center of any arguments that the two ladies had, and Violet spoke this truth in almost every letter she wrote Colleen.

And that truth was that Violet was offended she and Colleen had to hide their love from Sarah and Ava. Colleen always knew how Violet felt about Colleen's desire to not tell her daughters about their relationship. They had many an argument about it, but Colleen always squashed it as soon as the argument got going. Violet respected Colleen's wishes, even if she didn't agree with them, so she would never go behind Colleen's back to tell Sarah and Ava the truth.

Colleen ignored Violet's pleas while Violet was alive. She told Violet she didn't understand – Violet's parents were very accepting of her relationship with Colleen, and Violet didn't have children. How could Violet understand where Colleen was coming from? Colleen put the whole issue out of her mind, so, the first time she read those letters, at the time when the letters were actually written, Colleen didn't take the pleading words to heart.

Now, however, in light of how Colleen was feeling about Violet – a mix of nostalgia, grief, and joy at reading Violet's words again, for she felt Violet was there with her as she read her letters – she saw Violet's wishes in a different light.

After Colleen finished reading the last letter, she went to find her daughters.

She was ready to come clean at last.

CHAPTER 24

AVA

Ava was busy cleaning some bedrooms when her mother came to find her.

"Ava, why don't you and Sarah join me at The Straight Wharf this evening? It'll be my treat."

Ava just nodded her head. She didn't think her mother was ready to talk to her about anything serious. She thought her mother just wanted to hang out with them. The whole getting to know my daughter better, blah, blah, blah.

"Sounds good. I love that place. I usually quit working around seven in the evening. So make a reservation for around 7:30. And, thanks, mom."

****

Right at 7:30, Ava, Colleen, and Sarah were driving to The Straight Wharf for dinner. Ava always liked the Scottish salmon for her entrée, and oysters for her appetizer. Sarah usually liked to go more vegetarian for her entrée, so she usually ordered the Eggplant Parmesan, with the Spaghetti Carbonara as her appetizer. Their mother was a beef eater all the way – she got the beef carpaccio for her appetizer and the prime rib for her entrée.

Colleen ordered a bottle of wine for the table. Sarah recommended a Zinfandel for herself and Colleen, because, as she explained, medium-bodied red wine went well with both nightshades, such as eggplant, and red meat. Ava asked Sarah what kind of wine would go well with her seafood. Sarah recommended a Picpoul varietal, a light-bodied white wine, low on sweetness, with notes of green apple, citrus and thyme.

"It's made for fish," Sarah explained. "And quite rare. I'm impressed this place has it."

So, this Picpoul wine was what Ava ordered.

When the wine came and Ava took a sip, she knew Sarah had hit the nail on the head. It was different from any other wine she'd ever tasted, and the notes were unique. She knew it would go perfectly with her fish.

Sarah really had a gift for knowing what kind of wine to order for every meal. Colleen was right – her sister had a passion for wine, and it showed.

Over appetizers, Ava and Sarah made small talk with their mother. How did she like staying at the bed-and-breakfast, was she missing her work, how was the beach today, those kind of topics.

Then, when their meal came, Colleen actually addressed exactly why she wanted her daughters to join her for dinner.

"Okay," Colleen began. Then she took a deep breath. Ava thought her mother looked a bit nervous, which was very uncommon. "This conversation is 40-odd years in the making. But, I don't know how to say this, so I'll just say it. Violet was not my friend. She was the love of my life."

At that, Colleen took a sip of her wine and refused to look at either of her daughters.

Ava put her hand on her mother's. Sarah got up, came over to where Colleen was sitting, and gave her mother a hug.

"Mom," Ava began. "Thank you so much for sharing this with us. I'm sad Violet has passed on, but I'm happy you weren't alone all those years. Experiencing great love is a rare thing that needs to be cherished. You were lucky to have her in your life for as long as you had her."

Sarah was now sitting down, but was holding Colleen's other hand. "What Ava just said. Ditto. What I wouldn't give to have experienced a great love in my life."

Colleen looked at her two daughters. "That's it? You two girls aren't shocked or appalled?"

Ava tried to suppress her laughter. Why would her mother think she and Sarah would be appalled, of all things?

"No, mom, on the contrary," Ava said. "I'm envious. If you had a great and loving relationship with somebody for the past 40+ years, you're doing a lot better than I've ever done in the romantic department."

"Or me," Sarah said.

"Wow. Willow told me if I just got this big thing off my chest, I'd feel so much better. Lighter. She was right. I feel good. Perhaps for the first time in over a year, since I lost Violet, I feel really good. It's like this brick has been taken off of me. A huge brick that's been weighing me down. I wish I would've said something sooner."

Ava nodded her head. "Why didn't you?"

"I was afraid you girls would shun me, like my parents would've. My mom would've taken a hot fire poker to my behind if I ever wanted to bring a girl home to meet them. My dad probably would've shot us both where we stood. At any rate, I didn't think it would be this easy. I thought the two of you would have something to say about all this."

"Love is love," Ava said. "That's true now and it was just as true back when you were growing up. It's always been true, even if not everybody wants to see it that way."

Sarah cocked her head. "I agree completely with Ava. But Willow knew? How did she know about it?"

"That girl knows everything. She has a sixth sense, like some kind of character in a Stephen King novel. I never believed in that kind of thing, but she's made me a believer."

"Yes, Willow is the real deal," Sarah agreed.

"Mom," Ava began. "Violet was the love of your life. She died a little over a year ago. How are you handling that? I mean, I guess the two of you had been together for, what, 44 years or something?"

Ava and Sarah both knew what it was like to lose a partner. Ava's first husband was killed in a car accident. Sarah's boyfriend of many years died of ALS. In Sarah's case, the tragedy was she felt very little about her boyfriend's death. It turned out that Sarah and Nolan, her boyfriend, had a toxic relationship, to say the very least.

But Ava really loved her Daniel, who was the father of her triplets. Daniel was the love of her life, even if they were only together for five years before he died. So, she knew a little bit of how her mother was feeling. But only a little bit, because she and Daniel had such a tragically short relationship. She couldn't imagine going for over forty years with Daniel, only to lose him. To say she would be devastated would be an understatement.

Colleen looked sad. "I still can't believe it happened. I'm just now coming to terms with it. That was why the Chief Judge wanted me to take some time off – my grieving was affecting my work."

"Mom," Ava said. "I know we've had our problems over the years. But I want you to know that whatever I can do to help you through this, I'll do it."

Colleen smiled, but then grimaced. "Ava, you don't owe me a thing. I was horrible to you when you lost your husband all those years ago. I wouldn't blame you if you turned around and did the same thing to me. If you just told me to suck it up and don't bother you, I really wouldn't blame you."

"Water under the bridge," Ava said. "At some point, you have to let go of the past."

Sarah nodded her head. "Yes. I know you and Ava may have had your issues over the years, but now that you're more open with us about your life, maybe we can all get closer."

Colleen nodded her head. "Oh, I can't tell you how good this feels. I can let you girls into my life. I can tell you everything I've gone through. How my mind hasn't been right ever since my Violet died."

And then Colleen told Ava and Sarah everything. She told them about how she didn't accept Violet's death, and how she only authorized the autopsy because she thought it could bring Violet back somehow. About her anger at the doctors who didn't diagnose Violet properly. About how she lay awake just about every night, obsessing over how she found Violet, and ruminating over all the what-ifs.

By the time Colleen told her daughters everything about what she'd been feeling for the past year, it was 10 o'clock and the restaurant was ready to close. But Ava was feeling, for the first time, in a long time, she somewhat understood her mother.

Maybe understanding was a key to forgiveness and was a first step towards having a better relationship with her mother.

CHAPTER 25

AVA

After Ava found out about Colleen's relationship with Violet, she realized her mother took a chance on love. Against all the odds, her mother found the love of her life. Colleen was brave enough to silence the voices in her head and just go with it.

Ava knew she should do the same. When Deacon came to play the piano that evening, she was going to talk to him about her feelings. She had no idea if he still felt the same way about her, but she would ask him and see.

She called Quinn just before Deacon was going to come over.

"I'm freaking out," Ava said to Quinn. "I'm going to tell Deacon I changed my mind about our relationship, and I don't know how it'll be received."

"Sugar, you got this," Quinn assured her. "You have to just tell him your truth and let the chips fall where they may. I've a feeling, though, it's going to go great. And you deserve it. You've gone through hell, lady, in the past few years. The stress of opening that bed-and-breakfast, the pain of your husband leaving you high and dry, your mother showing up out of the blue. It's about time you pursue joy."

Pursue joy. Wouldn't that be a change for her? She realized true joy was something missing in her life and had been for a while. Oh, she was thrilled about the success of her bed and breakfast. But, it was almost empty because she couldn't share her high highs and low lows with somebody special. She was able to share all of that with her girls, of course, but she was also looking for a significant other to hold her hand through all of her challenges.

That evening, she was careful with putting on her makeup, she styled her hair by dragging a straight iron through it, and she took care to find the most flattering dress in her wardrobe. It was a teal number, a really good color for her and her flaming red hair. The cut, a halter bodice with a flared skirt, showed off her best assets – her square shoulders and toned arms - while minimizing her flared hips.

She nervously waited for Deacon to arrive.

He showed up right at 5:30, when he usually arrived at Ava's bed-and-breakfast. The dining room opened at six, and Deacon liked to get there a half-hour early to warm up. Emerson appeared at the same time, her violin in her hand.

He smiled at her. "Hiya, Ava. You look beautiful, if I must say so myself."

Emerson looked Ava up and down and then smiled. "Yeah, Deacon's right. You're looking good, lady."

She nodded and felt herself blush. "Deacon, you don't have any plans for after you quit playing tonight, do you?"

"I have a hot date lined up with Netflix. Does that count?"

She put her hands to her cheeks and felt they were warm. Why was she feeling this fluttering? Deacon was a friend, and he had been her friend for quite a while.

"Well, I was just hoping maybe you and I could hang out on the terrace this evening. Maybe go down to the beach. It's a beautiful night. I mean, it's going to be a beautiful night. The weatherman says so."

There she was, babbling at the mouth like a 13-year-old.

Hell, most 13-year-olds would probably have an easier time talking to the opposite sex. She was sure Emerson was much more fluent talking to boys than she was talking to Deacon.

"Sounds like as good of a plan as any," Deacon said. "It's the best invitation I've had in a while."

Ava felt her heart soar when Deacon said he would love to join her later on. However, when she thought about what she was going to say, and the very real possibility he would reject her, she felt sick.

Deacon and Emerson warmed up for their set, and people were already filling the dining room.

Ava waited on tables that night, fetching food and drinks all night long for her guests. Deacon and Emerson looked like they were having a ball, so Ava was happy.

Finally, at 10 o'clock, it was time for the duo to stop playing. The late guests were dispersing, and Ava finished cleaning off the tables.

After Ava was done with her work, she found Deacon, who was waiting for her in the foyer. She stopped to get a couple of beach chairs, and she handed him his. Her heart was pounding as she walked with him out the door, over the beach grass and sand dunes, and towards the beach. As usual, people were hanging out around bonfires, singing along to guitars, and there were even a few surfers out in the water.

Ava and Deacon set their chairs in the sand, and they both sat down.

"So," Deacon began. "How've you been? How are things going with your mum hanging about the house?"

"Actually, it's not going so bad. I think my mom and I had a breakthrough the other night. It sounds crazy, because I've never gotten along with her, but she's trying, for the first time in my life, to be nice to me. I'm not going to respond to her new attitude with my old bad attitude. At some point, you have to be the bigger person and let bygones be bygones. So, yeah, it's going really well."

"Good to hear it. I was hoping you and your mum could build a bridge. Sounds like that's what's happened. Congratulations."

"Yes," Ava said with a deep breath. "And I also found out my mother had a great love in her life." Ava chose not to tell Deacon her mom's great love was a woman, just because she didn't think it was her story to tell. "And, I don't know, I realize my mother was braver than I thought. She grabbed a chance to be in love, and she didn't let anybody stand in her way."

"That's a great thing to hear," Deacon said. "I know you always thought she was alone in her life. I guess you found out differently, huh?"

"Yes," Ava said. "I never knew about her love because she was such a private person. I mean, she didn't share much with me." Ava swallowed hard. "I started to understand maybe I was being premature in turning you down. Sometimes I get in my head, and I get in my own way. When I told you I didn't want to get involved, I was just being neurotic."

The look on Deacon's face told Ava everything she needed to know. He smiled, and his blue eyes looked into her own.

"Really? You want to see where this can go?"

"Yes. Although I do want to get one thing out of the way. I don't want to get involved with somebody who'll just be a fling. Which you will be if you have your heart set on having a family of your own at some point. So, is that something you desire in your life - children? If that's something you were looking forward to happening in your future, then it'll be pointless for us to get involved."

Deacon laughed. "Actually, mate, I've had a vasectomy. I've always known I didn't want children. So, no, that's definitely not part of my plans."

Ava felt relieved. She was shocked about how relieved she felt about that. "Good," she said. "That was one thing holding me back. I wanted to ask you about that earlier, but I thought I was getting way over my skis. You know, we haven't even gone on a date, and I'm already asking about your family plans."

"Or lack thereof," Deacon said with a smile. "As it happens, you're suited for me more than you know because most younger women want children at some point. At least, that's what I've found in my dating life. It's what led to my divorce. She wanted some ankle-biters, and I didn't. So we agreed to disagree. She went her way, and I went mine."

"I'm sorry to hear that," Ava said. "Divorce is never easy. I know from experience."

"Oh, it was years ago. Ages ago, really. Another lifetime, at this point. It wasn't a very long-lived marriage. But she helped me get my citizenship, so I'll always be grateful to her for that. Not that that was why I married her, to become a US citizen. Just don't want you calling the FBI on me," Deacon said with a smile.

"I was going to do just that, as a matter of fact. I was going to get on my cell phone and call them right up."

Deacon grinned and then leaned in for a kiss. Ava shut her eyes and lost her breath and just let the feeling of Deacon's lips on her own wash over her. His lips were warm and soft, and his tongue slowly explored inside her mouth. He tasted like cinnamon gum and strawberries, with just a hint of red wine.

Ava felt she was floating above the beach, looking down

at everybody huddled around bonfires and floating out in the ocean on huge surfboards.

Deacon stood up and motioned for Ava to hold his hand. "Let's walk, shall we, my sheila?"

Ava smiled as she recognized the term "sheila" as Aussie slang for an attractive woman or a pretty girl. And, as she walked along the beach with him that evening, holding his hand, she felt like a sheila.

Maybe for the first time in her life, she felt pretty.

CHAPTER 26

COLLEEN

After she talked to Sarah and Ava, Colleen felt a huge weight had been lifted off of her shoulders. Willow was right - she spoke her truth to her daughters and it wasn't as bad as she imagined it would be. In fact, their reaction to her bombshell news was very positive.

Now the air was cleared and she felt amazing. There was no longer that wall between her and her daughters. Her relationship with Ava was finally turning a corner.

Her story inspired Ava to pursue her own romantic relationship with a very attractive younger man, Deacon. So, as far as Colleen was concerned, all was right in her world.

She had her usual appointment with Willow that morning. She got there, and Willow was waiting for her.

"I did it. I told my daughters my secret. You were right. Once you tell your truth that you're terrified of saying, and it all turns out okay, there's nothing more liberating."

Willow raised an eyebrow. "You still haven't told your whole truth. And you know it. Don't get me wrong. I'm happy for you for telling your daughters about your loving relationship with your long-time significant other. But, I'm telling you, you need to tell Ava your whole truth. Otherwise, you're not being fair to her."

Colleen rolled her eyes. "I told all the truth I'm going to tell. There's no reason why Ava needs to know the truth about her father. None at all. It's just going to cause problems unnecessarily."

Truth be told, Colleen didn't want to tell Ava because she knew if she did, she'd be right back to square one with her daughter. She was finally starting to see a point where she and Ava could go forward in their relationship. Colleen was actively letting go of her irrational resentment of her daughter, and she was able to open herself up to her relationship with Ava for the first time in her life.

There was no way she would destroy that by telling her the truth about her dad.

CHAPTER 27

QUINN

After Emerson started playing for Ava's patrons, things settled down a bit. Emerson was focused on practicing her violin, because it turned out the young girl really loved the attention she got from the guests at the 'Sconset Inn, and she was motivated to play the best she could for the guests.

Quinn breathed a sigh of relief. She also insisted on meeting Joe, the kid Emerson was hanging out with, and one Thursday night, she had dinner at Joe's house. She was able to not only meet Joe but also his parents and two sisters.

They lived in a four-bedroom cottage a few blocks away from Quinn's home. Joe had a sister named Holly and another named Sailor. His mother was Hazel and his father was Ralph. The entire family, including Joe, had scads of curly bright red hair, pale skin, and tons of freckles.

Ralph was a web designer who worked from home and had a lucrative business, judging by the size of his house. His mother Hazel was a stay-at-home mom who had a side gardening hobby. There were books and magazines about the subject all over the house, and her garden was beautiful.

She grew lettuce, kale, carrots, radishes, tomatoes, sweet peppers, artichokes, Brussels sprouts and every herb imaginable. She also had flowers growing everywhere in the front and the back yards.

The Russells were friendly, jovial people that wanted nothing but the best for their son and daughters. And Joe, with his mop of curly red hair, freckles, and gangly body, looked like a typical 15-year-old boy who just got his braces off.

"I'm so excited to meet you!" Hazel said when Quinn and Emerson appeared on the doorstep of their Cape Cod home. Hazel impulsively gave both Quinn and Emerson a hug. "Your daughter has visited a few times over the weeks, and I've really enjoyed her company."

Quinn felt a little unsettled that she was only now meeting Joe, but apparently, Joe's family knew all about Emerson. Emerson had been stonewalling Quinn about meeting Joe up until this moment, never telling Quinn where Joe lived or even what his last name was. Emerson only recently gave Quinn the information about Joe.

"We've just decided we're going to start dating," Emerson had said. "So I guess you better meet the fam."

So much for not wanting to get involved. Quinn figured it was going in that direction, much as she didn't want it to.

The dinner went very well. Quinn felt more than comfortable with Joe's sweet and friendly parents. By the time the evening was over, they all talked like best friends.

And the kid himself really impressed Quinn. He was polite, respectful, smart and hilarious. "I'm just a gamer geek who looks like Ronald McDonald," he said, pointing to his mop of bright red curly hair.

Emerson just rolled her eyes. "Ronald McDonald's hair is a completely different kind of red, Joe. Your hair's like sunset. His is more fire engine."

Joe laughed and nudged Emerson sweetly. "That's what I love about her. She really knows how to describe things."

Emerson raised an eyebrow, took a drink of her water, and nudged him back. "Boy, is that a backhanded compliment or what? I really know how to describe things? Gee, thanks."

And so it went, the entire evening. Emerson and Joe were playing off each other like two best friends - which they kind of were if they weren't sleeping together, as Emerson assured Quinn would not happen.

"Emerson's just been a treat," Hazel said. "And I don't let them hang out in Joe's room. They have to stay in the den, where I can see them, and they just play games together. Sometimes other kids come around, and then this place is really a zoo. But it's a fun zoo."

The den was right next to the living room and in full view, as the house was an open floor plan. Quinn was relieved her daughter and Joe were never alone.

By the time the evening was over, Quinn felt much more comfortable about Emerson hanging out with Joe.

Things might not be as bad as it seemed, Quinn thought. She just had to trust the universe.

The universe, and Joe's parents.

CHAPTER 28

AVA

The weeks flew by, and Ava was starting to enjoy her mom's company. Her mother had taken to helping out around the house – she helped Ava clean the rooms, greeted guests, and booked reservations. She even helped in the kitchen a time or two when Ava was short because somebody had called in sick.

Then, one day, the ladies arranged a shopping trip.

"I'm going to a crystal shop in Hyannis," Colleen said to Ava. "Why don't you come with me? It'll be fun."

"A crystal shop, mom?" Ava asked, feeling amused. Her mother, going to a crystal shop? What was next – a tarot reading with Willow?

Turned out, Willow had actually done a tarot reading for her.

"Yes, and it was amazing," her mother told her when Ava asked if Willow ever did her tarot reading. "Willow brought out all my issues with that reading. She even uncovered things I didn't even know were in my psyche, but, once I thought about it, there they were." And then Colleen looked a little sad. "She also said Violet's proud of me. She said Violet was proud of me when she was alive, but she's really proud of me now. All Violet ever wanted was for you girls to know how we felt about each other. And now that you girls do, she's up there, feeling very proud."

Ava had to smile. "Mom, I love that you're seeing Willow. It sounds like she's been an amazing influence on you. But am I hearing my lifelong agnostic mother believing in the afterlife?"

Colleen just shrugged her shoulders. "You have to believe in something in this world. Otherwise, where's the meaning? And I do prefer to believe that Violet is somewhere, looking down and cheering for me. I also have to believe I'm going to see her again one day. So, yes, I guess I believe in the afterlife."

"So, you want us to go to Hyannis together? I'd love to go, but I can't leave the inn for the afternoon. I always have too much to do around here."

Colleen touched her nose and pointed at Ava. "Lady, I got you covered. Sarah's going to take over for you. She already said she would do everything you do to keep this place running. In fact, I talked to her, and she's anxious to take over for you whenever you need her to. At any rate, you need a day off. So, let's go."

At that, Sarah appeared in the living room, where Ava and Colleen were standing. "Sis," Sarah said. "I got this. You and mom, go have fun. Have a girl's day."

And then Colleen just nodded her head. "Actually, Ava, why don't we go all the way? Let's go to the airport, and let's go to Boston. They got some really great metaphysical crystals shop there, and I need a new pair of shoes. That's one thing I never have spent money on – shoes. Violet loved her shoes. She would spend $500 on a single pair. It used to make me so mad. I couldn't understand why she had to get a pair of Dior

THE BEACHFRONT SURPRISES.

shoes or Jimmy Choos. I was just as happy wearing a pair of Anne Kleins that cost less than $100. But, you know what, I might just buy myself a pair of fancy shoes in her honor."

"Boston," Ava said, nodding her head. "Okay, let's do it."

Sarah looked at Colleen. "Mom, if you and Ava want to stay overnight, that's okay with me. Go, live a little."

Colleen looked at Ava. "Well? What are you waiting for, go pack a bag. I'll go do the same."

"Okay. Let's do it."

It felt strange to pack a bag so she could stay overnight with her mother. Yet, at the same time, she needed to take a break. She was working seven days a week, and it was hard labor. Vacuuming, mopping, scrubbing down the bathtubs and toilets, shining up the mirrors, hauling bedsheets to the laundry room in the basement. It all added up, and Ava was looking forward to having 24 hours when she didn't have to worry about her bed and breakfast.

She and Deacon were slowly getting to know one another romantically. Since she had every evening off after 6 o'clock or, sometimes, 7 o'clock, she could see Deacon for a few hours every night. He would come over, and sometimes they would hang out in her room, build a fire and drink a glass of wine while making out like teenagers. Other times, they would go out to eat or occasionally to a bar. Often times, they would go down to the beach and hold hands while they walked along the shore, looking for unique seashells or maybe sand dollars.

So far, they didn't do much more physical than kiss, which was okay with Ava. She was over the days when her hormones would lead the way. These days, she was more than happy to lay on Deacon's lap in front of the fire and talk and get to know him.

Ava called Deacon to tell him she wouldn't be around that

evening. "I'm going with my mom to Boston for the day, coming back tomorrow."

"That's great!" Deacon said. "I guess I'll just be seeing you tomorrow then."

Ava would miss seeing him that evening, but she wanted to take advantage of any offer to better understand her mother. Sarah apparently had fun social moments over the years with their mother. Now, it was her turn.

Before Ava knew it, Sarah was driving the two ladies to the airport. A couple of hours later, they were in the air. 45 minutes after they got into the air, they landed in Boston.

"Now, what would you like to do?" Colleen asked her daughter. "This is my backyard. You showed me around Nantucket, and I can do the same for you in Boston."

"Well, mom, you mentioned you wanted to go to a crystal shop. And go shoe shopping. I'm good with doing both those things." Ava wanted to remind her mother that she went to Harvard, so she knew Boston very well, but she didn't want to embarrass Colleen. Besides, Colleen was acting like a school-girl, eager to show her daughter the place where she'd been living for the past 15 years.

"Let's get an Uber and go to the Hidden Jewel. I looked at the website online. It looks like a place with a pretty good collection of crystals and stones. And then maybe after we go to Hidden Jewel, we can go to Copley Place. That's the big shopping center that has all the high-end stores. I think I'd like to visit the Neiman Marcus, Jimmy Choo, Louboutin and Versace stores. Maybe you can find something at one of the stores, too. Not to mention, I need a new watch. Maybe I'll splurge and get a Rolex." She raised her eyebrows with delight after she talked about the possible new watch.

Ava started to laugh. Who was this person who'd taken over her mother's body? Her mother was always so frugal, so wanting to squeeze a dime until it begged for mercy. Now, here she was, talking about $500 shoes and a $10,000 watch.

The two ladies booked a room at the Doubletree Hotel. They called an Uber, who took them to the hotel. Then they dumped off their luggage in the hotel room and called another Uber to take them to the Hidden Jewel.

The Hidden Jewel was a metaphysical store on the south end and was only a half-mile away from Copley Place, which was their next stop. It was like a much larger version of Willow's old store, and it had a wonderful selection of beautiful gems, stones, and crystals.

Ava looked at the crystals with interest. Unlike her best friend Hallie and her sister Sarah, Ava had never really been into Willow's shop to look for crystals. She understood that certain people believed crystals had some kind of healing properties. Like tourmaline was protective, and amethyst supposedly calmed the mind.

"So, mom, what kind of crystals are you looking for?"

Colleen looked at Ava. "I'm looking for something that'll make me feel closer to Violet. Willow told me certain crystals can open up my third eye." And then Colleen pointed to her forehead. "This is where my third eye is. I'd like to open it up so that I can feel Violet's presence."

"What is the third eye?"

"It's apparently the part of our body that connects to the spiritual realm. Most people have a closed third eye. My third eye is definitely closed, but I'd like it not to be. So, I'm looking for some crystals to help me with that."

Ava nodded her head. She knew her mother was having a hard time with Violet's death. She just didn't know how hard her mother had it. All at once, Ava understood her mother's pain.

"You're really missing her, huh?" Ava asked as she looked at the beautiful stones.

Colleen just nodded her head. She, too, was staring at the crystals, looking at each one. "They say that you'll know it when you find the crystal for you. It calls out to you, or something like that. That's why I wanted to come to this shop. Willow sells a lot of crystals, but none of them actually attracted me. She suggested coming to this shop once I got back to Boston, because it has such a great collection."

A sales lady came over to talk to Colleen and Ava. She was tall and thin, her long brown hair tied back in a low ponytail. She was wearing a long and flowing white dress with flowers around the neckline. She wasn't wearing any makeup, and she had a very friendly expression on her face. Ava liked her immediately.

"May I help you ladies find anything?" she asked. "My name is Britt, and I'm here to help."

"I think I'd like to see that piece of rose quartz," Colleen said, pointing to a beautiful light pink crystal.

The lady took the piece of crystal out and gave it to Colleen. Colleen held the crystal in her hand and closed her eyes. She nodded her head. "Yes, I think this is the one." Then she smiled. "And I'd like to look at some other crystals that are supposed to be good for grieving. I'm going through the stages, and it's been messy. What do you recommend?"

Britt took out a crystal that had both brilliant flashes of red and deep, mossy green. "Rhodonite," she said. "It helps with gentle acceptance of your situation. Also Carnelian." Britt pointed to a brilliant orange stone. "This will balance out your energies, and chase away negative thoughts. It also will help you connect with the spiritual realm, like the rose quartz."

Colleen just nodded her head. "I'll take all of these. And one of those moonstones and one of your amethysts."

Britt smiled and took out one of the moonstones, which was a very pale crystal, and an amethyst, which was a bril-

THE BEACHFRONT SURPRISES.

liant purple. "These are very good choices. The amethyst will calm your mind. The moonstone will help you move through your cycle of grief, and make you realize there are tides to everything. The tide goes out, and it comes back in, over and over again. And we all will experience joy and grief in that same manner. So you know the pain you're experiencing right now will soon be balanced out by abundance and joy."

Colleen smiled and took a deep breath. "That's just what I want to hear - I'm not going to be stuck in this black hole forever."

The two ladies left the crystal shop after Colleen bought several crystals. Ava never imagined her mother would be getting into crystals, but if it helped her, that was all that mattered.

"I guess we're heading over to Copley Place," Ava said. "I'm really excited about going shopping with you."

"I know. Who would've ever thought I'd be looking forward to finding a really nice pair of shoes? Not to mention a totally frivolous pair."

That afternoon, Colleen and Ava went to Neiman Marcus, where Colleen picked up a Rolex watch. It was small and feminine, with a pink-colored round face with diamond studs all the way around. It set her mother back $9,000.

"I've never paid more than $200 for a watch in my life," Colleen said. "But I had to have this."

"You work hard for your money," Ava said with smile. "Live a little."

Colleen also bought a stunning pair of Manolo Blahniks. They were a pair of blue satin high-heeled pumps, with a jewel buckle, just like the pair Carrie Bradshaw wore for her courthouse wedding with Mr. Big in the first *Sex and the City* movie. And, for good measure, Colleen bought the same pair in hot pink.

"Violet loved the color pink," Colleen said as she tried on

the hot pink pair. "I think she would've absolutely loved these shoes."

Then the two ladies went over to the Versace store, where Colleen picked up a midnight blue wrap dress and a pair of rhinestone-encrusted stiletto sandals that looked amazing on her. And then over to the Dior store, where Colleen bought a beautiful floral dress and a pair of pink pumps that matched the dress to a T.

She also found Ava a dress at the Dior store. It was an off-the-shoulder number in dark green. Ava fell in love with it, but she didn't fall in love with the $3500 price tag. Colleen noticed Ava eyeing the dress and told the sales lady to put it on her credit card, as well.

Ava tried to protest because the dress was just too extravagant. But Colleen waved her away. "It's the least I can do, Ava, for being such a bitch to you all these years. Not that that fancy dress will ever make up for my behavior. But, I guess it couldn't hurt."

Ava smiled. "Well, mom, thank you."

"Now, why don't we go over to the Harvard campus? I can show you all my hangouts and haunts from back in the day, when I was a young and idealistic law student. You might be surprised about some of the things I did back then. We can grab some chow there, too."

"Mom, you went to school in the 60s. Nothing you can tell me about your wild and abandoned youth can shock me. But, I'm eager to share your memories with you. So, let's go."

CHAPTER 29

COLLEEN

Colleen was starting to feel good for the first time in over a year. It was partly because of Willow's treatments. She never fully believed in the power of acupuncture, although she'd always heard about the treatment. But, she was starting to believe there was something to the practice after all.

She was happy she bought the crystals at the Hidden Jewel place. She was starting to believe crystals helped with the healing process. At any rate, she didn't think the crystals would do any harm, so why not try? If there could ever be anything that could bring her closer to her Violet, Colleen would try it.

Shopping was a lot of fun, too. It felt good to be frivolous. She was shopping so carefree because that was her way of honoring Violet. Violet would've loved to have seen Colleen shop with such abandon. Colleen bought shoes she never would've even looked at before, but when she tried the shoes on, she knew she had to have them. Especially the hot pink Blahnik shoes with the jeweled buckle and the matching shoes in royal blue. They just sang to her.

She felt the same way about the Rolex and the dresses. She was going all girly girl like she never had before. Maybe there was part of Violet's spirit that had taken over her. She could almost hear Violet whispering in her ear when she tried on those dresses at the Dior store and the Versace store. The Versace dress was even a bit daring, as Versace dresses tended to be.

And now Ava and Colleen were heading over to her old Harvard stomping grounds. Before grabbing a bite, she would show Ava her first apartment, the bars she hung out at, and the place where she met her Violet.

She'd met Violet at a party in a classic Boston brownstone, hosted by a guy working on a Master's in English Lit at Harvard. A 21-year-old Violet was standing in the corner, her long blonde hair worn straight with a thick black headband holding it back. She was wearing a short plaid miniskirt jumper, a white turtleneck and high white boots. She was so fresh-faced, so dewy, with milky white skin and rosy cheeks. She had a smile that could light up a room.

Ava and Colleen made their way over to the Harvard campus.

"Oh, the memories," Ava said as she approached the campus. "And not all the memories were great. There was a lot of stress when I was here, but a lot of fun, too."

Colleen had forgotten that Ava, too, went to Harvard Law school. She was too embarrassed to say that to her daughter because what kind of mother forgets something like that?

The two ladies walked around the campus, and Colleen smelled the air. She could still imagine herself as a young law student there.

They walked over to the enormous Victorian home where Colleen rented a studio apartment just off campus.

"This is where I had my first hit of LSD," Colleen said with a wicked smile. "And everything you've heard about the

THE BEACHFRONT SURPRISES.

drug is true, and more. It really does expand your mind. It opens you up to possibilities you might never think of otherwise."

Ava looked at Colleen with a look of surprise. "Mom. You never told me you dropped acid. What was it like?"

"Dear, I started law school in 1966. What kind of self-respecting feminist law student would I've been if I didn't try LSD at least once? I did it a couple of times. Both times I did it, I was in a positive frame of mind going into it, so I had very good trips. That was one thing I learned – you never drop acid if you're feeling anxious or depressed, because you're going to have a bad trip if that's the case."

Ava started to laugh. "What kind of good trips did you have?"

"Lots of colors, and I could taste sounds. It was the weirdest thing - I think Jimi Hendrix was playing on the stereo, and the music tasted like strawberries to me. It was very distinctive. And then some Janis Joplin came on, somebody started playing one of her records, and I tasted chocolate. And then somebody started playing The Doors, and, wouldn't you know it, it was chocolate-covered strawberries. And the sofa came alive and danced around the room." Colleen started to laugh as she thought of that memory. "The other time I did it was at Woodstock."

Ava laughed along. "You were at Woodstock?" Ava's eyes got huge. "How was it?"

Colleen still stared at the brownstone, getting lost in the memories. "Woodstock was just how it looked. Half a million hippies and one pair of jean shorts between all of them. I forget who described Woodstock like that, but it was the truth. Mud, drugs galore, naked hippies, a bunch of bands you've never heard of and a bunch who are legends. The Dead was the best band there, but I also got into Jefferson Airplane and Joan Baez."

Ava's mouth was open. "Wow. The things I never knew about you. Woodstock. Drugs. I mean-"

"Ava, I came of age in the 60s. What do you think I did back then, weave baskets all day? It was the era of turn on, tune in, drop out. Everybody was experimenting with drugs in those days. You missed out. You went to college during the boring 80s. Your generation was caught up in the wrong things – getting ahead, going to business school so you can make your fortune, stupid drinking games with stupid boys and girls. I mean, bouncing quarters into beer glasses?" She shook her head. "Popped collars on the boys and bows in the girls' hair. Your big campus events centered around Bid Day bashes, Homecoming floats and Greek Week house decs. Our campus events centered around people with a bullhorn rousing us to action. We were about so much more than finding out where the next party was."

Ava raised an eyebrow and smiled. "Oh, but mom, your generation became the ones who made all the money on Wall Street during the go-go 80s. Your generation went from getting arrested protesting the Vietnam War to getting arrested for shady bond trading on Wall Street. Your generation was the one who voted for Ronald Reagan, for the love of God."

"And what was wrong with St. Ronnie?" Colleen asked ironically. She didn't like Reagan, either - she voted for Carter in 1980 and Mondale in 1984.

"Nothing, I guess. It's just that I don't know what happened to all that idealism you and your friends in the late 60s were about."

Colleen shrugged her shoulders. "I guess after Nixon, it all went to hell. The nation got cynical. As for me, personally, I just started seeing too much when I was on the bench. You become faced with the worst of humanity when you're a judge. Criminals, greedy corporate raiders, psychopaths and sociopaths of every stripe."

"Yeah, I know what you mean," Ava said. "I saw the same type of thing when working at my law firm. Just so many men who couldn't care less about their fellow man. All they ever cared about was the almighty dollar and how they could get more of it while screwing the government."

"And, you know, Ava, your generation didn't have to protest as much as my generation did, because we did it all for you. We got civil rights passed. We broke the glass ceiling and paved the way for women to get out of the kitchen and into the board room. Our movement ended the Vietnam War."

Ava smiled. "And there was a backlash against all of that. Two steps forward, two steps back. Your generation made change, and my generation pushed back against it. So, in many ways, we've stood in place."

The two ladies walked along the sidewalk, passing classic brownstone after classic brownstone. They were getting closer to where Colleen had met Violet all those years ago.

"So, mom, what else did you do at Harvard besides drop acid?" Ava asked with a grin.

"Oh, there was many a party where I got stuck talking to some guy who was hitting on me, and I only had eyes for a pretty girl in the corner. That's where I met Violet, you know - a party hosted by a grad student who wanted to get in my pants."

Ava laughed. "That sounds familiar. I think I went to a few Harvard parties like that myself."

Colleen just stared at the brownstone where she met Violet. "That Violet, she knew who she was from the beginning. She never tried to get a beard like I had with Kenny. And she was so beautiful. So fresh-faced and feminine. When I met her, I had no idea she was into girls. She didn't strike me as the kind who would've been. She was the kind of girl who turned every boy's head. Yet, she fell in love with me at first sight, and I did the same with her."

"So, you met Violet here at Harvard. But I didn't see her coming around until I was 10 years old. What happened?"

Colleen looked at Ava for a long moment. She was battling in her head on whether or not she should tell her daughter the full truth on why she didn't get together with Violet right away.

"I was married to Kenny."

"My father," Ava said with a nod of her head. "That's just a shame. I guess you were married to my father because you felt you had to hide who you were?"

Colleen just took a deep breath. "No. I was married to Kenny because I wanted a stable home for you."

"Oh. I guess you and my father got careless? I guess I don't understand, mom. Why were you ever with him in the first place?"

Colleen took another deep breath. "Because I fell in love with a man. But the man that I fell in love with wasn't Kenny. His name was James. James Bloch."

CHAPTER 30

AVA

Ava stood and stared at Colleen. Just when she thought she was getting to know her mother, all at once, she realized she didn't know Colleen at all.

If she read between the lines, it sounded like Colleen fell in love with the man who willed her the Nantucket house.

And, although Ava didn't want to make that connection, it sounded like James Bloch was her father.

"Okay, mom," Ava said calmly. She wasn't going to jump to conclusions. She was going to let her mother tell the story. Maybe there was something she was missing. "I'm very confused now. James Bloch? You mean *the* James Bloch who I became good friends with? The man who willed me his Nantucket house?"

Her mother started to look terrified. "Yes. That's the man, the only man, I've ever loved."

Ava's head felt like it was going to split into two. "So, mom, you loved a man?"

"Yes. I did love a man. Don't ask me why or how I fell in love with James, but I did. And my love for him was as all-consuming and passionate as my love for Violet." She paused for several minutes. "That was how you were conceived."

Ava felt like her heart was going to drop through the floor. She wasn't sure she wanted to hear anything more from her mother.

She knew there was little chance she would ever forgive her mother for hiding this piece of information from her all these years. She now didn't know who she was. She always thought she was Kenny Flynn's daughter. Not that she ever really knew the man, but she knew his reputation as a hard-charging attorney with Shook, Hardy and Bacon, the largest law firm in Kansas City. She also knew his reputation as a caring brother and friend.

She'd always craved knowing more about Kenny over the years. So she sought out people who knew him, people who could tell her what he was like. There was a period of several years when she called Kenny's brothers and sisters, along with calling his closest friends. And she got a portrait of him.

His friends and family saw him as a really good, upstanding guy. He was the guy who, when he played baseball and somebody broke a window with the ball, would go to the neighbor's house and make sure the window got repaired. Whenever his sister had a problem with a guy, he actually listened to her and gave her advice. When his other sister was going through an issue with an eating disorder, he told his parents she needed help. He was the kind of empathetic guy who Ava would've loved to have gotten to know, and it was a tragedy she never really did.

Unfortunately, he started smoking when he was 10 years old because he wanted to be cool like his friends. That was what killed him in the end.

And now, suddenly, the man who she desperately tried to get to know through other people's stories actually had no connection to her at all. Worse yet, the man who she did get to know, the man she adored, actually was her father. And she never even got the chance to know it while he was alive.

How could her mother do this? How could she just not tell her? Ava had a relationship with her real dad. It would've been nice to have known he was her dad whenever she had matzo ball soup with him at Frankel's Deli.

She always wondered why James would leave her a house, and she felt guilty for the extravagant gift. Now she knew he was probably just assuaging his guilt over not being in her life for years and years. After all, she only started to get to know him when she was 45 years old. That was when he hired Ava's law firm to get him out of a tax debt, and that was when she met him.

For 45 years, he didn't want to know her. For 45 years, he probably didn't even know what she looked like. What even caused him to come to her law firm, of all the law firms in New York City? Other white-shoe firms did the same thing as Collins and Lahy, tax law for scofflaws. Why did he choose her firm? Was it just a happy accident?

She now had so many questions that couldn't be answered in this lifetime. These were questions she had for her father, James Bloch. Her father! He was dead. But if she would've known he was her father, she could've asked the questions she had in her head while he was alive.

It was just so unfair. Her whole relationship with the kindly old man was brought into question.

She was so frustrated she felt like screaming.

Her mother was reaching for her, but Ava just waved her hands in front of her. "Just stop. You're not going to make this better. You can't possibly make up for what you did. Don't you understand that? Don't you understand I could've been asking my father, the man who gave his DNA to me, questions I've always wanted to ask the man who gave me life? I never thought I had a chance to question my actual father because I always assumed it was Kenny. Since he died when I was five, I obviously couldn't have sought him out. But you knew my father was alive and you hid that from me. Now it's too late for me to have a relationship with him."

Colleen was crying. "Ava, you did have a relationship with him. He sought you out, and the two of you got close."

"You don't understand. Obviously, if I would've known the truth, I could've had a different relationship with James. And, you know what, if I would've known the truth when I was younger, I would've found him long before the age of 45. I would've sought him out at the first chance. I could've had so many more years getting to know him, but you denied me that by your lying."

Ava wanted to strangle her mother where she stood. She tried to hold back tears, but, all at once, she was crying like she'd never cried before. She was crying for James and her lost relationship with him. She was also crying for her mother. Just when she thought she was turning a corner with her mother, it turned out that Colleen was just who Ava thought she was all along - a bitch. A duplicitous lying bitch at that.

Why did she ever think her mother could change? Why did she ever believe she could have a normal mother – daughter relationship with Colleen?

"Ava, please don't do this. We were having such a good day together. We were having such a normal mother-daughter day. Can't we forget this? Can't we pretend like I never said anything about your dad?"

Ava shook her head violently. "Hell to the no on that one. Hell no. Colleen, I've never liked you, but I've always loved you. You've always been so cold and cruel to me over the years. I've long since given up the idea that you and I would have a decent relationship. Now, I admit, in the past few weeks, I started to see a future where you and I were really good. But that's blown to hell now. I will never, and I mean never, forgive you for this."

At that, Ava called an Uber.

"Are we going back to the hotel?" Colleen asked hopefully.

Ava just shook her head. "Maybe you are. You need to call your own Uber. My Uber is taking me straight to the airport. I'm going back to Nantucket, but I'm not going home. That damn James gave that house to me just because he felt guilty about not being in my life for so many years. What, he thought he could just give me a $7 million home, and that was going to make up for him not acknowledging me? He thought that was going to make everything okay?"

Ava knew what she was going to do. She was going to look into the process of giving back that damn bequeathment. Let somebody else take over that house. Somebody who James actually acknowledged as being his relative during his life.

She didn't know what she would do in the meantime. It was complicated because Sarah, Quinn and Hallie were out on the island with her. She was the one who drew everybody together on Nantucket, and they were all thriving.

But she wasn't going to run that bed-and-breakfast for one more day.

She was going to see a lawyer about giving back the house, and then she would have to figure out her life from there. She might go back to New York, she might go back to Kansas City, or she might move to a place where nobody knew her. She wasn't quite sure.

All she was sure about was she had no idea who she was anymore. Everything she thought she knew was turned upside down in just a matter of hours.

No, everything she thought she knew was turned upside

down in just *seconds*. In the time it took for Colleen to tell her her father was James Bloch, that was the time it took for her world to turn upside down and inside out.

She knew she was never going to be the same again.

CHAPTER 31

AVA

Ava called an Uber and went straight to the airport. She didn't bother to go back to the hotel, even though she knew her overnight bag was there.

She sat on the short flight, shaking the entire time. Even the vodka tonic she ordered on the plane wasn't helping to calm her nerves.

She closed her eyes. Sarah had a different father. It figured. She and Sarah looked nothing alike, unfortunately for her. She guessed that maybe she took after James's side of the family, for he, like Ava, was constantly battling his weight.

She now had another family tree. All of James Bloch's kin was hers as well. He was Jewish. Did that mean she was too? She actually heard somewhere that Judaism is only passed down on the mother's side. She thought that meant she wasn't ethnically Jewish, but she wasn't sure about that, either.

Was there even such a thing as "ethnically Jewish?" So many questions...

James had other children, which meant she had half-brothers and sisters. And he'd been married for 64 years at the time he died. 64 years - he was married at the time she was conceived. That put yet another wrinkle into the whole sorry scenario. She was going to be coming out of the woodwork. She imagined that James Bloch's family wasn't going to welcome her with open arms, to say the least. Not only was she not Jewish, but she was agnostic, like her mother was at one time.

Her mother was gay. What was this about her falling in love with a guy?

Ava shook her head. She knew many straight people fell in love with somebody of the same sex and vice versa. Colleen loving a man was one bombshell Ava accepted without question.

She had so many questions for her mother, but she couldn't ask them. She didn't want to speak to her mother again, let alone have a long and in-depth conversation about Colleen and James and their love.

The plane touched down, and Ava got another Uber to take her to Quinn's home. She was going to call Sarah the next evening and ask her to meet her at Quinn's place. She'd tell her and everybody that she didn't want to set foot in that house again, and exactly why.

Before the plane disembarked, Ava did a quick Google search on the issue of declining a bequest, and found she couldn't do it. If she declined the bequest, the house would pass to her children.

Ava closed her eyes, thinking about her three irresponsible children suddenly owning a $7 million house. Samantha, her free-spirited child who had no sense of responsibility or ambition, would be 1/3 owner of it. Jackson wasn't nearly as irresponsible as Samantha, but, as a struggling actor trying to make it in Hollywood, he probably wouldn't want the burden of it.

That left Charlotte. She, too, was busy with her life. She had an infant child at home, so she probably wouldn't have any interest in running the house, either.

Ava sighed as she realized that if she rejected the bequeathment, and her children took control of the house, she was going to end up running the place anyway.

She was stuck with the house. She was stuck with a house she didn't want to step foot in ever again, because it was tainted by her mother's betrayal and her father's rejection.

Her mother had always rejected her. Now she knew her father did too. She wondered if she could ever get over feeling that both her parents turned their backs on her.

Her Uber took her to Quinn's home, and Ava knocked on her door.

Hallie opened the door, saw the look on Ava's face, and immediately put her arm around her. "Ava, what's wrong?" Hallie asked. "Sarah told me you and your mom were staying in Boston tonight. What happened?"

"Hey," Ava said. "You're staying here tonight?"

"Actually, I was going to go home at some point. Willow and I were over brainstorming with Quinn about some of our business plans, and she's gone to bed with a headache. Emerson's upstairs, too, playing video games."

"Oh." Ava shook her head and tried to stop the threatening tears. "I'm sorry to be barging in on you guys so late," Ava said. "But I can't go back to my house."

"Come on in," Hallie said. "You can stay in Sarah's bed tonight, since Sarah's over at your house."

Ava walked into the home, and saw Willow standing there. Ava immediately felt uncomfortable being around the young psychic. She was afraid Willow was going to have her number from the very beginning.

Her fears weren't unfounded, as she discovered shortly.

"Hey, Ava," Willow said to her. "I think I know what happened with your mother. She finally told you, didn't she?"

Ava put her hands on her head, and then pulled on her hair. "You already knew about it? Who else knew about it?" Ava demanded. "Did Hallie and Quinn know about it? What about Sarah? Am I the last one to find this out?"

Ava took a deep breath and looked at Hallie to see if she knew about her mother's betrayal. However, the look on Hallie's face told Ava she had no clue what was going on. Ava relaxed as she realized that.

"What's going on?" Hallie asked.

Ava took a deep breath and told Hallie everything.

"Oh my God," Hallie said. "I don't know what to say. How horrible for you to find out something so major in such a way. What are you going to do?"

"I don't know. I know about the HALT thing. You're not supposed to make any decisions when you're hungry, angry, lonely or tired. And, at this point, I'm all of those things. I got on a plane before mom and I were going to have dinner, and I haven't eaten yet, so I'm hungry. And God knows I'm angry. I'm also very tired. And I'm really lonely. I mean, I know things are going well between Deacon and me, and I have my friends and my sister in my life, but I feel this emptiness now. I thought I knew who my father was – and, even though I never got to know him, I accepted his absence in my life. I had to – he couldn't help that he died so young. But James – that's another story."

"Ava, did you ever consider that maybe James didn't know about you? Are you sure your mother told him she was pregnant when they broke up? It's possible he had no idea you were his daughter all along."

Ava smiled. Hallie was so sweet. She always tried to see a side to a bad situation that made it not so terrible. "No. I don't think that's possible. If he didn't know about me, then he just happened to hire our law firm, he just happened to have me assigned as his attorney, and he just happened to give me an extravagant house in his will. He knew about me."

Ava looked over at Willow, and she knew by the look on the young psychic's face that she was correct. In Ava's mind, there was no doubt that James always knew about her. Willow was tacitly confirming this.

"Ava," Willow said gently. "I can try to communicate with James if you like."

Willow was able to communicate with the dead? Ava actually wasn't surprised about this. In fact, she would've been surprised if Willow *wasn't* able to communicate with the dead. And, didn't her mother say something about Willow communicating with Violet?

"Okay. Do you need anything of his? If you do, just let me know. I can probably try to get an article of clothing or something of his from a member of his family." Ava knew when she said the words "a member of his family" that she was talking about a member of her own family, too. God, that was going to be weird. How was she going to approach this other family of hers?

Willow just shook her head. "Actually, no. I don't need any article of clothing or lock of hair or any of the things people think psychic mediums need. I just need to meditate and see if he's willing to communicate. I have a feeling he will be. Do you trust me?"

Ava nodded her head. She was feeling much calmer now than she felt in Boston with her mother, or on the plane on the way over. She wasn't ready to forgive her mother, not even for a second. But, at the same time, she was curious about James, so much so that she was willing to trust Willow when she said she could communicate with him.

"Okay," Willow said. "I'll go ahead and communicate with him, and I'll let you know what he says."

"How much do you charge?"

"I don't. I do it as a favor for people who are close to me or people who really need the information. If I charged for it, the information would be tainted in some way. You know, lots of folks would think I'm only doing it for the money, and they wouldn't believe the information I give them."

"But don't you need things? Candles, crystals, things like that?"

"Of course. But I already have those things, so it's not like I need to buy anything. You're good. Don't worry about it. I'll get back with you in a couple of days."

A couple of days. Ava was going to be on pins and needles, trying to figure out how James felt about her. She had to know whether or not he looked on her as a daughter. Did he really give her that house because he felt so guilty? Or did he do it because he loved her?

Ava was surprised that the answer to that question was so, so, so important to her.

Because it mattered to her to know that at least one of her parents loved her.

CHAPTER 32

COLLEEN

Why did she tell Ava? She knew why. She let her guard down. She and Ava were having such a good time, she just lost her head. She thought Ava would take it better than she did.

Why would she think Ava would take it well? How could *anybody* take something like that well? Everything her daughter took for granted in her life was a lie. Ava thought she knew her heritage, and, come to find out, she didn't.

She went back to the hotel, hoping against hope that Ava had changed her mind and would be waiting for her in the room. But she got there, saw the empty room, and felt despair. She sat down on the bed and hung her head.

Oh, she screwed up in so many ways. If she had a chance to live her life over again, she would do everything differently.

****

The next day, Colleen took an Uber to the cemetery. She had not yet visited Violet's final resting place, for the same reason why she didn't go to Violet's funeral – if she saw Violet's headstone, she would have to accept that her Violet was gone. She couldn't accept that for the longest time. But now, finally, she was ready to.

She got to the cemetery, and found Violet's stone. It was a very calm day. The birds were singing and there was a gentle breeze that swayed the trees. She'd brought some flowers to place by Violet's stone, and she laid them carefully on the grass.

"Violet, honey, I miss you so much. I know you're happy now, but you were always happy. I wish you were happy here on earth instead of wherever you are – I'm assuming you're in heaven, but you always believed in reincarnation, so maybe you're some brand-new baby somewhere, starting life all over again. Who knows? Wherever you are, you need to know I told my daughters about you because I knew that was the right thing to do, and I knew that's what you wanted from me."

Colleen paused, as if she was half expecting Violet to answer her.

She heard nothing but the birds and the breeze.

"I really messed up. I messed up with you all those years ago, when we fell in love and I didn't tell you about being married. And I messed up with Ava when I didn't tell her the truth about her father. And what do those two things have in common? Both of those huge mistakes in my life were because I couldn't tell my truth. I think if I would've told you the truth, you would've been hurt, but I think we could've worked it out if I would've divorced Kenny."

Colleen hung her head as she realized that she'd made the messes in her life. Nobody else. She always had the chance of living an authentic life, and if she had, she wouldn't have had the heartache she'd experienced along the way. She could've told Ava a long time ago the truth about her father. Ava was always a bright child, and she probably would've understood it when she was quite young. And she could've told her daughters a long time ago about her relationship with Violet. If she had, they all could've been a family, for real.

And if she just would've told her truth all along, she probably would've had a great relationship with Ava all this time.

So many regrets. So many forks along the road where she just took the wrong direction, where, if she would've gone in the other direction, everything would've turned out differently. Who knows? Maybe Violet would still be alive in this alternate universe where Colleen took different paths in her life. Maybe Sarah, who was so health-conscious, into yoga and eating right, would've set Violet on the same path if she was in Violet's life as a daughter.

Maybe her daughters would've chosen their own more positive paths along the line if Colleen wouldn't have shunned them so much, especially Ava. If Colleen would've had a proper mother-daughter relationship with Ava, she could've guided her on a better path than the one she took. Colleen would've been able to make Ava see that her job defending billionaires was going to make her unhappy, and maybe she could've convinced Ava to take a different job.

And maybe Sarah would've listened to her when she told her that Nolan was the wrong man for her. She always had a better relationship with Sarah than she did with Ava, but even with Sarah, there was often a strain. If there wasn't that strain, would Sarah have seen the light a long time ago and stayed with the architecture firm, which would undoubtedly have made her much happier than her chosen path?

Did her lack of bravery cause everyone around her much more heartache than if she would've been able to live her life out loud? That was unknowable, of course. The only way she would ever be able to know differently how things would've been if she would've had the bravery to be with Violet when she was young, and told Ava the truth about James, would be if she had the chance given to Nora in the book *The Midnight*

Library. Nora was able to, in that book, see how life would've been for her if she would've taken paths X, Y or Z, as opposed to the paths she took in her current life. And, in most of the scenarios Nora was given a chance to see, it didn't turn out like she'd expected.

Colleen couldn't overcome the guilt about her life choices. But there was no way she could turn back time and do things differently, so she just had to work with the situation she was in.

She had hope that Ava would forgive her, but that wasn't a given.

That wasn't a given at all.

CHAPTER 33

AVA

Ava talked to Sarah, who took the news well, considering. "I guess we're half-sisters," Sarah said matter-of-factly. "That doesn't change anything. We still love each other, just like if we shared the same mom and dad."

"I know," Ava said. "It still seems weird to know we don't share the same DNA, the way I always thought we did."

Sarah gave Ava a big hug. "Don't let it change anything between us," she said. "But what are you going to do now? Are you going to talk to James's family, the way you did with dad's family, to find out more about him?"

"I don't know yet. I don't want to do that to them. I mean, James was having an affair on his wife when I was conceived. How fair is it to drop that on their heads?"

That was yet one more reason for Ava to resent her mother. There would be no way for Ava to get to know her father's family without driving a stake through the heart of everybody in that family. But not getting to know her father's family was going to leave Ava feeling like she was only half a person.

Still, Ava knew if she contacted James' wife, it would be

for a very selfish reason. And she couldn't, in good conscience, let the Bloch family know that James was unfaithful. She was going to have to let that side of her family tree go.

"Is there anybody you can talk to who might know more about James? Somebody who isn't part of his family, who you might be able to trust not to tell his family about you?" Sarah asked Ava.

Ava nodded her head. "Yes, now that you mention it. James came to my law firm at the recommendation of a long-time client by the name of Morty Savich. Morty hired our firm whenever he was audited by the government, and, because he was a billionaire, he was audited quite a bit. But he wasn't shady, at all. I really liked that guy. I can probably talk to him about James."

"Well, go and find him," Sarah said. "I'll hold down the fort while you do what you need to do."

"Okay. But I'd like to do something for you, and I don't want any argument about it. On the days you take over the inn, I want you to keep all the money. That place makes money hand over fist. I bring in almost $3000 every day from my rooms. It's only fair you get to keep the money if you're going to be running the place for any period of time."

"Ava, I can't let you –"

Ava closed her eyes and counted to 10. Then, with gritted teeth, she said, "Sarah, I don't want any argument about this. You're keeping the money, and that's that. I need to go back to New York for a few days. I need to do what I can to find my roots. I need to learn about my father so I can feel more grounded."

Sarah just nodded her head. "Ava, thank you, for your generosity."

"It's only fair. Besides, you're trying to save money for a down-payment on a house out here. Your taking control of the inn while I'm gone will help you achieve that goal a lot quicker. You're helping me out, so I'm going to help you out as well."

"What about Deacon?" Hallie asked.

Deacon. Suddenly, Ava saw there was something more important than hanging out with Deacon, and that was her need to find herself.

"I don't know. At this point, I'm so confused, I don't really know what end is up. I don't have the bandwidth to deal with anything right now. I'm going to tell him I'm going to be gone for a few days, and hope he understands."

"Sugar, we're going to miss you," Quinn said. "But you do what you need to do to get straight. All of us have your back, of course, like usual. Keep in touch with us."

The four ladies got together in a group hug. Ava was crying and shaking her head. "I don't know if there's anything I can find out about my father that's going to make any of this feel right. But I have to try."

*****

After Ava had a talk with Deacon, she went to the airport. She was going back to New York and try to find out whatever she could about James. She didn't know how much good it was going to do, but she knew she had to make this sojourn.

She had to grasp onto whatever she could to make her feel whole. There was a gaping wound that needed closure.

The only way she could tend to that wound would be to find out as much as she could about her heritage.

CHAPTER 34

COLLEEN

Colleen got back to Ava's bed-and-breakfast and found Ava was no longer there. Sarah was there, of course, doing everything Ava always did to keep the place running. Her daughter looked at her when she came in the door, and motioned her to wait.

"Mom, I need to talk to you. I'm not mad at you, just so you know. But I need to find out more about this James. I'm curious about the two of you – how you met, why you fell in love with him, how you found out he was married, how you felt when you were pregnant with Ava. There's so much about your life I don't know, and I'd like to learn it."

Colleen smiled. At least one of her daughters didn't hate her at this point. That was a definite plus, to say the very least.

"Well, let's make a date for tonight after you're done," Colleen said. "I'll tell you everything you need to know. At least, everything from my side of the fence. I don't know how you or Ava are going to get the other side without dropping a bomb on James's widow. I hope to God Ava's not going to do that - go over to James's family and out him.

THE BEACHFRONT SURPRISES.

If she does, of course that's her right, but I hope she doesn't."

"I don't think she's going to do that," Sarah said. "In fact, Ava said she wasn't going to do that for the very reason you just said. She said she didn't want his widow to know he was having an affair."

Colleen sighed as she realized the pickle she put her daughter into. Ava was never going to know one-half of her heritage. That seemed very unfair to Colleen. She, herself, knew all her aunts and uncles and grandparents on both sides the family. She didn't know what she would do if she didn't know where she came from on both her mother and father's side. She knew her family tree, her ancestors. Sarah did too.

Ava was going to be denied all that. How fair was that for her? It wasn't. But, for Ava to know her family tree on that side, she was going to have to rip a family apart. She knew her daughter well enough to know that Ava wasn't going to do that.

******

That evening, Colleen was enjoying a glass of wine on the terrace. As usual, there were quite a few people milling about – drinking wine at different tables, a few were in the hot tub, still others were lounging on the chaises. It wasn't a very private place for her to talk to Sarah, but she loved this space so she wanted to talk to her there. Colleen could hear the ocean rolling in, and the words of Britt from the crystal store rang in her ears.

Britt told Colleen that life was like that ocean. The cycles of life were like the tide. The tide came in, but it would go right back out, and come back in again. Life was the same. Just when you think you're at a low ebb, you find yourself in a high flow. Right now, in Colleen's life, the tide was definitely out. But it was going to come back in again. She just had to wait and have faith that everything was going to turn out okay.

That was why she liked this terrace, because the ocean comforted her.

Sarah found her at 8 o'clock that evening. She had a small plate of food with her and a bottle of wine. The plate consisted of crackers, olives, dairy-free cheese made with cashew milk, sliced cucumbers, a small bowl of hummus and a small bowl of dry-roasted mixed nuts.

"If you're not hungry for dinner, this might do you," Sarah said. "Or, if you do feel hungry, we can go down to the dining room and grab some dinner. The kitchen's closed, but we can scrounge something up."

Colleen just shook her head. "My appetite's left me," she said. "When I'm under stress, I can't eat a thing. I think you got that from me, because you've always been that same way."

Sarah smiled and nodded her head. "Yep. That's the reason why I've stayed thin through the years. I haven't had too many happy days, at least until recently, when I came here and made up with Ava. I've been really happy since I've been here, on this island, so, for the first time in my life, I've had to watch what I eat. I'm no longer naturally eating like a bird like I when I lived with Nolan, and I was so miserable."

Colleen cocked her head, and munched on some of the crudités that Sarah had offered her. "Open up that bottle of wine," she said. "It's going to be a long evening."

Sarah poured her a glass, and poured one for herself, and sat down next to Colleen. "I really love it out here, on this island, and on this terrace. Did you ever used to watch *The Golden Girls?*" Sarah asked her.

"Of course. Didn't everybody in the 80s?" Colleen asked.

"I loved that show. I was in college when it used to air on Saturday nights. Whenever I didn't have a date or party to go to, and I was feeling down about that, I'd watch that show and it always made me laugh. Do you remember when they actually had good Saturday night programming?"

"Oh, yes. I do remember those days. You forget, *Mary Tyler Moore, Bob Newhart, All in the Family, M*A*S*H* and *The Carol Burnett Show* all used to air on Saturday nights. I remember watching those shows with you girls. But why did you think of the *Golden Girls*?"

"They ended most of their shows on the lanai. That's what they called their back patio. I used to watch that show and fantasize about having my own lanai to sit on and talk to my friends when I got older, just like Dorothy and everybody. This terrace reminds me of that."

Colleen snorted. "Sarah, in that mansion you lived in with Nolan, you had that amazing terrace. You could fit 100 people on that patio with room to spare."

"Yes, but even when I was living in Nolan's home, and I had that amazing terrace, like you say, I always thought about those *Golden Girl* episodes and how much more comfortable it seemed to have just a small space, outdoors, where you could just relax and gab with your girlfriends. You forget, I didn't have girlfriends when I was living out in Monterey. I had toxic women who I thought were my friends, but weren't. They were back-stabbers of the highest order. Now, out here, I have true friends, including my sister. Anyhow, we aren't here to talk about me. We're here to talk about you and James."

Colleen took a deep breath. "What do you want to ask me about him?" Colleen asked.

"Just talk. I'm fascinated to know about that period of your life. What drew you to him? How did you meet him? How did you find out he was married?"

"Well, you're just getting right on into it, aren't you? That's fine. To answer some of your questions, I met him when I was at Harvard, my first year of law school. He was my professor. And I was very confused in my life. You have to understand, it was the middle of the 60s, and I didn't know a single person who was gay. Of course, I probably knew plenty of people who were, but I just didn't know it at the time. I thought I was the only one."

"Your professor? I thought James was a rich guy."

"Oh, he was. He was like your Nolan – working for peanuts as a college professor, but came from a very wealthy family, so he inherited quite a bit of wealth. But he was my Con Law professor, and, I don't know, I was attracted to him right from the beginning."

Sarah munched on her snacks and took a sip of wine as she listened to Colleen. "Okay, so he was your professor and you were attracted to him. How did you get together with him?"

"He had a party at his house, and he invited the students. Nowadays, I'm sure that type of thing would be frowned upon, but, back then, things were just more freewheeling. I wasn't underaged. I was 23 years old, so I was able to drink alcohol at his party. I flirted with him. He flirted back. I stayed after the party to help him clean up. I never saw a woman around, and he never mentioned a wife, so I assumed he was unmarried. Turned out his wife was out of town, but I didn't know that."

Colleen took a sip of her own wine and listened to the surf roll in. *The tides roll in and they roll out. Life is the same way.*

"I started to see him in his office. I don't know, I think I was searching. I didn't get along with my parents, because I liked girls and I knew they would hate me if they knew that. I was searching for somebody who would accept me. He and I became friends, and I was going to tell him about my love of women."

Sarah smiled. "So, ironically I guess you got to know him because you were going to tell them about your feelings about being gay, but –"

"I never got a chance to tell him about why I really wanted to talk to him, because he kissed me. That kiss completely blew my socks off. I thought he was my solution. Oh my God! There I was, feeling this burning attraction to my male professor, and I really thought he was going to save me."

"Save you," Sarah said. "I understand what you mean."

"Yes. When he kissed me, and the fireworks were going off in my head, I immediately had visions of sugar plums dancing. I thought he was going to be The One. I thought I was going to be saved from my lifetime of humiliation I knew I was going to feel when I met the girl of my dreams and settled down. Because you just didn't do that in those days - settle down with a member of your own sex. Not if you wanted to be respectable."

"Such a different time," Sarah said.

"To say the least," Colleen said. "But, yes, it was a very different time. I wanted more than anything to be straight, and here was this man who I thought was offering me that chance. I thought we were going to have babies together and have a family. I was picturing my picket fence, my 2.5 babies and my station wagon with this guy. The suburban dream with the *Father Knows Best* guy I was raised to want. I thought my parents could come over and have dinner with us on Sundays and everybody would be happy."

"But it didn't quite work out that way, did it?"

"No, it didn't. We were careless, because we were kind of forced to be. Birth control was illegal back then to unmarried folks. I lied to him and said I was able to get the pill. Told him my mother helped me get it. I knew I would've lost him if he knew the truth. I went along, hoped for the best, didn't prepare for the worst, and came down pregnant with Ava."

Sarah shook her head. "The things we women take for granted now, huh? My generation always assumed birth control was a thing and always had been, but I guess it wasn't always that way."

"No. It wasn't. It wasn't until 1972 that it became unconstitutional to ban birth control to unmarried people. In 1965 it became unconstitutional to ban birth control for married people, so, if James and I were married, we could've gotten birth control. But, we weren't, and I just didn't know how to get a hold of the pill. You can imagine how James took it when I told him about having a bun in the oven."

"Let me guess. He freaked out."

"Oh, yes," Colleen said. "He told me he was married, and my heart sunk to the floor, let me tell you. Because, you know, I assumed if I was going to have his kid, he was going to marry me. You can imagine how I felt when I found out that no, he wasn't going to marry me, because he was already married, and he had no intention of leaving his wife. And, even if he wasn't married, he told me he still wouldn't have married me, because I was a goy."

"Oh, dear," Sarah said with a shake of her head. "What a mess."

"Yes. I had no leg to stand on because I lied to him and told him I was on the pill, so he thought everything was safe. I had to admit to him that I never was on the pill, and did that piece of information start World War III, let me tell you."

"Wait, didn't that happen with Ava's kid, Charlotte?"

"Yes, history repeated itself with young Charlotte," Colleen said. "She did the same damn thing, in a way. In her case, she took herself off the pill and lied about it." Colleen took a deep breath. "Anyhow, there I was. Pregnant with Ava and not knowing where to turn. Kenny was a friend of mine.

Turned out he was in love with me. When he found out I was pregnant with Ava, he said he'd marry me and tell everybody Ava was his. You didn't have to convince me that that was the way to go. I was desperate and I liked Kenny as a good buddy. So, I went for it."

"You liked my father, but you didn't love him," Sarah said.

Colleen touched her nose. "You got it. But I figured I could learn to love him. And then I met Violet. I took one look at her and knew. We fell in love immediately. And it was so complicated. The situation was, my feelings weren't. I knew the girl was the love of my life right from the start. And we started seeing each other, behind Kenny's back."

"Where was Ava while you were seeing Violet?"

"She was with a nanny. I was studying all the time, so I had to have a nanny. Anyhow, Violet and I had only been seeing each other for a month, and it was the most glorious month of my life, when I admitted I was married. I couldn't leave Kenny for her because I needed a stable home for Ava. I wanted to keep seeing her. But, she told me to choose, and I chose Kenny because I didn't see any other choice. If Ava weren't in the picture, I never would've gotten married to Kenny in the first place, and I would've been with Violet from the word go." Then Colleen made a face.

"So, you chose to stay put," Sarah said.

"Yes. That was my choice, because I had to do right by my little girl. And then I got pregnant with you, but, as much as I wanted to make things work with my husband, because I really wanted my family, I never stopped thinking about Violet. Never. I wanted more than anything to turn back time so that Ava never came into the picture, and I could've been free to be with the woman who captured my heart from first glance. But I'd chosen my path, and I was going to stick with it."

"And then dad died…"

"Yes, Kenny died. And the first thing I did after he died was go to Violet. She was with another woman and had no interest in what I had to say. She loved me but couldn't trust me because I lied to her about being married. And that was that. It wasn't until I ran into her when Ava was 10 that she and I finally got together for real. We saw each other again when I went back to Cambridge to visit some friends. She was single by then, and we talked through the night. By the time the sun came up, she had agreed to move to Kansas City to be with me."

Sarah looked like she understood. "So that's why you always resented Ava," she said. "Because you were angry with her father…"

"Not angry, irate. Defcon one irate. Wanting to kill him with my bare hands irate. Get the picture? But, yes, I think I resented Ava because I hated her father so much."

"And also, because if she never existed…"

"Yes. If she never existed, I would've been free to follow my heart when I met Violet."

"But, mom, I wouldn't have been born either," Sarah said. "Why didn't you resent me, too?"

"Because I liked your dad. And, you weren't the one that held me back. Ava was. You just came along once I decided I was going to commit myself to Kenny, in spite of my heart being with Violet. I know that doesn't really make sense to you, but that's how I looked at it. So, in my irrational brain, Ava was the cause of my unhappiness. Also, I hated her father for lying to me. He told me he wasn't married when he was. He took advantage of me and I hated him for it. I couldn't look at Ava without seeing his face, so I irrationally resented your sister for that, too."

Sarah just took a deep breath. "Mom, I know Ava's having a real problem right now with the news. Just give her time. She'll come around."

THE BEACHFRONT SURPRISES.

"Where is she?" Colleen asked.

"She's in New York. Don't worry, she told me she wasn't going to contact James's family when she got there. But she was going to talk to this guy by the name of Morty Savich. I guess that Morty was a good friend of James. I think Ava's going to pick his brain on James, find out as much as she can about him from Morty."

"I really screwed the pooch, didn't I?" Colleen asked.

"I won't lie. Yes, you did. But I don't think that you screwed the pooch on a permanent basis. To tell you the truth, I think that your telling her this is probably going to bring you guys closer in the end. There's not going to be the wall up anymore. There's going to be a new honesty between the two of you. That's going to go a long way towards repairing your relationship. I know your trip to Boston with her was supposed to be some kind of a bonding thing, and it probably was. But you're really going to be bonded with her now that everything is out in the open. I really believe that."

Colleen sighed. " I hope you're right. I really do. Because it would be a damn shame if I've come this far to try to make nice with my daughter and she shuns me after all. I'm not getting any younger, you know. I really don't want to check out of this world knowing my daughter hates me."

Sarah took Colleen's hand. "Believe it or not, I think Ava realizes that time is getting short with you. I know, you're healthy and you walk 4 miles a day, but it's just a reality that…"

Sarah didn't want to say it, so Colleen finished the sentence for her. "I could go at any time, and I know that. Look at Violet – she was four years younger than me, and she just died out of nowhere. Out of nowhere."

Colleen thought again about how she found Violet on bathroom floor, and immediately felt that stabbing pain in her chest she felt when she found her. When she closed her eyes, she could see Violet lying on the cold tile. That image was so burned in her brain that she could never fall asleep before seeing it. She wondered if she could ever get that image out of her head.

She knew the same could happen for her. Violet, too, walked 4 miles a day, because the two ladies walked together every day. They both had a Fitbit on the wrist, that measured resting heart rate, steps taken, the total hours they slept, activity and so forth. They both had a resting heart rate in the low 60s. And they both slept between six and eight hours a night, just like you're supposed to.

Colleen thought maybe the difference between her and Violet was that Violet must've had a family history of heart disease. But that was cold comfort for Colleen, because Colleen loved life and it was frightening for her to know she could go lights out one evening, just like Violet did.

It *really* frightened Colleen that she could go out one day, lights out, never having truly made amends with Ava.

"Mom, don't worry. I'm going to talk to Ava. She was upset when I talked to her, but I've a feeling that when she gets back from New York, she's going to have a different attitude. So, mom, I don't want you to worry. Ava has always loved you. Nothing that you said to her, nothing that you've done, will change that."

"I hope you're right. I hope you're right."

CHAPTER 35

AVA

When Ava landed in New York, she had to go to the one place she hoped she would never have to set foot in again - Collins and Lahy. That was where she was fired for insulting a billionaire who richly deserved her tame words and much more.

She knew she would have to find somebody there who could help her track down Morton Savich. The client list was proprietary, of course. As a former employee of Collins and Lahy, she wouldn't be privy to that information. She was going to have to approach the situation delicately.

She still had an ally in one guy. His name was Lars Thatcher, and he'd recently reached out to Ava to see how she was holding up. He'd sent her an email to let her know what was going on with the firm and that he agreed with her when she insulted John Wilson.

She walked into the firm and saw Jennifer Hart, a 23-year-old receptionist who Ava always got along with. When she walked in, Jennifer looked up from her computer and smiled.

"Hey, Ava!" she said. "Long time no see. What's new?"

Ava was nervous. She felt like she was doing something wrong, although she wasn't. She was just trying to get the phone number for Morty Savich. She needed it for a very good reason – her sanity. She simply had to talk to Morty because Morty knew her father so very well. From what she understood, Morty and James were somewhat like her and Hallie. They went back to their freshman year at Harvard, and even before that, they were best friends during their teenage years in Brooklyn. If anybody could tell Ava anything about James, it would be Morty.

"Is Lars in?" Ava asked.

Jennifer looked at her computer and then looked up at Ava. "Yes, he is. It looks like he's in his office working on a legal brief. Why?"

"I need to talk to him. Can you call him?" Ava looked around nervously. So far, she hadn't run into anybody she knew from the firm. She didn't know what she would do if she did run into anybody. She'd probably feel embarrassed, but she wasn't breaking any laws because the terms of her termination agreement didn't preclude her from coming into the firm at any time.

Jennifer rang Lars, and, five minutes later, he was coming to the lobby to meet Ava. "Ava Flynn, as I live and breathe. How come you never answered my email?"

"I'm so sorry. Things have been really hectic. Can I take you out to lunch?"

"I've never had a better offer. Let me go back and get my wallet, and we can go to the restaurant around the corner."

Ava waited for him to come back out, still looking around nervously. It was only 10:30. Regardless, she would have an early lunch with this guy because she needed to pick his brain.

Lars came back out. "Okay, lady, what do you say you and I go grab an early lunch?"

"Sounds good."

Ava and Lars went to a steakhouse around the corner. Mark Joseph's Steakhouse was an elegant yet traditional restaurant that served everything from burgers to seafood to steak. Ava wasn't starving, so she planned on getting a salad, and this place had some good ones.

Ava and Lars ordered their food, and Ava ordered a glass of wine. Lars ordered a beer.

"So, what brings you here?" Lars asked, getting his head close to Ava's. Lars was an attractive guy, around Ava's age, with salt-and-pepper hair, blue eyes and a body that he had apparently kept fit and trim over the years. The guy was married. Otherwise, before she met Deacon, Ava would've been interested in him. He was always nice to her, and Ava considered him her best friend in the firm.

"I need an address. That's all I need. Well, no, I also need a phone number."

Lars cocked his head. "I'm assuming you need a phone number for a client."

"You got it. The guy's name is Morty Savich. He's a long-time client. Would you be able to get that for me?"

Lars raised an eyebrow and said, quite flirtatiously, "It depends on what you can give me in exchange." And then he raised both of his eyebrows and smiled.

"I don't know what you're getting at," Ava said. "But tell me what you want from me, and I'll give it to you, within reason. If your request is something your wife won't approve of, then I don't know what to tell you."

Lars just laughed. "I was just teasing. Actually, I'm not married anymore. I've been divorced for the past six months."

"So you're single, ready to mingle, is that it?"

"Something like that. And Ava, I think you know we've

always had a thing for each other. Much as you've liked to deny it."

"Of course, I've denied it," Ava said. "Because you've always been married."

"Not married now," he said.

"Regardless, I think that ship has sailed. But, listen, here's what I can do. I own a bed-and-breakfast on Nantucket Island. It's right on the beach. You can come and stay at my bed-and-breakfast anytime you want to. Just let me know when you plan on coming. I can give you up to five nights. That's a gift worth $2000. That's how important it is to me to get this phone number."

He nodded his head. "Will dinner be included with that offer?" he asked.

Ava thought about Deacon when Lars suggested dinner. However, this guy was doing her a solid, so it would be wrong for her to turn him down.

"Sure, I'll take you to the best restaurant on the island. So, what do you say? Five day stay at my bed-and-breakfast and dinner?"

"That sounds like an offer that's too good to be true. All of that for one phone number?" Lars asked playfully.

"All of that for one phone number. Listen, I know you're taking a chance by giving me this phone number. I'm not overlooking this fact at all. You could get in trouble giving out this kind of proprietary information to someone like me, who has been on the outs with the firm, to say the very least."

Lars shook his head. "I'm just teasing you, Ava. I'd like to go ahead and stay at your bed-and-breakfast, but I'm not going to stay there for free, and I won't let you give me a room for free. So don't even ask me. But I could really use a vacation, and Nantucket sounds like a great place to visit. So, count me in for a reservation there. I'd like to go out to dinner with you once I get out there. I won't let you buy me dinner, though. It'll be my treat."

Lars took a swig of his beer, and Ava felt the look he was giving her was more than friendly. Still, Ava needed the information, and he was a very attractive guy. She wondered what happened to his marriage, though. Was it just one of those things where he was working too much? Or was there something more nefarious that led to the demise of his relationship with his wife? Then again, it could be something as simple as what happened with Deacon – somebody wanted kids and somebody didn't. That might have been the case, as Lars was married to a much younger woman.

"Well, we'll just have to see. Now, what about it? Are you going to get that phone number for me?"

"Sure. I'm curious about why you want it so badly, though."

"I need to ask him a few questions about James Bloch. As you might've heard, he was the one who willed me that house on Nantucket."

Lars nodded his head. "Yeah. That was one lucky stroke for you, wasn't it?"

"It was. And, you know, I have some questions about him. I'm still looking for answers about why I was so deserving of that house. That's all. Morty was best friends with James for many years, so I'd imagine he might be the person who can answer my questions."

"That's legit," Lars said. "I admit, if some client just randomly willed me a $7 million house, I'd be suspicious. I don't know exactly what I would be suspicious about, but it would seem weird. I'm a naturally cynical person, though. I don't blame you for wondering."

"Yes. Anyhow, I'd really appreciate you giving me that phone number. You can text it to me when you go back to the office and find it on the client list."

Lars nodded his head. "Okay. Now, that's the only reason you asked me to lunch?"

"I have to be honest, yes. I mean, I also wanted to catch up with you. You were always a good friend in the office, and I miss talking to you."

That was a lie. Once Ava left the firm, she didn't look back. She no longer thought about Lars or anybody else in the firm. It was a painful part of her past she'd like to forget.

But a little white lie never hurt anyone.

"I miss talking to you, too. I always kind of thought of you as my office girlfriend. Isn't that silly?"

"Office girlfriend? What do you mean by that?"

"It's just a term for a guy and a girl who act like boyfriend and girlfriend, but only at the office, and they're just friends. Obviously, it would be an office affair if they were more than friends. I'm sorry, I just get these terms from my kids. They're millennials, and they're much more up on the lingo than I am."

"Oh, you have kids. Somehow, I didn't know that. I guess I haven't been a very good office girlfriend, have I?"

"Nope. Guess not. Anyhow, I'm glad I could help you out. Just don't give this phone number out to anybody else. You could be giving the number out to someone who wants to stalk the guy. If that's the case, I'll have my butt in hot water in two seconds."

Ava laughed at that. "Well, actually, that's why I offered you a stay at my bed-and-breakfast. I know you're going out on a limb to get me this phone number, so I wanted to give you something in return."

"As I said, Ava, I'd love to stay at your bed-and-breakfast. But I'm going to pay my own way. I'll give you that phone number when I get back to the office. And, while I'm at it, I'll go ahead and book a reservation at your place. What's it called?"

THE BEACHFRONT SURPRISES.

"The 'Sconset Inn. It's on the Siasconset beach. The locals call Siasconset' Sconset, so that's where I got the name of my little inn."

All at once, Ava felt nervous about inviting Lars to stay with her. He was flirting with her quite a bit. She didn't recall him being flirtatious before because he was married, but he did refer to her as his "office girlfriend."

She didn't want a barrier between her and Deacon. It was bad enough she'd left him back on Nantucket, didn't invite him to New York with her, and didn't tell him why she was coming to New York. There were already a few roadblocks she'd thrown up in front of Deacon, so she didn't know how she felt about this attractive Lars, who seemed to be into her, coming to stay.

Yet, she couldn't go back on it now. She made the offer, and Lars had agreed to help her.

"Okay, I'll let you know what Morty's phone number is," he said.

The food came around. Ava eagerly dug into her salad while eyeing Lars's burger with envy. What she wouldn't give to be able to order what she wanted without having to worry about it showing up on her hips later on. She was agnostic, but if she did believe in the afterlife, she knew her afterlife would be the ability to eat anything she wanted with abandon and not worry about a thing.

After Ava and Lars finished their lunch, they settled up the bill, and Ava walked back to the office building with him. "Thank you so much for helping me," she said to him. "I can't tell you how important this is to me."

Lars kissed Ava on the cheek, and she noticed the color of his eyes for the first time. She always thought they were just brown, but she just noticed they had flecks of green and even blue, which made the eye color so much more interesting.

Ava walked away from the office building more confused

than ever. Was she now going to have to question her feelings for Deacon? She thought maybe her relationship with Deacon would be sturdy for her, but now she was questioning whether or not that was going to be true.

Just like that, Ava felt there was one more pillar of her life going soft. She would have to pull it together like she had many times before. Otherwise, she was going to go under. And she couldn't do that.

She had just too much riding on her ability to stay sane.

CHAPTER 36

COLLEEN

Colleen went to her regular appointment with Willow. She had mixed emotions about the young psychic. On the one hand, she was angry with her for pushing her to tell Ava the truth about her father. On the other, she knew Willow was right, and she was absolutely wrong when she thought she should go to her grave with that secret.

Because Willow was correct about one thing – the secret was tearing her apart, and it was coming between her relationship between her and her daughter. Now that it was all in the open, she could concentrate on building a foundation with Ava, a foundation that not built upon shifting sand.

"Hello," Colleen said to Willow frostily.

Willow raised an eyebrow. "Congratulations," she said. "What you did took guts, and, don't worry, it will turn out okay."

"How do you know?" Colleen asked her.

"Because I know. And, by the way, I communicated with James the other night. I did that for Ava. But, I don't think Ava will need my help because I know she'll get the same information she would've gotten from me from somebody else. I'm getting a vision that she'll be meeting with an older guy who has answers for her. Once she gets those answers, it'll be time for the two of you to really come to terms."

"Who is she going to see?" Colleen asked.

"I'm not sure. I'm getting a message that it's a man named Marty or Mark."

"Morty?" Colleen asked. "Morty Savich?"

"Could be. I'm not entirely sure. I know he's an older man, completely bald, quite tall and broad. He was good friends with James."

"Then it's Morty. I guess that's a good thing. James and Morty were best friends from way back."

Willow just nodded her head. "I think your daughter will get some closure when she talks to this guy."

"I hope so. God, I made so many mistakes in my life. At what point do you say you're too damn old to be so dumb? I don't want to go to my grave with so many regrets, so I hope you're right – Ava will get the answers she needs."

"She will. Now, come on back, and we'll get started with your treatment."

Colleen went back to the acupuncture room with Willow and lay down while Willow put the needles in. She closed her eyes and tried to concentrate on anything other than how many screw-ups she committed in her life.

She wondered if she ever could get over her regrets.

CHAPTER 37

AVA

Ava got in touch with Morty. They arranged to meet at Palma, a historic Italian restaurant in the West Village. The restaurant was located in a 200-year-old carriage house and had a beautiful garden outdoor seating area. The tables were surrounded by flowers and ivy-covered walls, and the tablecloths were whimsical - white with red and green flowers stitched into the fabric. The menu featured fresh Italian food made with organic produce and offered gluten-free pasta options.

Ava got there early and ordered a glass of wine. She took a deep breath. It was June, so it was extremely warm, but she was comforted by the sounds of the birds and the beauty surrounding her. A lovely woman, around 25, with black hair and large brown eyes, came and took her order. She was Isabella, and Ava deduced she was a member of the family that owned this place.

Ava leaned back in her chair and took a deep breath. She smelled the flowers and closed her eyes. What was Morty going to tell her? She was nervous about this meeting, to say the least.

Morty appeared, a large and strapping 92-year-old man with a completely bald head, tiny wireframe glasses, and a ready smile. Ava didn't know Morty all that well. She'd only met him a few times, but she liked what she knew of him.

She stood up, and Morty gave her a hug. "Ava Flynn," he said with a twinkle in his green eyes. "I have to say, I was surprised you got in contact with me. But, I'm glad you did."

Ava had explained over the phone why she wanted to talk to him. She got the impression he knew about her all along. Maybe he was just waiting for her phone call. She also thought he wasn't going to stonewall her about James. After all, there was no reason to.

Ava smiled. "I'm happy you agreed to meet with me. I chose this place because it's so peaceful. That's what I really need in my life – peace. I thought I had it, but I got this bombshell dropped on my head, and now I don't know if I'm coming or going."

Morty smiled and sat down. "I'm glad you chose this place," he said. "I love it too, for the same reason you do, and the food is good."

Ava knew that Morty was a Holocaust survivor. He was in Bergen Belsen when he was 15 years old, and was in the camp for several months before it was liberated by the Allies. He survived and his father didn't.

Apparently, Morty had a positive outlook on life because he knew how precious it was. In the camp, he was surrounded by death, so he always said that every day he was on this earth was a good one. Far too many of the people he knew in Germany were no longer on this earth and hadn't been for at least 77 years.

Morty ordered a glass of Pinot and then turned to Ava. "Do you like calamari? They have some really good calamari here."

"Love it. Go ahead, order it."

THE BEACHFRONT SURPRISES.

Morty nodded his head and ordered the calamari in fluent Italian. Then he smiled again at Ava. "Sorry, I'm not trying to show off. I lose my head when I'm around such a fantasy setting. Whenever I come here, I feel like Alice in Wonderland. Don't you?"

Ava cocked her head. She knew Morty was fluent in German, of course, because that's where he lived when he was a teenager and child. She was surprised he also was fluent in Italian, but she really shouldn't have been. Morty was such an intelligent man, and, because he spent his formative years in Europe, he probably was able to travel quite a bit. His family was well-to-do - they owned a château in the German village of Luebeck, and his father was a prominent lawyer in the town. They lost everything in the Holocaust, and Morty and his mother had to start completely over when they arrived in New York and moved in with Morty's Aunt Hannah.

Ava thought about Morty's life as she sat across from him. She realized she really didn't have any complaints. Yes, her mother lied to her, and was never nice to her, but what right did she have to complain about anything? Morty's father was murdered by the Nazis and his family lost everything. Yet he was able to go to Harvard Law school and follow in his father's footsteps in becoming a prominent lawyer. He thought of life as a gift, and he was such a sunny person that he felt like he was Alice in Wonderland when he sat at that restaurant.

Suddenly, all of Ava's problems seemed so petty. Yes, she didn't like her mother very much, but her mother was alive and wanted a relationship with her. Morty couldn't say the same about his father, yet he wasn't bitter about that.

Ava smiled. "Yes, actually, I do feel like Alice in Wonderland. I'd love to have lunch with the Mad Hatter because he was always a lot of fun. And strange, so very strange." She read that book when she was a kid and loved it.

"Yes, he was. Now, let's talk about James. What do you want to know about him?"

"Well, I know a lot about him because we used to go to lunch all the time. And maybe I should've questioned why he was so eager to get to know me as a person when I was just his lawyer. But, you know, I never even thought about it. Ironically, I wanted to have a relationship with him because I was looking for a father figure, and he provided that."

Oh, the irony. She was looking for a father figure. She had one all along, but she didn't know it.

"You want to know how he felt about you," he said. "Well, that's a complicated thing. I've known James since I was a teen. He was one of the first guys on my block to come to our house and ask me to play baseball with him and his friends. I still remember the first time he knocked on my door, a baseball in one of his hands, a bat in the other. I was new to America and terrified. It's disorienting for a teen to leave everything he's ever known to come to a completely strange land. But my mother and I were lucky to have a place to go after we got out of that camp."

Ava just nodded. She so wanted to hear about James, and she was also fascinated with Morty's story.

"Well, here comes James, inviting me to play baseball with him and his friends. I thought it was the greatest invitation ever. I wanted more than anything to have a normal life, and I wasn't sure if that would be possible. I felt like a freak. But, from that day on, when I played baseball with those boys, I felt like one of them. And, let me tell you, my mother was thrilled beyond belief that I made a friend so quickly."

Isabella came around and took their orders for their lunch, after depositing the crispy calamari on the table. She smiled at the charming Morty, and said something to him in

Italian, and he spoke back to her in the same language. Then he smiled at Isabella, and Ava could tell he was flirting with her. He was such a sweet older gentleman and Isabella was evidently charmed by him. She giggled sweetly and then took their orders.

Ava ordered the *fettuccine ai funghi* - handmade fettuccine served with mushroom and black truffle. Morty ordered the *cotoletta di pollo alla Milanese* - pan-fried organic chicken breast served with lemon and a market salad.

Ava's mouth watered as she thought about her delicious meal that would be coming up. She took a bite of the calamari and rolled her eyes with pleasure. She knew there was a reason why she loved this place, and it wasn't just because it was such a beautiful space to eat.

"You met James when you first moved to Brooklyn," Ava said. "What happened next?"

"We became thick as thieves," he said. "Both of us got into Harvard, so we decided to go ahead and live together in the dorms. We double-dated all through college, we got in trouble together for pulling several pranks on some of the faculty, we went to parties together, we crammed for exams together. We were just extremely close. I introduced him to Esther."

Esther was James's wife of 64 years.

"Esther," Ava said. For some odd reason, just saying the name "Esther" aloud filled Ava with dread. She knew that if Esther knew about her, the older woman's heart would just break. She felt sorry for the woman, and she didn't even know who she was. "Tell me about his relationship with her."

"Well, it was a relationship not without problems. Obviously, since your mother was stepping out with James way back when. I think Esther and James were going through growing pains when he met Colleen. They'd been married for less than 10 years and had two children at home. James wasn't home a lot because he was usually at the university. Esther's mother was sick, so Esther spent a great deal of time in New York during that time. James and Esther grew apart. They were even talking about divorce."

Ava took a sip of her wine. So, at one time, James was going to divorce his wife. It was around the same time he was seeing her mother. She wondered if that was a coincidence.

"So, they just grew apart? Or were they ready to divorce because my mother was in the picture?"

"No. Your mother was in the picture because they were about to divorce. She wasn't the cause of anything, only the symptom. And I don't want to hurt your feelings, but he was never serious about her. She was a pleasant diversion, a pretty girl who turned his head and took his mind off his marital problems. But your mother isn't Jewish, so he could never get serious about her. Also, he had children with Esther, so any decision to leave the family would never have been taken lightly."

Just when Ava was starting to feel a bit relaxed around Morty, she felt her hackles rise. She felt for her mother, who apparently fell head-over-heels in love with James. Colleen apparently never knew, and as far as Ava was concerned would never know, that James felt so casually about her.

She thought it was a good idea to talk to Morty, but she was starting to question that wisdom. Did she really need to know for sure her parents were never really in love? Or, rather, her father never loved her mother? No, she didn't need to know this, and she wished she'd never found it out.

Ava must've had a look on her face that showed her distress, because Morty put his hand on hers and squeezed it. "I'm sorry I'm telling you this, but it was reality. If your mother was Jewish, Morty probably would've fallen in love with her, the way she fell in love with him. But she wasn't, so he couldn't fall in love like that. You have to understand that Judaism was very important to James. He could never be with somebody who was not of his faith."

"Well, my mom is agnostic. She never really followed a religion, so she probably would've been willing to convert." Ava knew she was talking out of turn when she said that because she could never imagine her mother following any religion. Yet, the way her mother described her relationship with James, Ava got the impression that Colleen would've done anything to have kept him in her life.

Morty smiled. "It doesn't work like that. A woman has to convert to the religion for her own reasons, not because she's trying to land a man. If she doesn't, she ends up not converting in her heart and soul. Judaism is not just about the holidays, about reading the Torah without an understanding of the words, about lighting the candles on Shabbat and saying the blessing. Anybody can do those things. But James absorbed his faith. He lived it every day of his life. Your mother might've been able to take the conversion classes and gone through the mikveh bath to ritually cleanse her soul. But would she have become a Jew? From what I've known of her, I'd say the answer would be no."

Ava knew Morty was probably right about that. Her mother was just too cynical. She used to always tell Ava that she questioned the existence of God because of all the evil and sadness she constantly saw in her courtroom. She saw the worst of humanity in that courtroom, and she used to tell Ava that no God would allow those things to happen to His children.

"So, why would James have gotten involved with my mom? If he knew there would be no future, why did he get started with her?"

"As I said, James was going through a rough time with Esther. He needed something to take his mind off that." He sighed. "Esther was also having an affair at that same time. It all came out during marital counseling. She was seeing a man in New York while James was living in Cambridge, teaching at the law school. And it came out that their son, Elijah, wasn't actually his."

Wait - Esther had a son by somebody else? "How old is Elijah?"

"He's about your age now. He just turned 55."

Ava would be 55 in two more months.

"Oh," Ava said. "So, I wasn't the only, uh, mistake, to come out of the marriage."

"No, you weren't." Morty shook his head. "As I said, James and Esther almost divorced. It took a strong will for them to stay together. A strong will and an even stronger therapist. Marriage is work, and they put in the hard work because they both wanted to stay married for the rest of their lives."

Ava took another bite of the calamari and another sip of the wine. "So-"

"If you're wondering if you're what saved the marriage, I would have to say yes."

Ava scrunched up her eyebrows. "Huh?"

"Think about it. Esther had a child who had a different father. If the same hadn't happened on James's side, there would be no coming back from that for her. James would've never forgiven her. But, as it was, he couldn't say one word about it, because he was guilty of the same thing. You could say that their mutual indiscretions canceled each other out, and they were able to start over for that reason alone."

Ava thought that was weird moral reasoning. At the same time, she could see the twisted logic in it. "But Elijah was being raised by James and Esther," Ava said. "That was a different thing than what happened with me."

"It was different, but the same, too. At any rate, Esther

and James were able to start over because they both did the same thing to each other. Do you see?"

"Yes, I do see," Ava said.

The food arrived, and Ava took a bite of her pasta. "Oh, a slice of heaven," she said with delight. She would never stop appreciating really good food, and this pasta dish definitely qualified as that.

Morty smiled as he cut into his chicken. "A slice of heaven, indeed," he said. "There's really nothing like good food, is there?"

"No, I was just thinking that," Ava said. "So, tell me more about James."

"You mean, tell you more about James and how he felt about you," Morty said. "He thought of you as his daughter. That was why he was interested in getting to know you."

Ava took a deep breath. "He couldn't have thought of me as a daughter," she said. "He didn't seek me out for 45 years. That's when I met him - when I was 45, and I argued his case in front of the appellate court."

Morty raised an eyebrow. "Well, that was complicated, you know. James and Esther decided to put the past behind them and start fresh, so James tried to put you out of his mind. But you were never far from his mind, I can tell you. He talked about you all the time, but only to me. He got your school pictures from Colleen and got updates on what you were doing. He cheered when you got into Harvard."

"He didn't have anything to do with that, did he?" Ava asked. "My getting into Harvard?"

"Ava, you scored a 172 on your LSAT, and you graduated *magna cum laude* from MU," Morty said. "I think it's safe to say you got into Harvard on your own steam."

"But he didn't tip the scales in my favor, did he?" Ava asked.

Morty didn't answer, but took a sip of his wine.

"Oh my God, he did tip the scales," Ava said. "Harvard was one of the biggest benefactors of his family's wealth. His father gave the school millions and there are wings named after the Blochs there. James could've gotten a moron into Harvard if he really wanted to."

All at once, Ava felt sick to her stomach. She'd always thought she'd gotten into Harvard completely on her own. Yes, her mother was a legacy, but her mother didn't give any money to the school, so Colleen couldn't have had much pull with the admissions officers.

But, as a former faculty member, combined with the fact his family gave the school so much money, James had a lot of pull there. And, apparently, he used some of that pull to get her into that school.

"Ava, you had the credentials to get into Harvard," Morty said. "And you probably would've been chosen even if James didn't intervene. But, yes, he did put in a word with the admissions officer to make sure you got in. I can't lie about that, even though I wish I could."

So, Ava was running a bed-and-breakfast because James willed her a house. And she was a Harvard-educated lawyer because James put his thumb on the scale.

Did she do anything on her own?

She was irrationally angry now. How dare James do those things while never acknowledging her? Instead of influencing the admissions board at Harvard to let her in, he should've come out of the woodwork and announced to the world he was her dad. Ava would've preferred that, even if she had to settle for a lesser law school.

"Ava, don't dwell on this. You got into Harvard on your own steam. He just made sure you would be accepted. It's not like you had a 3.0 grade point average and a 160 on your LSAT, both of which are exceptional by any measure, but

THE BEACHFRONT SURPRISES.

neither of which would've gotten you into Harvard. No, Ava, you had a 3.9 GPA and an excellent LSAT score."

Ava closed her eyes. "Lots of students had those two things, and they didn't get in. I'm not positive of that, but I'm pretty sure of it. It's not enough to have a stellar LSAT score and GPA to get into Harvard. Apparently, you also need an older gentleman who doesn't want to admit you're his daughter, but wants to make up for his lack of acknowledgment by doing other things. And these other things – making sure I got into Harvard, willing me a very extravagant house – don't make up for the fact that I never knew my actual father. "

Ava took a deep breath. She was going to lose it, right then and there, and it wasn't fair to Morty that he would get the brunt of her anger. The best thing to do would be to cut the lunch short, thank Morty for his time, and…

She was going to have to make another pit stop. Kenny Flynn's sister, Moira, was alive and living in Kansas City. Ava always got along with her Aunt Moira, so she could rely on her to tell the truth about what she knew. And Ava somehow knew she would need Moira's perspective on this before she could turn the corner on her rage.

"Ava, I wish there were words I could use to make this easier for you," Morty said.

Ava just nodded her head. This kindly older gentleman, who was clearly in the twilight of his life, took the time to meet with her and answer her questions. It would be the height of unfairness if she spoke to him in a hostile tone. So, she was just going to have to calm down.

"Morty, you've been such a dear for coming out and meeting with me. You had nothing to do with any of this, and you've been extremely helpful. I'm having trouble with this, that's all. I have a couple of other questions, though."

Morty nodded his head in a tacit encouragement for her to go on.

"Am I considered to be Jewish?" Ava asked.

Morty chuckled a little. "Oh, now you're opening a can of worms. The short answer is that Judaism is not hereditary, so, no, you don't automatically become a Jew just because your father is. I know Hitler defined Jews as being a race of people, so, if you have a drop of Jewish blood, you're considered a Jew. But, no, simply having Jewish blood doesn't make you a Jew. Of course, you're free to convert to Judaism, just like anybody is, but being born to a Jewish father isn't enough. It's the same as any other religion. If you're were born to a Catholic mother and father, do you automatically consider yourself to be Catholic? Or do you become Catholic because you take communion, you go to services, and you're baptized that way?"

Ava nodded her head. "You're right. I guess I'm just confused. But because my father was Jewish, I might study the religion. Maybe it's for me."

"Maybe it is, and maybe it's not. Either way, you need to make the choice for yourself."

Ava took a deep breath. "Another question - why did James give me that house? Was it because he felt guilty for not acknowledging me as his child? Or was there some other reason?"

Morty cocked his head to one side and then put his hand on Ava's. "Ava, you might not want to believe this, but James loved you very much. He told me he was ashamed he didn't get in touch with you for all those years, but, once you came into his life, he couldn't have been more delighted. He cherished those lunches with you. Cherished them. He looked forward to them like nothing else in his life at that time. And he was so proud of you. You just can't imagine it. He was thrilled that his daughter did so well for herself in her life.

THE BEACHFRONT SURPRISES.

He was tickled pink about your Harvard career and how you wrote for *Law Review*, and he was so happy you were doing so well in your chosen profession."

"But what did he think about me flaming out like I did?"

"He was cheering for that, too," Morty said with a smile. "Even though he had a case that got him into hot water, he paid his taxes, and he took great pride in doing so. As you know, he got in trouble that one year because his accountant dropped the ball. Other than that, James was thrilled to write a check to the IRS every year because he knew how important taxes are to the running of the country. So, when you told that John Wilson off, when you gave him what-for, he said, and I quote, 'good for her. That's my daughter.'"

Ava smiled. "Well, I'm glad I made him proud by doing that."

"Oh, he was proud of you for a lot of things. When you wrote a brief for the Supreme Court, he got ahold of a copy of the brief. He read it and dogeared it and called me all the time, reading to me over the phone some of the more brilliant arguments you made. But he thought the entire brief was brilliant. He thought *you* were brilliant. If he could've put your brief on gold-leaf paper and framed it, he would've. At any rate, I'm not surprised your argument won the day in front of the Supreme Court because he was right – you are a brilliant lawyer. It was a shame your firm didn't understand that."

"Well, it might've been a shame, but I'm much happier now than I ever was before when I was at that firm. And my happiness is because of James and his generous gift."

Ava was happy James loved her after all. He didn't give her that house just because he felt guilty. He did it out of love, and that was important to her.

Ava and Morty spent the better part of the afternoon

talking about James, and Ava felt she came away from the lunch with a much better idea of who her father was.

Now, it was time for Ava to move on to the next person she wanted to talk to – Moira. And she had very definite questions for her aunt.

Ava was going to get closure on her heritage if it killed her.

CHAPTER 38

AVA

Ava traveled to Kansas City, the city of her youth. She'd not been back to the city for quite a few years, and she was somewhat astounded by the city's changes in the past 30 years or so.

When she had last been in the city, the downtown area was a ghost town on the evenings and weekends. While there were quite a few businesses in the downtown area, once everybody got off work at five, they went home. There were no real bars, restaurants or shops for people to go to.

However, the downtown area was now a vibrant place even on the evenings and weekends. There was a beautiful modern arena, called the T-Mobile Center, in the heart of the downtown area, and hundreds of bars and restaurants surrounded the arena. The T-Mobile Center was so luxurious and modern that major acts lined up to perform concerts, and Garth Brooks performed a series of exclusive concerts for the good people of Kansas City when the arena opened.

On the edge of downtown, hundreds of artists had opened studios and galleries, all within a few block radius called the Crossroads District. So, on the first Friday of every month, the streets were filled with people going from one gallery to the next, drinking wine, eating from food trucks, and buying art.

Another huge change that occurred since Ava had left the city was that the football team, the Kansas City Chiefs, went from a laughingstock to going to back-to-back Super Bowls, and hosting the AFC championship game four years in a row. That was mainly due to the superstar quarterback, Patrick Mahomes, who was young and hopefully could carry a dynasty on his shoulders into the future. When Ava lived in Kansas City, she wanted a good football team to root for, and now, wherever she lived, she rooted for the Kansas City Chiefs. She was a Kansas City girl through and through in her heart, and that hadn't changed over the years.

The New York teams could go to the World Series or the Super Bowl, but Ava never got excited about those teams going. But when the Royals went to the World Series, Ava painted one of her walls Royal Blue in honor of her team. When the Chiefs went to the Super Bowl, twice in a row, Ava got a red and yellow manicure, and went to a local bar where fellow Kansas City ex-pats gathered, and cheered them on at the top of her lungs.

Ava adored her hometown. She loved the beautiful old mansions in the Northeast area. They were mainly in the Queen Ann style in that area, with the turrets and enormous stone porches. And many neighborhoods sported turn-of-the-century mansions, most of them built in sturdy brick or stone, in different styles such as Tudor, Queen Anne, Colonnade, Federalist, and many large homes influenced by the renowned architect, Frank Lloyd Wright.

Ava loved the hidden neighborhoods, where little shops and restaurants were tucked away amongst the older brick apart-

THE BEACHFRONT SURPRISES.

ment buildings and homes. She loved the history of the place – Pretty Boy Floyd once ran the city, a Kansas City mob war led to bombings near the river, and the grand Union Station was the site of an infamous mob massacre called, appropriately enough, the Kansas City massacre or the Union Station massacre.

Ava didn't just love the violent history of the place, although that fascinated her, but she also loved to hear about the famous jazz musicians who got their start in Kansas City, such as Charlie Parker, and about the many other famous jazz musicians who pioneered the Kansas City jazz sound. Count Basie and Jay McShann were just two of the great jazz musicians who played in Kansas City bars back in the day. Those great musicians back in the '30s and '40s were responsible for putting Kansas City on the map, along with the barbecuers that attracted people from around the nation to sample Kansas City-style barbecue.

Although Ava was thrilled to be back in her hometown, and she really wanted to explore the city – go to the world-class art museum, investigate the beautiful conch-shell-shaped Performing Arts Center, go to some of the old bars she used to haunt when she was young and home from a college break, or maybe visit the beautiful gardens in a town just east of the city - she wasn't there for a pleasure visit. She was there to visit her aunt, who would give her answers she craved.

When she called Aunt Moira, her aunt excitedly invited her over to her home for a little lunch in her garden. Moira lived in Brookside, a neighborhood where large turn-of-the-century homes shared space with little shops, bakeries, restaurants, and a pub or two. Moira lived in a two-story stone home built in 1908, that featured an enormous wrap-around porch and a beautiful backyard garden filled with roses, peonies, lilies, marigolds and sunflowers. There was also a 50-foot-tall oak tree in the front yard with a tire swing Ava used to play on.

Ava was thrilled to be having lunch in yet another gorgeous garden and was also extremely happy to see her beloved aunt. Moira was like Ava's mother - blunt-speaking, sarcastic, funny.

Moira was around 75 years old, but she didn't look it because she dyed her hair jet black. She apparently had excellent genes because, even though she'd gotten out the sun in her youth, her face was remarkably unlined.

Moira gave Ava a huge hug when Ava came to the door of her home.

"Ava, come here you," she said, as she spread her arms open wide. "How the hell have you been? You know, you can come around a few times a year. I don't bite."

Ava just nodded her head. She knew she'd been negligent in visiting her aunt over the years. She felt terrible she was only there to talk to her about Kenny.

Ava followed Moira into the garden, where a couple of dirty martinis were sitting on the table. "Let's have a couple of cocktails before lunch, huh?" she said. "Tommy's out playing golf somewhere, as usual, so if you weren't here, I probably would be watching my stories. Too bad they took off all the good ones, like *One Life to Live* and *All My Children.* Now I have to settle for watching *Days of our Lives,* of all things. Oh, ABC, why have you forsaken me?"

Moira shook her fist mockingly at the sky and then grinned at Ava.

"Aunt Moira, it's good to see you. And I'm really happy to be back in my hometown. I'm so sorry I haven't been around for a few years."

Moira waved her hand at Ava dismissively. "Oh, I know you've been extremely busy," she said. "To say the least. What's been going on with you these days?"

Ava told her all about losing her job and getting the house in Nantucket. As she spoke, Moira looked at Ava like she was trying to concentrate on what she was saying, but also trying to hide that she probably knew who gave Ava that house.

Moira nodded her head. "Well, Ava, I'm not going to pretend I don't know why you're here. I mean, other than the fact that you want to see your wonderful Aunt Moira, I'm pretty sure you found out the truth about your dad."

"Yes. I did." Ava took a deep breath. "I don't really know what I'm looking for here, but I'm trying to cover all the bases because I'm still searching."

Moira took a sip of her martini and shook her head. "I wanted your mom to tell the truth a long time ago. But I was shouted down by both your dad and your mom."

Ava started to open her mouth to protest that the man Moira called her dad wasn't, but her aunt didn't let her say anything. Moira apparently knew what Ava wanted to say, and she shut it down.

"Yes, Kenny Flynn was your father. He was much more your father than the random sperm donor was. Look at it this way – if a woman goes to the sperm bank and gets knocked up by a turkey baster, or however it is they do that type of thing, who's the father? The guy who whacked off into a cup, or the guy who changes the new baby's diapers and stays up with her when she's sick? Because Kenny did both of those things for you."

"But-"

"But, nothing. What did James do for you other than give you his DNA? Was he there when you spiked a fever of 103 and had to be rushed to the hospital? Where was he when you took your first steps, said your first word, and threw your first fit in the middle of the shopping mall? Was he the one who dropped you off for kindergarten, even though you cried, begged and pleaded not to go? Was he the one who got up in the middle of the night because you were hollering in your crib? You could wake the dead with your hollering, let me tell you. I know because I watched you when I was young."

Moira shook her head. "I still remember the weekend your parents dropped you off for me to watch you because they wanted to take a vacation to The Elms hotel. I don't think you stopped screaming the entire time. I had Sarah, too, but she was a perfect angel that weekend. But you. I knew you were trouble when you were born with all that red hair."

Ava chuckled. She knew her aunt was teasing her, as she often did. That was one of the things she loved about Moira.

"Obviously, Kenny was the one who cared for me. James wasn't around," Ava said.

"No, he wasn't. The reason why he wasn't was because he chose not to be. Don't let anybody ever tell you differently. He chose not to be in your life, and Kenny stepped up to the plate. Kenny knew Colleen was pregnant with James's baby, and that was why he married her. He loved her. I know Colleen didn't love him back, and I know why. And that's not for me to judge, except that your mother crushed my Kenny."

Ava was starting to think maybe it was a bad idea to see her aunt. Moira was trash-talking the only still-living person who Ava could call her parent.

"But," Moira went on. "The heart wants what it wants, and sometimes the head cannot stop the twisted thoughts. I know Colleen struggled with finding love with my brother, but she did try."

"That's a good thing," Ava said.

"Yes, it is. And if Kenny wouldn't have died so young, stupid boy smoking so much, what was he thinking, maybe your mother would've fallen in love with Kenny at some point. But I know how frustrated Colleen was with her life back then. It's not your fault, it was never your fault, but Colleen's twisted mind made it your fault."

"What wasn't my fault?" Ava asked.

"It wasn't your fault that Colleen couldn't be with her girlfriend back in the day. But, somehow, she thought that it was."

"I don't understand?"

Moira sighed. "Here's the thing. Your mother was only married to my brother because she got pregnant with you. She was so scared of her parents, just so frightened of them. She knew if she turned up pregnant and unmarried, her parents would've just cut her out of their lives. Colleen couldn't face that. Believe it or not, your mother wasn't always the bad-ass federal judge she is today. When she was in her early 20s, she had the same insecurities many young women had then and now. You know, she wanted to please her parents."

Ava just nodded her head. "Okay, so…"

"Well, like I said, your mother only married my brother so she could stay in her parent's good graces. The timing was suspicious, of course, because Colleen was two months pregnant on their wedding day, so you were born only 7 months after they got married. Colleen and Kenny told everybody you were born prematurely, and she must've gotten pregnant on her wedding night. Nobody ever questioned it. Everybody thought you were two months premature. I knew better. You were way too big and healthy when you were born to have been a preemie. But Colleen's parents bought her story, and nobody was ever the wiser."

Ava was starting to get the picture, but it was still a little hazy. She still didn't know exactly why Colleen blamed her for an unhappy life.

"Along comes Violet. And Colleen is gaga. But, she

couldn't have her because she was married to my brother. Are you starting to understand now?"

It finally hit Ava what her aunt was trying to get at. "She hated me because she couldn't be with the love of her life from the moment they met. Is that what you're telling me?"

"Bingo. And also, Colleen hated your real dad for lying to her like that and getting her into that situation. So, she also resented you because you reminded her of James. And you know, I always wanted to tell you why your mom was mean to you, but I never had the green light. Now, Colleen gave me the green light, in a way, because she told you the truth."

"I don't understand. My mom was able to be with Violet early on. So why was she still so hateful to me?"

"Who understands the human brain and the twisted thoughts that reside there? Her unhappiness in her marriage with my brother and her bitterness towards James got heaped on your head. It wasn't fair, it wasn't right, but it was what it was."

All at once, Ava started to understand her mother's animosity towards her. While she didn't feel sympathy for her, she was starting to understand why her mother was so cold to her. It had nothing to do with her. Nothing at all. She always thought her mother was hard to please. She never understood what she did wrong. Now, however, she realized she did nothing wrong. Her mother just irrationally blamed her for things beyond her control.

Regardless, even if her rift with her mother wasn't her fault, she had a much better understanding of what her mother went through when she was very young.

Would she have felt the same if somebody had kept her from Daniel? Her feelings for Daniel were much like Moira described her mother's feelings for Violet. She fell in love with Daniel at first sight, and they had a wonderful relationship. He was definitely the love of her life. He was taken too soon, but that didn't make him less of a great love. Would she have irrationally hated a daughter who kept her away from Daniel for years? Maybe.

She didn't know. What she did know was she still had one parent left. And, yes, that parent lied to her about where she came from. That wasn't right. But, at the same time, nothing could be done about it now. She was just going to have to accept that she would never really know one side of her family. She would have to get past all that and forgive her mother.

Moira was studying Ava. She was scrutinizing her, her eyebrows scrunched up, and the look on her face was questioning.

"What's going on in that head of yours?" Moira asked Ava.

"I finally understand why mom was never very nice to me. It doesn't mean I'm not angry about it, but I can finally stop blaming myself. I always just thought I was such a disappointment to her. I never imagined her hostility was something that had nothing to do with me. You helped me understand that, so I thank you for that."

Moira shook her head. "Well, I hope you can forgive your mother. It's no good going through life at odds with a parent. And, if the two of you can come to terms, I think you'll both be happier."

"Yes. I know you're right. I think if we stop being so angry at each other, we'd both be happier. I'm going to work on that. It doesn't necessarily mean that I can forgive her for not telling me the truth about my father, but I found out he loved me, so that means a lot."

"Kenny loved you too, very much. I know, I know, you were very young when he died. What do you remember about that time, by the way?"

"Not much. I remember my parents talking in very low

voices all the time. And I remember that my father was gone for long periods. I guess he was gone a lot because he was in the hospital. I visited him there a time or two. The times when I saw him, he looked okay. But there were also long periods when I couldn't see him. My mom would go to the hospital and leave us with a nanny."

Ava took a deep breath as she remembered that time. She and Sarah were so frightened because they didn't know what was happening. They only knew their father was very sick, he was in the hospital, and their mother was gone all the time because she was visiting their dad. Their mother never talked to them about their father and what was wrong with him.

"And then, one day, our mother said our father died," Ava continued. "I don't really remember much more about that time. I guess mom wanted to shield Sarah and me from him when he was looking really bad. When we got older, our mother told us he lost a lot of weight towards the end, and that was the reason why we couldn't see him before he died. I guess that's okay. I used to be angry with her about that, as well. But I've long since come to terms with it and I've understood for a long time that she was protecting us."

"That's a good thing," Moira said. "Your mother cared about you girls. She was doing the right thing for you, at that time, even if, in retrospect, you would've rather gotten the chance to say goodbye to my brother."

Ava just nodded. "Yes. I would've liked to have gotten the chance to say goodbye to my father and to my birth father. I never got the chance to say goodbye to either one."

As Ava said those words, she realized she didn't want to make the same mistake with her mother. She wanted to be there when her mother took her last breath. If her mother got sick in the future, Ava would help take care of her and would ease her into the next world. She didn't get that chance with her two fathers, and she dearly wanted that chance with her mother.

Ava and Moira spoke at length for the rest of the afternoon about everything. Ava was beginning to understand that her mother was a very flawed human being. But that's what she was – a human being who couldn't really control how she thought or felt. Ava couldn't hold her mother's feelings against her.

As she left Kansas City later that day to fly back to Boston, where she would catch the commuter plane to Nantucket, she realized one thing. She got the closure she wanted.

She was ready to go home.

CHAPTER 39

QUINN

The weeks had flown by since Emerson had started playing for Ava's patrons and had introduced Quinn to her new boyfriend, Joe. Things were settling down, and Emerson was no longer sneaking out the window. She was behaving like a normal teenager – she asked permission to see Joe, or to see one of her other new friends, and usually Quinn gave her blessing. After all, Joe seemed like a nice kid, and his family was wonderful.

And, just like a teenager, whenever Quinn refused Emerson to see Joe or do whatever she wanted to do, Emerson pouted, stomped her feet, begged, cajoled, harassed, blackmailed and used every trick in the book to try to get Quinn to change her mind. What she didn't do, however, was sneak out the window anyways.

Emerson was also eating the food Quinn fixed for her. Quinn was getting quite skilled at hiding vegetables and other healthy ingredients in various cakes, puddings, pies, breads, and the like. Emerson gobbled black bean Brownies; carrot cupcakes made with walnuts, carrots, raisins and dates; muffins made with sweet potato and nut butter;

blondies made with pumpkin and carrots; and banana breads filled with chia and sunflower seeds, walnuts and flax. She made chicken nuggets with beet puree and flaxseed meal and made pesto with peas.

She was actually enjoying the process of trying to creatively find ways to sneak in veggies, seeds and nuts into food and make it all taste delicious. Dr. Woodley was still seeing Emerson once a week, and, so far, no breakthroughs. But Dr. Woodley was the one who gave Quinn the invaluable advice to buy *The Sneaky Chef* cookbook. That one act changed her life. She was afraid Emerson would die of starvation, but she no longer feared that.

So, things were smoothing out, and Quinn was starting to enjoy her daughter's company. For the first time, Quinn started to feel like she had some control over the situation.

Of course, as they always say, the best-laid plans…

Emerson told Quinn she was spending the night with a friend named Amber. Quinn called Amber's mother, Neela, to confirm Emerson was to stay with them that night, and Neela did so. Quinn dropped Emerson off at 2.

But, at 5 o'clock that Wednesday evening, Neela called Quinn to tell her Emerson was gone.

"What do you mean gone?" Quinn asked, panic rising in her throat. *Not this again.*

"Amber and Emerson went to the beach, and Amber returned by herself. She said Emerson went to say hello to some other friends while Amber was in the water. Amber came out of the water, and Emerson was nowhere to be found. Amber came back, hysterical, and I went to the beach to look for Emerson. I asked every lifeguard there about her. I questioned everyone I knew and talked to every group there. Nobody has seen her. I'm so sorry. Oh, God, I'm so sorry."

Quinn was really panicking now. It was one thing for

Emerson to sneak out the window. She'd done that many times. But to disappear on the beach? Quinn's thoughts immediately went to a very dark place.

How easy would it have been for somebody to kidnap her daughter from the beach?

"What beach? What beach?"

"'Sconset beach," Neela said. "I should've gone with them. I knew I shouldn't have let them go on their own. I had a feeling. A gut feeling something was going to go wrong."

"I'll talk to you later," Quinn said.

She called Joe and asked him if he knew where Emerson was. He said he hadn't seen her for a couple of days. She then called all of the friends she knew Emerson had on the island, and none of them had seen her either.

Then she headed over to Ava's inn. She wanted to find Sarah to help her look for her daughter.

She felt absolutely nauseated when she walked into the inn and saw Sarah checking in a young couple. She felt tears start to flow, and she tried not to get hysterical.

Before she could talk to Sarah, though, Colleen came up to her. The older woman had been sitting in the living room area, reading a book. When she saw Quinn, she walked up to her.

"Quinn, can I help you? You look like you've just seen a ghost," Colleen said.

Quinn then broke down into tears. "My daughter, she's gone. She's gone, and I don't know what happened to her."

Colleen just put her hands on Quinn's shoulders. "Breathe. Deep breaths. Now, tell me what happened."

"I don't know what happened. She went to the beach with a friend. Only the friend came back." Quinn then explained about how Emerson went to spend the night with Amber, the two girls went to the beach, and Amber came back without Emerson, saying she couldn't find her anywhere.

THE BEACHFRONT SURPRISES.

"What beach?"

"This beach. 'Sconset. I need to go down there and see if I can find her myself."

"Okay. I know just who to call."

"Who?"

"Willow."

CHAPTER 40

QUINN

"Willow? What good is she going to do?"

"That girl is psychic. You may or may not believe in it, I didn't before I met her, but she's the real deal. You can go down to the beach and look for your daughter, but it doesn't sound good if her friend showed up without her. Every moment you waste is another moment that's slipping away from you."

Quinn felt sick. "What do you mean by that?"

"I've been a judge for far too long. I know how devious and cruel some people can be. Let's just leave it at that."

Quinn didn't press her because she didn't want to know the things Colleen had seen during her years on the bench.

Sarah finally noticed Quinn was there and came over to her. "Quinn, what's wrong?"

Colleen raised an eyebrow at Sarah. "We're going to go see Willow. I'd invite you along, but you have a lot of work to do here."

Sarah nodded her head. "Okay. I have no idea why the two of you are going to see Willow, but I'm sure I'll hear the story later."

THE BEACHFRONT SURPRISES.

As Colleen drove to Willow's spa, Quinn looked out the window.

Where was Emerson? What could've happened to her?

It was just the craziest thing. A few weeks ago, she'd rarely thought about the daughter she gave up for adoption. It was just a dark period in her life she tried to forget. She assumed she'd never see her little girl, which was fine with her.

Now, she somehow couldn't imagine life without Emerson.

She never wanted to be a mother, but it was forced on her.

Now, she could never imagine not being a mother again.

Colleen glanced over at Quinn from time to time. "Now, now, don't jump to conclusions. Not until you talk to Willow."

Quinn didn't believe Willow had any kind of special insight. Psychics were charlatans in her book. She never said as much, because she knew her friends, Sarah and Hallie at least, believed Willow was the real deal. She didn't want to insult them by saying out loud that Willow was probably a fraud. But she believed Willow wasn't going to help.

Yet, she knew Colleen was correct. Going to the beach wouldn't have done any good. Amber and her mother both went to the beach and looked for her and she was just gone. Going to the beach would just make her crazier than an outhouse rat.

They got to Willow's spa. Hallie was there, working the reservation desk. She looked up, saw Quinn's face, and immediately got up and hugged her. "What's going on?"

"She needs to talk to Willow," Colleen said calmly. "Now."

"I'll get her," Hallie said. "She should be finishing up with an astrological reading shortly. I'll tell her it's an emergency."

"Please," Colleen said with a nod of her head. "And thank you."

Willow came out five minutes later. She took one of Quinn's hands. "Your daughter is fine. I'm getting that she's on her way to Hyannis and then she's going onto Boston."

Quinn just shook her head. She didn't tell Hallie why she was there. How did Willow know she was looking for her daughter? And why would Emerson be on her way to Boston? How did she make it over to the ferry? And how would she end up in Boston by herself?

She knew now. The same way Emerson ended up on her doorstep the first time but in reverse. Using her dead mother's Uber account that apparently was still active.

In spite of her misgivings about Willow, she found herself asking questions about Emerson. She didn't believe in Willow, but, at the same time, she was impressed the young woman immediately knew she was looking for her daughter. And she was fresh out of ideas about how to find Emerson. She had to have faith in something, even if that something was a psychic.

"On her way to Hyannis? Is she on the ferry boat yet?" All at once, Quinn wanted to head down to the ferry terminal to try to intercept her daughter.

"Not sure. I'm just getting that that's where she's headed. To Hyannis and then onto Boston. She's trying to find answers about her adoptive mother. That's all I know."

Colleen nodded her head. "Let's go," she said. "Thanks, Willow."

Willow raised her eyebrows. "Anytime. Good luck to both of you. Quinn, you'll need all the luck you can get with this."

******

Quinn got to the ferry terminal and almost melted onto the floor with relief when she saw her daughter sitting on a bench. Emerson's arms were crossed in front of her, and her face was cast down to the floor. She was wearing a pair of Daisy Dukes and a t-shirt that said *Pro-Level Multitasker: I can halfway listen, kinda ignore, totally forget, all at the same time!* Her beach bag was next to her on the bench.

Quinn couldn't believe it. Emerson apparently had been crying. Quinn never thought she'd see her daughter crying because she was not that kind of girl.

Quinn saw, all at once, the pain Emerson was going through. Her daughter suddenly seemed like a 13-year-old girl, not like the 25-year-old woman she was trying to portray herself as.

Quinn approached her. Emerson saw her for the first time, and the mask was immediately back up.

"Quinn. What are you doing here?" she asked. Then she looked at Colleen. "Who's that?"

"I'm Colleen," Colleen said. "Ava's mom."

Emerson raised her eyebrows. "Great. Quinn, you always need to find somebody to help you out. What's up with that? What's next, you gonna grab a bum off the street to help you come look for me?"

Quinn couldn't explain exactly why Colleen was with her. It was just that Colleen was the one who suggested Willow, and Quinn, out of desperation, went along with the suggestion. Thank God. Willow saved her life. She had no idea how Willow knew what Emerson was up to, except that Colleen was right.

Willow was the real deal.

"Emerson," Quinn said calmly. "It's time to go home."

Emerson shook her head. "Not doing it. Not until I find what really happened to my mom. I'm going to Mass Gen, where she died, and I'm gonna find out."

"I don't understand," Quinn said. "You know what happened to your mom. She died of heart failure."

Emerson continued to keep her arms crossed in front of

her, and her feet with the neon green polish on them, which were clothed in a simple pair of rhinestone-studded thongs, started to sweep the floor.

"Maybe. Maybe not. I wanna know for sure."

Quinn was confused. "Emerson, I don't know what you need from me."

"Quinn, I need nothing from you. I just need to do this."

"Why now? Why did you just leave the beach to come here? What's the rush?"

Emerson just shrugged her shoulders, and Quinn wanted to strangle her. There was something about the shrug of the shoulders that made her go ballistic. Defcon one.

Colleen put her hand on Quinn's shoulder. "I got this. I know what this little girl's going through."

Then Colleen turned to Emerson. "Okay, kid. You're going to Boston, and you're going with me."

Quinn just looked at Colleen like she grew another head. Unfortunately, Quinn hadn't gotten to know Colleen very well. And, what she knew about her, she didn't necessarily like. She hated that Colleen had lied to Ava about her father.

Could she trust her?

"Colleen, thank you so much for your suggestion to see Willow about this. If I didn't see Willow, I'd be spinning like The Tasmanian Devil right now. But I'm her mother. I'll handle this."

Then Quinn turned to her daughter. "You're coming home with me."

"No, I'm not. You'll have to call the cops if you want me to go with you because I know you can't pick me up and carry me to your car. You're not that strong."

Quinn closed her eyes and counted to 10. "Emerson, if you don't come home with me right now, you'll be grounded for the rest of the year."

Emerson raised an eyebrow. "You gonna be getting bars

THE BEACHFRONT SURPRISES.

on my window? Because if you ground me, I'll escape out that window so fast, and you'll never find me again. Willow or no Willow."

Colleen took Quinn's arm. "Quinn, I need to speak with you."

Quinn just shook her head. "I'm not leaving Emerson unattended."

"Okay. Then I'll just talk to you right here in front of your daughter. Emerson obviously needs some information. We don't know why she needs it, but she needs it. She needs to see the medical records for her mom. She'd have to get a court order to see them, but I have a lot of pull, in Boston especially. I'll be able to get a copy of them."

At that, Emerson's eyes brightened. "You can do that? You can see a copy of my mom's records?"

"Yes. How did *you* plan on finding out this information?" Colleen asked.

Emerson shrugged her shoulders again. "Didn't get that far. Just thought I'd go to the hospital where she died and ask around."

Colleen chuckled. "Dear, one thing I've learned over the years is that life is not like the movies. Maybe in the movies you'd be able to somehow put on a white coat and sneak around and distract a record keeper and then somehow log onto their computers before anybody can catch you. Life doesn't work like that, kid. You need a grown-up with pull to get what you want in this case."

Emerson smiled. "Quinn, I'm going to like this old lady. She might be my new best friend."

Quinn took a deep breath. "I'm going with you."

Colleen put her hand on Quinn's shoulder. "Of course, you're the mother. But, if you trust me, I'd like to do this one on one. As I said, I know what this girl's going through. I know it deep in my bones. And, unless you've lost someone dear to you recently, you might not be able to relate as much."

Quinn thought back to the year after she lost James. The darkest period of her life, because she not only had to grieve the loss of her brother, but she had to deal with the aftermath of rape and the trauma of giving her baby up for adoption. All in the same year.

She wasn't right that year. She was filled with obsessive thoughts, praying for God to take her if it meant her death could bring James back somehow. Filled with regrets, convinced it was somehow her fault James died. He had brain cancer, there was no way it was her fault, but she still thought maybe it somehow was.

She barely got out of bed that year. If it weren't for Hallie and Ava, she would've withered away and died. And she was filled with rage. Not just at her rapist Charles, but at God for taking James so young. And at James himself. How could he let himself get sick and die and leave her? It wasn't rational, but she wasn't rational.

Oh, she knew about grief. But that was so long ago. She'd long since gotten over her intense pain from that year. She'd long since moved into the acceptance phase, and now she smiled and laughed when she thought of James. There was no more pain associated with his memory.

But Colleen apparently was going through active grief. Quinn wasn't sure about the circumstances that brought about Colleen's grief, but it was obvious the older woman was processing a huge loss herself.

"Okay, Colleen, if you think it's best you take Emerson to Boston, just the two of you, then you have my blessing."

Colleen nodded her head. "Thank you."

Emerson's eyes were bright. "Mom, thank you."

It took Quinn a second to notice one thing.

Emerson just called her mom.

CHAPTER 41

COLLEEN

Colleen was grateful Quinn took the leap of faith and allowed her to take Emerson to Boston. It was important she help Emerson with her grief. She understood it so well. She had a feeling Emerson was in the remorse stage of her grief.

Most people know the five stages of grief. Denial, depression, anger, bargaining, acceptance. Colleen knew there was at least one other stage: the remorse stage. That was the stage where you become obsessed about how you could have prevented the death and where you blame yourself for the person dying.

Something about Emerson made Colleen believe the young girl was convinced she was the cause of her mother's death. Something in the records would either ease her mind or make her remorse more vivid. Either way, Emerson needed to know, and Colleen had the right connections to make sure Emerson could find out. Colleen just had to make a phone call to the records clerk at Mass Gen, and she'd get the medical records immediately.

"So," Quinn said anxiously. "You and Emerson will take the ferry to Hyannis and then Uber it to Boston?"

"No. I'm going to see if there are any flights from Nantucket to Boston. It'll take too long to get to Boston the old-fashioned way."

Colleen punched up the site for Cape Air, which was the commuter plane that jumped from Nantucket to Boston. "Last flight leaves at 6:40. It's 6 o'clock now. We better get a move on."

At that, the two ladies and Emerson ran to Colleen's car. "Quinn, you drive. I gotta buy some tickets."

While Quinn drove, Colleen bought two tickets. In a matter of minutes, the trio were at the airport. Colleen and Emerson got out of the car. "Thanks, mom," Emerson said, giving Quinn a quick hug. "You're the best."

"Thank you, Colleen for doing this. I'll Venmo you the payment for the plane ticket, okay?"

"Sure, whatever you want to do," Colleen said. "I'll text you my Venmo info. It's $369 round trip."

A few minutes later, Colleen and Emerson were through security and sitting down and waiting for their flight.

"So," Colleen said. "You want to tell me what the rush was here?"

"What do you mean?" Emerson asked.

"I mean, you absconded from the beach, without even telling your friend where you were going. You panicked your mother. Trust me, there's a mean world out there. You don't want to be panicking your mother like that. Some bug got up your rear. What was it?"

Emerson narrowed her eyes. "Absconded. Long time since I've heard that word. Most adults don't use that word in a sentence."

"You're avoiding the question. Sorry, I'm a judge, sometimes fancy legal words just stick in my head and they come out. But it's an appropriate word here. Absconded means-"

"I know what it means. It's like when you jump bail or something like that."

"Right. That's what it refers to in my courtroom. It means to leave in a hurry and in secret. So, what's the deal? Why did you abscond?"

Emerson took a deep breath. "There's a guy I know, Frank. He's a friend, hangs out with Joe, who's my really good friend. Just found out his mother died of heart failure. Joe just told me that. Saw Frank on the beach, talked to him. Asked him what caused his mom's heart failure. He said her high blood pressure."

"Okay. What am I missing?"

Emerson just shrugged her shoulders. "You're not missing nothing. I just really have to find out how my mom died. That's all."

Colleen sat back. There was a big piece of the puzzle she wasn't seeing. Emerson held that puzzle piece, but she held it close to her vest.

"Okay," Colleen began.

"I wasn't sure what caused heart failure. I didn't know it could be caused by things like diabetes, high blood pressure, and sometimes you're born with a bad heart."

Emerson looked at her hands.

"And what are the medical records going to show you?" Colleen asked.

Emerson started to cry. "I don't know. I'm afraid to find out, but I need to."

"I see."

The two sat in silence until it was time to board the plane.
******

Less than an hour later, Emerson and Colleen were on the ground.

"Okay. Time to pay a visit to my good friend, Sven Gardner. He's the chief records clerk for Mass Gen. Let me just give him a quick call now. What's your mom's name?"

"Natalie Brown."

Colleen called Sven, who recognized her number. "Judge Flynn," he said when he picked up. "How are you?"

"Good. Need some records. Tonight."

"Okay. What's the name?"

"Natalie Brown. Hope it's not a problem."

Colleen heard Sven typing. "Got it. You want to pick them up here?"

"You got it. I'll be there in less than half an hour. Gotta call an Uber. See you soon."

Emerson beamed from ear to ear. "We're going to see the medical report tonight?" she asked.

"Yeah, kid, we are. You ready for this?"

Emerson shrugged her shoulders, but her face got white. "Yes. I guess so. No. I'm not ready for it."

Colleen put her hand on Emerson's shoulder. "Kid, we don't have to do this. We've come this far, but we can just as easily turn back."

"No. Let's do it."

"Okay. Remember, we can turn back at any time. Just say the word, and we're on the plane back to Nantucket. Last flight leaves at 7:55. All we gotta do is not leave this airport and get a flight back. Just say the word."

"No, Colleen, let's do it."

CHAPTER 42

COLLEEN

Colleen and Emerson arrived at Sven's less than an hour after landing in Boston. Sven lived in a classic Beacon Hill brownstone. Colleen rang the doorbell, and he answered.

"Come in, come in," he said. "Judge Flynn."

"Now, now. You know you don't have to call me Judge Flynn unless I'm on the bench."

He smiled. "Come in, Colleen." And then he looked at Emerson. "Who is this?"

"This is Natalie Brown's daughter." Colleen raised an eyebrow.

"I assume she doesn't have the proper paperwork from the estate's executor."

"You assume correctly. This is a big favor I'm asking. But I'm asking it. I know, we can do it the old-fashioned way. Get the estate's executor to sign off on a request or have Natalie's representative go to court. But this little girl needs it now. As a friend and as a Federal judge, I'm asking you to give me this."

"Okay. I'll give it to you, but this better not come back to bite me. If I get sued, I'm bringing you down with me. Fair warning."

"I'll take that chance. Now, the records."

Sven handed Colleen a stack of records. "Here they are."

"Thanks. St. Peter will smile on you for this."

******

Less than an hour later, Colleen and Emerson were in a hotel room, Natalie's records spread out on the table. Emerson was reading through them carefully.

Colleen had no idea what she was looking for. So, she didn't bother her. She just let her study them.

About an hour later, Emerson looked at Colleen with tears in her eyes. "I didn't kill her. I had nothing to do with it."

"I see. And why did you think you were responsible for her death?"

Emerson took a deep breath. "I went to a party. It was a couple of years ago, when I was 11. My mom had grounded me. Told me I couldn't go, but I went anyways. Snuck out the window, like I do to Quinn all the time. My mom didn't know where the party was because she wouldn't let me go anyways. So, she had no idea where I was that night. It was a slumber party, and I couldn't miss it. Everyone I knew was there."

"Okay. Go on."

"I came home the next day. My mom was frantic. Filed a missing person report. When she saw me, boy, did she hit the roof. But it was worth it to me because that party was epic. Epic. I didn't regret a thing."

Colleen waited for her to go on. Emerson got up and started pacing the floor.

"Turned out, I caught the flu. Everybody got the flu who

was at the party. And it was a bad one, too. I could barely get out of bed for three days. My mom said it served me right. I defied her, I got sick, and that was my punishment. She actually laughed about it."

"Okay. So you got sick, and –"

"Well, while I was sick, I watched a lot of television. A movie came on. I forget what channel it was on, but it looked good to me. Two little girls meet on the beach, a redhead and a dark-haired one. They're friends all their life. The dark-haired one dies of heart failure. Somehow, the disease she caught stuck in my head. Viral cardiomyopathy."

Colleen was starting to get the picture. "Let me guess. Your mother was diagnosed with heart failure soon after your getting the flu."

"Right. She got the flu, too. It was later than me, but I knew I gave it to her. And, after she recovered from the flu, she started getting very tired. She would swell up, lose her breath. She went to a bunch of doctors, and she told me one day she had heart failure."

Colleen nodded her head. "I know the movie you're talking about. It's called *Beaches*. One of my favorite movies, actually. Which is weird, because I don't usually like the tear-jerkers. That one got me, though. You'd have to be made of stone to not cry at that one."

Emerson nodded her head, tears trickling down her cheeks. "I'd just seen that movie, and when my mom told me she had heart failure, I looked up the words viral cardiomyopathy. I found out it can be caused by a virus like the flu attacking the heart. I thought the flu I gave her attacked her heart and caused it to fail. I assumed she'd get better because that's what the Internet said. Most people get better. But her heart failure was bad, really bad. She would have to have a transplant, it was so bad. And losing my dad just like that."

Emerson snapped her fingers. "That was too much for her heart."

"But the records show-"

"The records show she was born with a weak heart, but nobody knew about it. Then she got diabetes, but she didn't know that, either. Nobody knew she had a weak heart or diabetes until her heart started to fail. My mom never saw a doctor. She never went in for checkups, so she didn't know she was sick. Mom never told me the doctor found she had diabetes and a weak heart from birth. She just told me she had heart failure, but she would manage it until they found her a new heart."

"And the records said nothing about a virus causing the heart failure?"

"No. I looked at those records, reading every single word. I never saw the word virus or flu or cardiomyopathy or myocarditis or nothing like that." Then she smiled. "I didn't kill her. All this time, I thought I did. But I didn't."

Colleen smiled. "Kid, most of us find ways to blame ourselves when something bad happens. It's normal to have regrets when someone close to you dies. 'If only I did this, if only I did that. If only I didn't go to that party. If only I would've pounded on the bathroom door.' It's hard to accept that sometimes things just happen."

Emerson smiled. "You know, Quinn's a funny one. She makes these brownies out of black beans that are the bomb diggity. She makes macaroni and cheese out of squash. She puts vegetables into everything she gives me. And I love her for it. Now I know why Quinn does that. My mom, she ate nothing but junk. And so did I. And that's what killed her if you think about it."

"What's so funny about that?"

"She thinks I don't know about it." Emerson started to

laugh. "She thinks she's being sneaky. I don't tell her I know. I want her to think she's smarter than me."

Colleen raised her eyebrows. "Kid, I mean this with sincerity, not many people are smarter than you."

And that was the truth.

CHAPTER 43

QUINN

Quinn was on the back patio with her girls surrounding her when Colleen and Emerson came back. Quinn let out a sigh of relief when she saw them. She'd been on pins and needles the entire time they were gone, which was less than 24 hours.

Ava was back, too. She was with Quinn on the patio, with Hallie and Sarah. Colleen took one look at Ava, and Ava quietly got up and went to her mother and gave her a big hug.

"Mom," Ava said to Colleen. "I'm glad to see you."

Colleen had tears in her eyes. Quinn didn't know Colleen well, but she did know Colleen was not one to cry. Ava said that.

"Ava, I'm glad to see you too."

Emerson came over to Quinn. "Mom, what's for dinner?" she said with a big smile.

Quinn looked at her daughter. "I can take you to Foggy Nantucket to get a greasy pizza. Does that sound good?"

"Actually, I was thinking something healthier. Like a big

salad, with lots of vegetables and fruit. Maybe a big piece of fish."

Quinn wondered what had gotten into her daughter. "You pulling my leg? Because it's not funny."

"Nope. I just learned what junk food can do to you. That stuff can kill you, literally." Then Emerson smiled. "I also learned I didn't kill my mom. And you didn't either. I'm sorry for thinking you were responsible for her dying and I was too. I mean, I thought I killed her, and you also killed her because you put me up for adoption, and if I never went to live with her, I wouldn't have given her the flu. Turned out the flu didn't kill her though. So, yay! We're both off the hook."

Quinn was extremely confused. "You're making as much sense as a screen door on a submarine."

Emerson just laughed. "Long story, mom. I'll tell you the story over a nice big salad and a glass of almond milk."

"Deal," Quinn said with a smile.

CHAPTER 44

AVA

When Ava saw her mom, she knew it was time to make amends. All her anger had long since left her, and she was only left with regrets that she and her mom didn't get along for so many years.

She gave Colleen a hug, and her mom hugged her back.

Her mom was crying.

She'd never seen that before.

"Mom, let's go down to the beach."

They said their goodbyes to Quinn, and the two ladies went back to the house, grabbed their beach chairs, and headed down. It was early evening by then, but the sun was still out. People were still there - swimming, building sandcastles, laying on colorful blankets under even more colorful umbrellas.

The sun was going down, and the sound of the water calmed Ava's heart. "Mom, I finally understand why you've always treated me differently from Sarah. You resented my father because let's face it, he was a jerk to you. And I made things hard for you, my birth."

Colleen shook her head. "Ava, I need to apologize to you.

You're right. I really was so angry with James. So, so angry with him for stringing me along like that, lying to me, giving me the hope I could live in a normal relationship. Then snatching the rug out from under me. And, I'm sure you're right. My hostility towards him bled onto you."

"Right. And Violet played a part, too."

"Yes. I couldn't be with Violet for many years because I was married to Kenny, and I never would've married him if it weren't for you. I resented you for all that. I admit it. You're not to blame, of course. I wish I'd examined myself a bit better all along. If I would've figured it out before, I could've tried to correct it."

Ava put her hand on Colleen's hand. "I know, mom. I understand it all."

"I'm sorry, Ava. I am so, so, so sorry for how I've always treated you." Colleen shook her head. "So many years wasted."

"Oh, but mom, with any luck we might have many more years together. The past is past. Nothing we can do about it now. Tomorrow's a mystery, yesterday is history."

Colleen laughed. "Did you just quote Justin Timberlake to me?"

Ava laughed as well. "Guess I did."

Colleen shrugged. "Bob Dylan got the Nobel Prize for his songs, you know. Don't think Justin Timberlake's in that same category, but that line is a good one, I'll admit."

"Emerson's therapist apparently quoted Tears for Fears to Quinn, so I guess it's a thing now, quoting silly song lyrics."

Colleen took Ava's hand. "Okay. Tomorrow is a mystery, yesterday is history. Guess that's a good way of looking at it. Much as I'd like to turn back time and do it all differently, that's not an option. So, I'd like to make a gesture to you. I'm going to do this, Ava, so don't even try to stop me. But I'm redoing our agreement. I don't need money from your house.

And I really don't need you worrying about owing me money on a loan. I'm going to have my attorney void all of it. Think of the money I gave you as a gift, nothing more."

What? Did her mother take leave of her senses? "Mom, that's very generous, but-"

"Ava, don't argue with me. It's the least I can do. I want you to be a raging success. I'll be cheering you on from the sidelines every step of the way. But I don't need a cut. Just seeing you succeed is enough for me."

"But, mom-"

"I love you, Ava. I don't think I've ever told you that. And that's on me. But I'm telling you now. I love you."

Ava felt a lump in her throat. "Mom, I don't know what to say. Thank you. And I'm not just thanking you for the money and your generous decision not to be an investor but to treat it as a gift. I'm thanking you for finally telling me the words I've always wanted to hear, that you love me. Because I love you too."

The two ladies sat and watched the ocean in silence for a while. The sun had already set by that time, and the moon was high in the sky. As Ava breathed in the salty air, she'd never felt more at peace.

She and her mother were finally good.

All was right with the world.

CHAPTER 45

AVA

Colleen finally had to be back on the bench. Her six-week vacation was over, and it was time to face the real world. But Ava knew she would do something special for her mother before she left.

She came to know that Colleen never attended Violet's celebration of life. Colleen explained why she didn't attend it - she didn't want to believe Violet was gone. Ava knew Colleen being able to formally say goodbye to her longtime love would mean the world to her. So Ava decided to hold another celebration of Violet's life right there at the inn.

She got the guest list together with the help of Colleen, and, on the day, 50 people gathered together to remember Violet's life once more. This was an important part of Colleen's healing process, because Colleen got to speak the words she wanted to speak about Violet. She told Ava she had regrets that she didn't get to tell everyone who loved Violet how she felt about her. And now, she was ready to do just that.

Everybody gathered together, laughing and talking, and, when the time came, Colleen got up and addressed the group. "Thanks for coming to this second celebration of life. I guess it's kinda like a renewal of wedding vows, except you're supposed to renew your vows years and years after the first ceremony. This is coming less than a year after Violet's first service, so I guess the analogy breaks down."

Everybody laughed at her little joke.

"Truth is, I didn't go to the first celebration of life. I didn't want to face life without my Violet. I wasn't ready to say goodbye. Now, I am. I'm ready to say goodbye to Violet, but not to the memories. I'll never say goodbye to those. I still have her voice in my head every single day. I still see her sobbing after having watched *Titanic* on the big screen for the seventh time. Aye, yi, yi. Once watching that cornball film was enough for me, but Violet loved it. Tragic love stories were kind of her jam. Not mine, though. Give me Liam Neeson with a gun and a sneer over namby-pamby Leo any day of the week."

More laughter.

"Anyhow, Violet was the yin to my yang. The alpha to my omega. When she died, I felt like one of those charm necklaces that was cut in half, like you used to buy at the five and dime. One person gets half of the charm, the other person gets the other half. You take one of the halves away, and you're left without the whole charm. I felt like I was only half a person. The other half was gone."

The room was silent.

Colleen took a deep breath. "She was my angel on earth. And now she's an angel in heaven." Colleen kissed her two fingers and pointed to the ceiling. "Goodbye, my angel. Until we meet again."

******

Ava found Colleen later, talking to several of her friends. "Mom, that was a beautiful speech you gave. Short and sweet, but packed a punch."

THE BEACHFRONT SURPRISES.

"I guess."

"Anyhow, mom, I was talking to a lady over there. About your age, single, just your type. Maybe you'd like to meet her?"

Colleen put her hands on her hips. "Ava, are you trying to set me up? Do you think that I'm gay and this other lady's also gay, so let's make a match? Doesn't work like that."

Ava felt confused. "What do you mean?"

"I mean, do you go for every man you see? No. You have to be attracted to him. There has to be a spark. Same thing with lesbian women. Just because another woman is gay doesn't mean I'm going to like her."

Ava nodded her head, and felt embarrassed. Truth be told, that was what she was thinking. She thought she'd be able to match her mom up with somebody else, no problem.

"Oh. I'm sorry. I just thought...Well, I want you to be happy. That's all. I didn't mean to offend you."

Colleen just laughed. "Dear, you're not offending me. Bring her over. You never know."

Ava went to find the lady she met, whose name was Arlene Chambrille. She found her, and led her to Colleen. "Mom, this is Arlene. Arlene, this is my mom. Judge Colleen Flynn."

Arlene smiled and shook Colleen's hand. "Nice to meet you."

Colleen smiled at Ava, raised her eyebrows and nodded her head.

Ava knew she had done good.

******

Later on, Ava and Deacon had some quiet time. Ava had told Deacon everything about what had happened in New York and Kansas City.

"I was going a little nuts. Spinning like a top. I'm sorry for not letting you in on all that."

"Sheila, it's okay. I'm not spewing. You're going through a lot, and that's going to happen. Sometimes life deals you a curveball, and you just gotta roll with it."

He kissed her, and she melted. She closed her eyes and let the feeling of being with her man wash over her.

This was it. This was one of the moments that made life worth it. It was the tide coming back in after having been way out. She knew the tide would go back out again, but she was going to weather it next time, much better than she did this time.

Colleen was finally her mother, for real.

And all was right with the world.

Want to know what happens next? *The Nantucket Reunion* **is available for preorder NOW!** https://amzn.to/36xvARV

The Nantucket Reunion Synopsis

Samantha Flynn, Ava's daughter, is now on the island, as flighty as ever. She's determined to snag a rich guy who can whisk her away like Cinderella. She meets a billionaire's son, Adrian, who just might fit the bill. But is Adrian a toad instead of a prince? And might her prince be awaiting her after all?

Samantha also has a secret dream she's never shared and a creative soul that needs to be realized. Can she realize her dream before it's too late?

Charlotte, Ava's other daughter, is experiencing a fork in the road. Her husband wants a divorce, she has a newborn at home, and she needs her mom more than ever. She, like Samantha, is trying to find herself. An unexpected encounter leads her to follow her first passion, art, and a dramatic, life-threatening illness forces her to re-evaluate everything.

Ava is torn between two men. Deacon, the hot younger

man who was Ava's crush fulfilled. And Lars, an old friend who wants to be more. Then Ava's world is rocked by the appearance of yet another man - Christopher, the man who broke Ava's heart and bank account. With so many suitors vying for her attention, Ava doesn't know if she's coming or going. A nice problem to have, maybe, but not for an earthy Virgo like Ava, who likes things uncomplicated.

Her life becomes anything but uncomplicated, though. How will she handle it?

Join Ava, her friends and family, as they take you on a journey of tears, laughter, pain and promise. For readers who like their heart-warming tales with just a touch of magick, spice and humor.

AND IF YOU **want to know when the next books will be out, then sign up for my mailing list!**

Sign Up:https://mailchi.mp/1e4784c41707/ainsley-keaton-mailing-sign-up

And please leave a review! Reviews help get the word out and are invaluable. Just click the link, scroll down to the "Write a customer review button" and go!

https://amzn.to/3tyzqDE

OR CHECK OUT MY WEBSITE! You can find what's coming soon and check out books I've written under different pen names and different genres. If you like romances and legal thrillers, then check out my site!

https://attorneykc.wixsite.com/my-site-2

THANKS FOR READING!

Made in the USA
Middletown, DE
29 June 2024

56551353R00159